"FOR OBVIOUS REASONS, I AM UNABLE TO HIRE A HUMAN INVESTIGATOR—"

"I work with moreys. I don't work with human problems. You got the wrong P.I." Nohar told the frank.

"Binder pressures the police, they close the case. I need to know if someone in my company is responsible for Johnson's death. No qualified human is willing to talk to me. My company is privately owned. The board is formed of South African refugees—"

"All like you?"

"Yes, like me. To succeed, the owners need to remain hidden, unnoticed. The company will not survive if our existence is widely known."

"You said Binder's blocking the investigation. What are you worried about?"

"One kills once, one kills again. I have no idea who of my colleagues are involved. And I am closely watched—"

Nohar stood up. "I don't deal with anything involving murder."

"I have a five thousand retainer, and I will pay five times your usual rate."

Nohar froze. *No*, he told himself, *it's a bad job all over. You don't get involved with killings. You don't get involved with things bigger than you are.* Against his will, he found himself saying, "Double the retainer."

The frank would never go for it. He'd be able to walk away clean.

"Agreed."

Nohar had trapped himself. . . .

FORESTS OF THE NIGHT

S. ANDREW SWANN

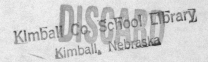
DAW BOOKS, INC.

DONALD A. WOLLHEIM, FOUNDER

375 Hudson Street, New York, NY 10014

ELIZABETH R. WOLLHEIM
SHEILA E. GILBERT
PUBLISHERS

First Printing, July 1993

3 4 5 6 7 8 9

DAW TRADEMARK REGISTERED
U.S. PAT. OFF. AND FOREIGN COUNTRIES
—MARCA REGISTRADA
HECHO EN U.S.A.

PRINTED IN THE U.S.A.

This is for John, Heather, and their kid(s?)

ACKNOWLEDGMENTS

Thanks to a number of people who left their mark on this manuscript. To Dan Eloff, who knows he got me writing again, and to R. M. Meluch, who doesn't. To the members of the Cleveland SF Writer's Workshop, who helped me get the burrs and toolmarks off this novel. To Stacy Newman, who offered to proof this. To Anastacia H. Brightfox, for naming one of the characters. And thanks to Amy, who, if nothing else, helped to give me something to write about.

Tyger! Tyger! burning bright
In the forests of the night,
What immortal hand or eye
Could frame thy fearful symmetry?

In what distant deeps or skies
Burnt the fire of thine eyes?
On what wings dare he aspire?
What the hand, dare seize the fire?

And what shoulder, and what art,
Could twist the sinews of thy heart?
And when thy heart began to beat,
What dread hand? And what dread feet?

What the hammer? What the chain?
In what furnace was thy brain?
What the anvil? what dread grasp
Dare its deadly terrors clasp?

When the stars threw down their spears,
And water'd heaven with their tears,
Did he smile his work to see?
Did he who made the Lamb make thee?

Tyger! Tyger! burning bright
In the forests of the night,
What immortal hand or eye
Could frame thy fearful symmetry?

—William Blake

CHAPTER 1

"One day, Nugoya, you're going to screw the wrong person." Nohar Rajasthan raked his claws across the seat of his booth, wishing it was Nugoya's face. Like the rest of *Zero's*, the vinyl on the seat was flashy, shiny, and cheap. The seat shredded.

Nugoya grabbed the collar of the black jacket that was draped over his left shoulder, shaking his head. He looked human, but only at first glance. A close examination of the graying Japanese would reveal joints large beyond normal human proportions and muscles that snaked like steel cable. The light above the booth glinted off the chrome irises of Nugoya's artificial Japanese eyes. "I hire you to find my girl. You find me a corpse. A corpse is worthless. I owe you nothing."

Nohar shouldn't have had the bad sense to let Nugoya hire him. It was becoming hard to contain his anger. "Expenses, and four days of legwork."

Nohar shouldn't have trusted a frank. Japan had been one of the few countries to ever defy the U.N. ban on the manipulation of human genetic material. The INS had tight restrictions on letting human frankensteins into the country, and those that made it here found that they had few, if any rights. That kind of bitterness tended to turn people into assholes—and Nugoya didn't need any help on that score.

Even moreaus like Nohar had a constitutional amendment in their favor.

"I owe you nothing. I should ask back the thousand

I paid you. You are an arrogant cat. Were we elsewhere, you would have to show some respect, and pay for your failure.'' Nugoya held up his mutilated right hand. It was missing two fingers.

Nohar was already scanning the rest of the bar. He picked out Nugoya's people easily. They were all moreaus—a human would not be caught dead working for a frank.

"Twenty-five hundred, Nugoya. Pay me."

It was Tuesday, two in the morning. There were only a half-dozen other people. The civilians—all human since they were downtown—were giving Nugoya's booth a wide berth. No surprise, since two of Nugoya's soldiers were hovering near the table. One was a tiger, like Nohar. The other was a dark brown, nearly black ursine that couldn't quite stand upright even with the relatively high ceiling. Nugoya had a vulpine manning the bar, and a trio of white rabbits sat near the entrance. Nohar knew there was a canine somewhere out of sight, probably in the kitchen. Nohar could catch a hint of the dog's scent.

"You failed. No money."

Nohar told himself that he should just walk out of there. Shut up, leave, and cut his losses. He didn't.

"I found the bitch, peddling her ass on the side for the flush *you* hooked her on. I don't know if it was cut with angel dust or drain cleaner, but her last trip splatted her all over Morey Hill. It's *your* fault she's dead."

Nugoya's jaw clenched, and Nohar could smell his anger. Nugoya stood up. His jacket slid off his shoulder, revealing his artificial left arm and some scarring on his neck. "How dare you, *an animal,* presume—"

That was enough. "And what are you, Nugoya, but a half-pint, half pink sleazeball?"

Nugoya sputtered something incomprehensible. Probably Japanese.

Nohar was glad he was the one facing the rest of the bar. He could feel all hell was about to break loose. Why couldn't he keep his damn mouth shut? One more try at being reasonable. "I just want my money, Nugoya. You aren't going to shake me down like one of your girls."

Nugoya's problem was he couldn't ever be anything but a small-time pimp. He wasn't human and he wasn't a moreau, so neither world would let him have more than a few scraps of the power he thought he deserved.

"I will not take any more insolence. Leave or I will have you removed."

Nugoya motioned with his left arm at the other tiger and the bear. The tiger started moving forward. The bear reached under a table and took a hold of something large and presumably deadly. He kept it out of sight of the patrons.

"It's insolence to think the world owes you respect because some defunct Jap corporation built you like a disposable radio."

That did it. Nugoya had a killer ego, and could only take a little needling before he jumped. In his prime, a Japanese corporate samurai could take Nohar in a fair fight. Nugoya's ego would never let him admit that he was well past his prime. Tokyo was nuked by China a long time ago, and Nugoya had been sitting on his butt for longer than that.

The frank ripped the table from the wall and threw it to the side. The advancing tiger almost tripped over it. Nohar stayed seated and Nugoya went for his neck. Nugoya was fast, faster than any normal human, faster than most moreaus.

Nohar was faster.

As the other tiger manhandled the remains of the table out of his way and the bear pulled out a Russian-make assault rifle, Nohar's right hand shot up and clamped on Nugoya's mechanical wrist. At the same time, Nohar wrapped his left arm around Nugoya's right arm. The frank's three-fingered hand ended up clamped under Nohar's armpit. Nohar had his forearm levered under Nugoya's upper arm, his hand resting on the shoulder.

Nohar pushed down and heard the bone crack.

Nugoya yelled, washing Nohar's face with his sour breath, and tried to escape. But Nohar had lifted the frank off the ground by the mechanical arm. Nugoya didn't have the leverage.

Predictably, one of the civilians screamed.

"That will heal. If I did that to your other arm, who's around to fix it? Call off the muscle."

Nugoya showed some reluctance, so Nohar bore down on the broken arm. Nohar could hear the bones grate together. Nugoya shook his head violently and screamed something back at his people in Japanese. The tiger stopped moving, and the bear set the rifle down on the ground.

The tiger slowly drew his gun from a shoulder holster and dropped it.

"You're dead, Rajasthan."

"Hundred years we'll all be dead. I just want my money."

It was a standoff. Nohar had Nugoya as a shield, but there were six of Nugoya's people between him and the door. The rabbits weren't an immediate problem, the press of exiting civilians were pinning them by the door. The bartending fox had pulled out a shotgun, but he had the sense not to point it at his boss. Even so, Nohar couldn't move away from the wall without exposing himself.

He might be 260 centimeters tall and weigh 300 kilos. He might be able to whip anything but that bear and a few franks in a fair fight. But guns were guns.

Nohar stood up, lifting Nugoya by his mechanical arm. The little pimp barely gave his torso cover. Nohar would have preferred kevlar—he would have preferred not being there in the first place.

Nohar could smell the canine, stronger now. The other tiger's nose twitched. The bear started turning toward the bar. The civilians were gone.

So were the rabbits.

What?

Nugoya was still yelling. "Dead!"

The tiger turned toward the entrance. Nohar was smelling it now, too. The copper odor of blood. Rabbit blood. It drifted in from the open door to the empty bar with the algae smell from the river. Nugoya stopped yelling.

The fox started turning around to face the long mirror behind the bar. The canine's smell was rank in the bar now. Nohar began to realize that the dog might not be one of Nugoya's people. The fox must have heard something because he was raising the shotgun toward the mirror.

"Let me down!" There was the hint of panic in Nugoya's voice and more than a hint of it in his smell.

Someone turned on a glass jackhammer and the mirror for the length of the bar exploded outward in a wave, from left to right. It was some sort of silenced submachine gun. The vulpine got in the way of at least three shots, and large chunks of fox flew out over the bar. The shotgun went off, blowing away a case of Guinness that was sitting behind the bar. The fox fell half over the bar and bled.

The smell of cordite, beer, and melted teflon wafted over. Whoever was shooting was using glazer rounds. If the internal injuries didn't get you, the blood poisoning would.

The other tiger was ducking for cover in a booth across from Nohar and Nugoya. There wasn't cover for the bear. All the ursine could do was reach back for the rifle and hope the guy with the machine gun missed.

The bear was bending over. Nohar had an unobstructed view of the assassin jumping out of the broken mirror and on to the bar. Canine. A dog with a shaggy gray coat that tagged him as an Afghani. The dog wore a long black coat over a black jumpsuit that bulged with the kevlar vest he wore under it. The gun was small, the silencer was twice as long as the weapon itself. The clip was the length of the dog's forearm.

The bear was intimidating, but size was the bear's downfall. What was terrifying on the battlefields of Asia was a deadly handicap in the small confines of the rear of *Zero's*. The ursine couldn't turn around fast enough to shoot the canine.

The canine emptied a burst into the bear's back and Nohar got a good look and a good smell of the inside of the bear's chest as the ursine splatted on to the ground.

The tiger had a problem. His gun was on the ground, by the rifle. Nohar could smell the bloodlust rising from the other cat. *No,* Nohar thought, *you don't jump a guy with an automatic weapon.* But the cat was already hyped on adrenaline and Nohar could see the muscles in the tiger's haunches tense, even under the human clothing.

The dog was waiting for the tiger to pounce. Three bullets hit the cat before it got halfway. Blood sprayed the wall and the tiger slammed into a booth, smashing a table and scattering glassware.

Then the dog turned his attention to Nohar and Nugoya.

Nugoya was thrashing like a fish out of water. "Get me out of this, you have your money, you have three times your money—"

The dog licked his nose. The smell of his musk made Nohar want to sneeze. "Drop the pimp."

Nohar didn't argue.

Nugoya hit the ground and collapsed, cradling his arm. He turned toward the dog. "Hassan . . ."

The canine shook his head. "Too late. You were warned last time."

"Can't we deal—"

"No. You knew the rules. Do not tread on our business. Flush is our business. We say who sells, and who to."

Nugoya staggered to his feet. "I needed the money to keep my girls supplied. You're charging too much—"

"Others will be quite glad not to get off as cheaply

as you.'' The canine fired one shot that hit Nugoya in the face. The pimp's head jerked back hard enough that Nohar heard the neck crack. Nugoya fell backward at Nohar's feet, looking upward with only half a face. Only one chrome iris looked up. The other eye had become electronic shrapnel buried deep in what was left of Nugoya's brain.

Nohar looked up from the corpse, and at Hassan. ''Me now?''

The dog shook his head and raised his gun. ''Not today. This was a lesson. Lessons need witnesses.''

Hassan began backing away, keeping his eyes on Nohar.

When Hassan reached the door, he gave the carnage a brief inspection. Then he looked back up at Nohar, who was still standing by the rear wall. ''Advice, tiger. Next time be more careful who you work for.''

No shit.

It took all of fifteen minutes for the first police to descend on the party side of the flats. In twenty minutes the east side of the Cuyahoga River was illuminated by a wash of dozens of flashing blue and red lights. Even though Nohar was the one who called in the shooting, he had to sit on his tail in the back of a very cramped Chevy Caldera sedan. At least the pink uniforms didn't cuff him—not that they hadn't tried, but this far out of Moreytown they didn't have cuffs that would fit him. They simply deposited him in the back seat and kept their distance.

Nohar squirmed to get his tail in a comfortable position and looked out the windows facing the river. Not much to see, water for a few hundred meters reflecting the police flashers. The water terminated at the concrete base of the West Side office complex. The office buildings were so dark at this time of night that they seemed to be trapezoidal holes cut in the night sky, revealing something blacker behind it.

There wasn't much else to watch out the other window. The forensics people were all in *Zero's*. He'd end up talking to Manny later anyway. Not that there was anything to discuss. It wasn't like he was on a case any more.

Twenty-five hundred dollars. Gone. The first of the month was at the end of the week, and he only had about two hundred in the bank. Served him right for working for a pimp.

Nohar had his pride. He didn't want to have to ask Manny about his old room—

He shook his head. Things would work out. They usually did.

A soft rain began to fall. It broke up the reflections on the river.

Nohar heard the scream of abused brakes. He turned around to face the entrance of the parking lot. A puke-green Dodge Havier that was missing one front fender jumped the curb and skidded to a halt in a handi-capped parking spot.

It had to be Harsk.

Indeed, Irwin Harsk's bald head emerged from the driver's side door of the unmarked sedan. Harsk stormed out like an avalanche. Many standards of pink beauty escaped Nohar, but some forms of ugly transcended species. Harsk's black face resembled a cinder block.

It had been only a matter of time before Harsk got involved. He was the detective in charge of Morey-town. He had jurisdiction over anything involving mo-reaus, and, by extension, any product of genetic engineering. In the case of the shoot-out at *Zero's* that covered the victims, the suspect, and the witness.

This obviously didn't please the detective.

Harsk stood a moment in the rain, looking over the scene—the ambulances, the forensics van, Manny's Medical Examiner's van, the seven marked and two unmarked police cars. Even over the twenty-meter dis-tance between them, Nohar could hear Harsk grunt.

After giving the scene the once-over, Harsk targeted

a lone uniform who was standing by the door to *Zero's*. Harsk looked like he wanted to unload on someone. The cop by the door was the unlucky one. Nohar supposed Harsk chose his victim because of the cup of coffee the guy was drinking. Harsk walked up to the guy, and even though Nohar wasn't great at reading human expressions, the way the poor cop bit his lip and gave forced nods indicated that Harsk wasn't having a nice day and was doing his best to share the experience.

Harsk pointed at the Caldera that Nohar was sitting in and yelled something that Nohar couldn't quite make out. The cop shrugged and tried to say something, and Harsk cut him off. Harsk grabbed the guy's coffee and pointed back into *Zero's*.

Nohar wished he could read lips.

The cop went inside and Harsk started walking toward the Caldera. He took a sip from the uniform's coffee and grimaced. He looked into the cup, shook his head, and dumped it on the asphalt.

Harsk walked up to the door and opened it. "Rajasthan, how did I know you'd be involved in this crap?"

"Deductive reasoning?"

Harsk grunted. "Get the fuck out of that patrol car. The city just bought those and we don't want you shedding on them."

Nohar ducked out the door and stretched. The misting rain started to dampen his fur immediately. He wished he had worn his trench coat to the meeting. "No apology for treating me like a suspect? I didn't *have* to call this in."

"Be glad that some downtown cowboy didn't shoot you. Half these kids are just out of the academy and tend to shit if they see a moreau. This ain't your neighborhood. What the fuck are you doing here?"

"Nugoya was a client."

Harsk looked at Nohar. "So when are you going to start selling yourself to the flush peddlers?"

Nohar had his right hand up, claws fully extended, before he knew what he was doing. Harsk's face cracked into an ugly grin. "Do it, you fucking alley cat. I would love to put you away and get you out of my hair."

Nohar took a few deep breaths and lowered his arm. "What hair?"

A lithe nonhuman form left *Zero's*. The moreau wore a lab coat and carried a notebook-sized computer, the display of which he was reading.

Nohar called out, "Manny."

Manny—his full name was Mandvi Gujerat—looked up from the display, twitched his nose, and started across the parking lot toward Nohar and Harsk. Manny was a small guy with a thin, whiplike body. He had short brown fur, a lean, aerodynamic head, and small black eyes. People who saw Manny usually guessed he was designed from a rat, or a ferret. Both were wrong. Manny was a mongoose.

Manny reached them and Harsk interrupted before Nohar could say anything. "Gujerat, what have you got on the bodies?"

Manny gave Nohar an undulating shrug and looked down at his notebook. "I have a tentative species on six of seven. The three bodies outside were all a Peruvian Lepus strain. From the white fur and the characteristic skull profile I'd say Pajonal '35 or '36. They all have unit tattoos, and some heavy scarring. Infantry, and they saw combat."

Manny tapped the screen and the page changed. "The bartender was definitely vulpine. Brit fox, Ulster antiterrorist. I think second generation, but I can't be sure. The British ID their forces under the tongue and most of the fox's head is gone.

"The tiger—" Manny looked at Nohar briefly. "Second-generation Rajasthan. Indian Special Forces.

"The bear, I would guess Turkmen, Russia, or Kazakhstahn. That's only on my previous experience in ursoid strains. Her species—"

"Her?" asked Harsk.

"Yes. I think she was a parthenogenetic adaption. But as I was saying, *her* species isn't cataloged. She's either a unique experiment, or one of the few dozen species that fell through the cracks during the war. From the corpse, for all I know, she could be Canadian."

Nohar snorted.

Manny shrugged again. "I suppose you already have a file on the one engineered human. But his strain checks out against what we have on Sony's late human-enhancement projects. The one we have here underwent a massive reconstruction after some major trauma. The hardware in his body was worth a few million when there were people who could make and install the stuff."

Harsk nodded. "Any leads on the suspect?"

"Some hairs from the mirror check out as canine. From that and a description, purebred Afghani, Qandahar '24. Attack strain, one the Kabul government 'discontinued' after the war."

"Enough. Rajasthan, I'll get your statement from the uniforms. Get out of here before you attract more trouble. Gujerat, dump the rest into the precinct mainframe." Harsk started to go toward *Zero's* and paused. "The *Moreytown* precinct."

Manny nodded. "Where else?"

Harsk left.

Manny folded up the computer and twitched his nose. "So, stranger, what the hell are you doing at this bloodbath?"

"Bad sense to let Nugoya hire me—"

"Let me guess. Female Vietnamese canine who shot herself so full of flush that she thought she was avian? The one you asked me to ID for you?"

Nohar nodded.

"I know you don't like my advice—"

"Then don't give me any."

"—*but* something dangerous is going on. I don't

think you want to be involved, even tangentially, with anything that has to do with the flush industry.''

Nohar leaned against the Caldera. His fur was beginning to itch. "Sounds like you know something you think I don't.''

"Something's in the air. The DEA is crawling all over downtown, and the gangs in Moreytown are acting up. Most of the bodies I'm looking at the past few weeks are young, second-generation street kids.''

"I can handle myself.''

"So I worry. You were once one of those second-generation street kids.''

"I can handle myself," Nohar said a little more forcefully.

Manny backed off. "Anyway, we do have to stop meeting like this. When are you going to come back and let me cook you some dinner?''

You've been trying to get me back there for fifteen years, Nohar thought. "I'll make it over one of these days.''

"The door's always open.''

"I know.''

Manny turned and started back to *Zero's,* where a gaggle of pink EMTs were trying to manhandle the ursine's corpse out the door.

Nohar sighed.

"I know," he whispered to himself.

Nohar uselessly turned the collar up on the irritating pink-designed jacket and headed for his car. There wasn't anything left for him to do here.

CHAPTER 2

Nohar's apartment had holes in the wall, a leaky roof, a sagging floor in the kitchen, and wiring that hadn't been up to code when it was put in forty years ago. However, the place had one redeeming feature. Someone had installed a huge stainless-steel shower that Nohar could fit into. Four in the morning was a godawful time to take a shower, but Nohar wanted to get the city off of him—as well as pieces of bear and Nugoya.

Nohar stood under a blast of warm water, feeling the grit melt off his fur. Through the open door of the bathroom, he listened to the news coming off his comm and tried to forget the fiasco he had left downtown.

". . . major demonstrations through the Economic Community. However, despite public pressure and threats of violence, the European parliament followed through on its vote to eliminate most internal restrictions on nonhuman movement. The French and German states are braced for a massive influx of unemployed nonhumans from the rest of the economically troubled European nation."

"The French and German interior ministers issued a joint statement condemning the parliament's decision to outlaw screening across internal borders."

Nohar sighed. The pinks in Paris and Berlin were worried about a few thousand moreaus—relatively benign moreaus for the most part. The EEC had a few combat designs in reaction to the war, but it never produced many moreaus. Most of their nonhumans were designed for police and hazardous industrial work.

The European parliament probably would still have considered their moreaus as no better than slaves or machines if the Vatican hadn't screwed everything up with the pope's decision that moreys had souls. The EEC was still dealing with the repercussions of that, even fifteen years after the production lines stopped.

"In a related story, a car bomb exploded in Bern, Switzerland, today outside of the Bensheim Genetic Repository Building. No injuries were reported, and no one has claimed responsibility. Damage to the Bensheim building was estimated at a quarter of a million dollars. The Bensheim Foundation issued a statement to reassure their clients that no damage was done to their inventory of genetic material which is kept in an undisclosed location. The building that was bombed housed only administrative offices. The Foundation says that this will in no way affect its worldwide collection and distribution of semen.

"Dr. Bensheim himself issued a statement from Stockholm deploring the attack, and saying, 'The right to reproduce is fundamental and should not be denied on the basis of species.'

"In local news . . ."

Nohar turned off the water and leaned his back against the cool metal wall of the shower. He couldn't get that two and a half grand out of his mind. How the hell was he going to pay the rent—how the hell was he going to eat? He knew too many moreaus who lived out on the street, and he had already done time there himself.

Nohar slid the shower door aside and Cat looked up quizzically. The yellow tomcat was curled up on top of the john and was looking annoyingly serene. Sometimes Nohar thought there was something to the idea that you shouldn't have pets too close to your own species.

Nohar turned on the dryer and Cat made a satisfying

leap out the bathroom door. Served the little fuzzball right for not having the sense to worry about where his next meal was coming from. After a few minutes, Cat peeked around the doorjamb and gave Nohar a peeved expression.

Nohar allowed himself the luxury of standing in front of the dryer until his entire body had aired out. Who gave a shit what this month's utility bill cost. Moot if he couldn't pay it. He needed the time to relax. He was too tense to think rationally.

". . . buried tomorrow. Graveside services to be held at Lakeview Cemetery. The police have no suspects as of yet, and the Binder campaign has yet to issue an official statement other than appointing Congressman Binder's legal counsel, Edwin Harrison, as acting campaign manager.

"Former Cleveland mayor, Russell Gardner, expressed sympathy for his opponent and said that he did not to intend to make rumors of alleged financial irregularities in Binder's fund-raising a campaign issue.

"Binder finance chairman, Philip Young, could not be reached for comment."

Nohar turned off the dryer and walked out of the bathroom. He collapsed on the nearly-dead couch in the living room. There was the sound of protesting wood and permanently compressed springs. He shifted on his back, and Cat ran up and pounced on his chest. Nohar winced as four *cold* little feet kneaded his fur. Cat curled up to take a nap.

Nohar lifted his hand to push him off, but a loud purring made him stop and simply pet the creature.

". . . more violence on the East Side today. There was an apparent clash between nonhuman gang members on Murray Hill—"

Only newscasters and politicians still called it Murray Hill. It was Morey Hill now, had been for nearly a decade. Nohar sighed. The guy on the news couldn't even bring himself to say the word morey—or even

moreau. Nohar looked at the guy on the comm. Pink—
what else—slick black hair, a nothing Midwestern accent, dead gray eyes, all the animation of a cheap computer graphic. The bodies on the screen behind him
were more lively.

"—fifteen dead, all of various species, making this
the most bloody incidence of cross-species violence
since the 'Dark August' riots of 2042. Local community leaders have expressed concern over the latest es-
calation of violence in the nonhuman community . . ."

To prove the point, the newscast started to show
clips of interviews with said "community leaders."
Nohar snorted, with the token morey exception—
Father Sean Murphy, a Brit fox who defected to the
Irish Catholics, one of two ordained morey priests in
the United States—the "community leaders" were all
human.

The newscast then went into the obligatory human
fear/responsibility versus moreau poverty/empower-
ment segment. Same shit, different day. Nohar closed
his eyes and listened for something interesting to come
on.

Nohar woke to the sound of the comm buzzing for
his attention. Grayish daylight streamed through the
windows. The comm's display was still on the news
channel. More gang violence, even worse this time. It
barely registered on Nohar that it had gone down only
three blocks from his apartment. Flashing text informed him he had slept through two other calls and
nearly eight hours.

The incoming call was from Robert Dittrich. Nohar
called out to the comm. "Got it."

The newscast winked out and was replaced by a red-
bearded human face. "I wish you'd put on some
clothes before you answer the phone."

Nohar growled. "What the hell do you want,
Bobby?"

"Tough night?"

Nohar closed his eyes and sighed. "What do you think?"

"Heard about Nugoya. Tough break—"

"Tough all over. What do you want?"

Bobby coughed. "If you're going to be like that. I was going to give you the background I hacked on Nugoya—"

"Great, real useful."

"Did anyone ever tell you that you can be a real asshole at times, Nohar? As I was saying—" Bobby paused. Nohar didn't interrupt. "As I was saying, I was going to give you that data when the Fed landed on my doorstep."

Nohar sat up, fully awake now. Cat tumbled off his chest and ran off into the kitchen. "Shit. You in trouble?"

Bobby laughed and shook his head. "No, apparently I'm still clean. As we all know, everything I do on my computer is perfectly legal."

Nohar shook his head at that.

Bobby went on. "Wasn't me at all. They were asking about you. That's how I heard about Nugoya and last night."

"Me?"

"Yes, thought I'd call you. They wanted to know about your politics, of all things." Bobby put his hand to his forehead and chuckled. "They had this *babe* with them. Was she a hard case—"

"Skip the commentary, what were they looking for?"

"Some hired gun, I think. Named Hassan. I think they wanted to know if they could link the two of you."

"An Afghan canine and an Indian tiger—do they know how silly that sounds?"

"The war's been over for eighteen years. Things change. Just wanted you to know the Fed's interested in you. I got to go. Still want the data on Nugoya?"

"Keep it."

"Don't let the Fed screw you."

"I try to avoid it."

Bobby's face winked out and the news came back on.

Wonderful stuff to wake up to. Not only was he broke and one day closer to eviction, but now the FBI was curious about him.

The comm was talking about dead politicians. Nohar told it to shut up.

There were still two messages on his comm, waiting for his attention. One had been forwarded from his office—

Maybe it was a client.

Yeah, real likely, and maybe a morey would get elected president. Nohar told the comm, "Classify. Phone messages."

"two messages. july twenty-ninth. message one, ten-oh-five a. m. unlisted number—"

The voice of the computer was a flat, neutral monotone. Nohar never understood the urge people had to make computers sound like anything but. He told the comm, "Play."

Nohar didn't like calls that didn't ID themselves. People who called from unlisted locations generally had something to hide.

This caller definitely had something to hide, the screen came up a generic test pattern. This guy either didn't have a video pickup, or had turned his camera off.

"I hope to reach you, Mr. Rajasthan." The voice that came over the comm sounded like it was at the bottom of a well. It sounded bubbly. The words oozed. "I have need of the service of a private investigator. Please meet me at Lakeview Cemetery today at one-thirty p.m. This is not something I can discuss on a phone. I look for you by the grave of Eliza Wilkins."

That was the end of the message.

"Damn. It *was* a client."

"instructions unclear." The comm thought Nohar was talking to it.

Nohar told it, "Comm off," and the comm shut off obligingly.

It was a client, and a damn secretive one at that. Nohar didn't trust the situation one bit. There was little he could do about it. Nohar was so low on cash that he would have to at least meet the guy—

Nohar suddenly realized that it was already fifteen after one.

It took him two minutes to dress and another five to call Lakeview and get a plot number for Wilkins. Nohar did it with the video off, because if they saw he was a moreau it would have taken five times as long.

The first thing to greet him as he walked out into the misting rain was the acrid smell of burning plastic. The smoke made his nose itch. He realized the smell was coming from a burning car up by the traffic barriers.

Across the street from his apartment was an abandoned bus. There was a fresh graffiti logo on it. "ZIPPERHEAD—Off The Pink."

Another gang with it in for humans.

He walked up Mayfield, toward the cemetery, passing a knot of pink cops at the traffic barrier. Apparently this was the latest violence the news was going on about when he woke up. The fire was burning a prewar Japanese compact, an ancient Subaru. The car was wrapped around one of the concrete pylons. The way the thing had gone up—was still going; the cops were letting it burn itself out in the middle of the street—it had to have been wired with explosives. Inductors might explode, but they don't burn very well.

The cops didn't stop him—any other part of town and they probably would have on general principles.

The car wasn't all. It had been a busy morning. A block past the cops, things got ugly. Upwind of the burning plastic, Nohar could smell the scent of some-

one, multiple someones, who had bought it nasty. He
smelled blood, fear, and cordite. The victims smelled
canine.

He rounded the old cemetery gate—sealed by a solid
four meter concrete wall behind the flaking wrought
iron—and headed down toward Coventry. When he
turned the corner, he could see the medics loading
body-bags—three vans' worth of body-bags. Canine
had been a good guess. Nohar caught sight of one of
the victims before the black plastic was zipped over
the face. The body was a vulpine female with a small
caliber gunshot wound to the right eye. One of the
hispanic medics saw him looking over. There was the
fresh smell of fear from the pink.

Another day, Nohar would have ignored it. Today,
however, he had just had a case blow up in his face,
the Fed was taking an unhealthy interest in him, the
record July heat and the misting rain were making his
fur itch under his trench coat, and—if his luck held—
he was going to be late and miss his potential client.
Today he was in a particularly bad mood.

Nohar could not resist the urge to smile.

Some moreaus don't have the facial equipment to
produce a convincing smile, but Nohar's evolved feline cheeks could pull his mouth into a quite percep-
tible arc. The same gesture also bared an impressive
set of teeth. Predominant among which were two
glistening-white canines the size of a man's thumb.

The poor guy didn't deserve it. Nohar could tell he
was nervous enough just *being* in Moreytown. He
didn't need to have a huge predatory morey looking at
him like he was lunch.

Nohar didn't hang around for the reaction. He was
still running late. Two blocks further down, at the intersection of Mayfield and Coventry, was the only open
gate on this side of Lakeview Cemetery—seemed appropriate that it was into the Jewish section.

When he reached the right monument, "Eliza Wilkins, 1966–2042, beloved wife of Harold," it was

thirty-two after. He was in time for the show. A funeral was progressing below him.

He was out of sight of most of them, and it was probably a good thing. They were planting someone of consequence, and from his vantage, it was pinks only. He thought he saw a morey in the crowd, but— damn his bad day-vision—it turned out to be a black pink with a heavy beard.

Not a morey in the lot, and the *whitest* bunch of pinks he had ever seen. Especially under the canopy. There, he figured on fifty people who got to use the folding chairs, at least another fifty standing back under cover, and a hundred or so milling about beyond some sort of private security line in back of the paying customers. Even with his poor eyesight he could make the types. The pinks who knew the corpse were obvious, they wore their money—he could see the glints of their shoes and jewelry whenever they moved—and they were, with few exceptions, white. The pinks who wanted to know the corpse were just as easily made, and they were closer to the normal mix of human coloring, a few blacks, orientals, hispanics. The black cops were totally out of it, with their cheap suits and their attention on everything but the service. The private security goons—they were white—were better dressed than the cops and were intent on keeping the flow of riffraff behind the tent. Then, in the back with the crowd, were the vids. Cameras and mikes at the ready . . .

Some of the riffraff—mostly blacks and orientals— were carrying signs. Looked like a full-fledged protest was going on. The vids were paying as much, if not more, attention to the riffraff than to the service. Nohar wished he could make out more of the signs, but the best he could do was read the occasional word. Lots of isms, "Racism," "Sexism," "Speciesism." The signs that weren't isms seemed to mention capital-R Rights.

The Right to what, Nohar couldn't read.

Nohar wondered who had died—irritating, because he thought he had heard something about this, and the job his anonymous client had in mind probably involved the stiff. Perhaps the guy left all his money to some morey squeeze and they needed to track her down.

Nohar heard a truck, and hoped it wasn't security. The pinks might take offense at a morey walking around the human part of the cemetery. But instead of security, Nohar saw an unmarked cargo van. A Dodge Electroline painted institution-green. It was windowless, boxy, cheap, and either remote-driven or programmed. It wasn't the kind of vehicle Nohar expected to see in a cemetery. It pulled on to the shoulder and backed toward him. When it stopped, the rear doors opened with a pneumatic hiss.

The smell was overpowering. His sensitive nose was suddenly exposed to an open sewer. Nohar was enveloped by the odor of sweat, and bile, and ammonia. Even a pink would've been able to sense it.

He had no idea what this guy was supposed to look like, or who he was—but Nohar did *not* expect another frank. They were supposed to be rare. Despite that, what the opening door revealed *couldn't* be anything *but* a frank.

And a failure at that.

Once Nohar's eyes had adjusted to the nearly black interior of the cargo van, he could see it. The frank was vaguely humanoid and had a pasty white color to its rubbery skin. Its limbs seemed tubular and boneless, and its fingers were fused into a mittenlike hand. It wore a pink's clothes, but its pale bulk was fighting them. Rolls of white flesh cascaded over its belt, its collar, even its shoes. Glassy eyes, a lump of a nose, and a lipless mouth were collected together on a pear-shaped head. Its face seemed incapable of showing any expression. It seemed that, if the clothes were removed, the frank would just slide down and form a puddle on the ground.

The frank also massed more than Nohar did though it was a meter shorter.

Whatever gene-tech had designed this monstrosity had screwed-up bigtime. Until now, Nohar could never quite fathom the reason for the pinks' horror at the franks. It seemed bizarre to him that humans, who took all the genetic tinkering with other species in stride, were so aghast when someone tinkered with their own. If this was a sample of what happened, Nohar could begin to understand. *Maybe,* thought Nohar, *pink genes didn't take kindly to fiddling.*

The voice was the same as the one over the comm—deep, bubbly, and, somehow, slimy. "Are you the detective, Nohar Rajasthan?"

Briefly, Nohar wondered if he needed the money this badly—he did. "Yes."

Nohar began to feel warmth coming from the back of the van. Nohar realized that the frank had the heat on in the van, all the way. Back where the frank was sitting it could be fifty degrees. An unpleasant sound emerged from the frank's mass. It could have been a belch. "We have fifteen minutes before van goes to next stop, forgive. I need to smuggle myself out. Have to keep meeting secret."

Nohar shrugged. "Then you better get on with it."

At least the frank took Nohar's appearance in stride. In most of the directories it didn't mention that Nohar was the only moreau in the city with a private investigator's license. For some people, his address wasn't a big enough clue. Of course a *pink* detective would have a problem with this guy, even more so than with Nugoya. At least with Nugoya, a pink could pretend the guy had been human.

"What kind of job? Surveillance or missing persons?"

Nohar heard flesh shifting as the frank moved. "Do you know who is being buried down the hill?"

Chalk one up for obvious conclusions. The stiff was involved. "Rich, human, lots of friends."

Another ugly sound emerged from the mass of white

flesh. It might have been a laugh. "The dead man is a politician. His name is Daryl Johnson. He is the campaign manager for twelfth district congressman, Joseph Binder."

Nohar was wondering about the frank's weird accent when he realized that the frank had ducked his first question. "What's the *job?*"

"I must know who killed Daryl Johnson."

Nohar almost laughed, but he knew the frank was serious. "Outside my specialty." So much for the money he needed. "I don't mess with police investigations—"

"There is no police investigation."

Nohar was getting irritated with the frank's bubbling monotone. "I work with moreys. I don't work with human problems. You got the wrong P.I."

"Binder pressures the police, they close the case. I need to know if someone in my company is responsible for Johnson's death . . ."

Nohar looked straight into the frank's eyes. That usually unnerved people, but the frank was as expressionless as ever. "Did you hear what I said?" It took Nohar a while to realize that the reason he didn't like the frank's eyes was because they didn't blink.

"Let me finish, Mr. Rajasthan. You are the only person I can contact for this job. For obvious reasons, I am unable to hire a human investigator—"

"No solidarity shit."

"Practical matter. No qualified human is willing to talk to me. My company is Midwest Lapidary Imports. We're privately owned. We import gemstones from South Africa. The board is formed of South African refugees—"

"All like you?"

The frank showed no offense at the question. "Yes, like me. We retain contacts in the mining industry—" Nohar got a picture of the South African gene-techs trying to create a modified human miner. Hell, maybe the frank's appearance wasn't a mistake. For all Nohar knew, this guy was perfectly adapted for work in a five-mile-deep hole. Nohar stopped musing and waited for the frank to get to the point. "To succeed, the owners of Midwest Lapidary Imports, MLI, need to remain hidden, unnoticed, private. The company will not survive if our existence is widely known.

"With Johnson's death there is the possibility that one of our number is behind the murder . . ."

Nohar sighed. Learn something new every day. A bunch of franks were importing diamonds from South Africa, probably illegally. The pinks would just *love* that idea. The Supreme Court was still debating if the 29th amendment even covered the franks. No one knew yet if the franks were covered by the Bill of Rights, the limited morey amendment, or nothing at all. Before the pinks in this country had even locked down the legal status of engineered humans, here were a few, acting just like eager little capitalists. "You said Binder's blocking the investigation. What are you worried about?"

"One kills once, one kills again. You have no idea what it would mean if one of our number is directly involved in a human's death. The company is a worthy project, but someone may commit atrocities in its name. I cannot, nor can anyone else, abide our secrecy, our existence, if one of us kills to further our ends."

"How is your organization involved?"

"The police call it a robbery-murder because there are over three million dollars in campaign funds missing from his house—"

"Sounds plausible." Nohar realized that he was just leading the frank on. He had some natural curiosity, but there was no sane way he could touch this case.

The frank's bulk groaned and rippled as he leaned toward Nohar. The heat and stench that floated off of the frank's body almost made Nohar wince. "I am the accountant for MLI. The three million that is missing is never there. Campaign records the police use are wrong about this. The money comes from MLI, and *should* be there. But I handle the books and such a sum never leaves our accounts, or, if it does, it returns before the sum is debited.

"I do not go to the police. For now I must retain the secrecy. I can be wrong. I cannot damage the company until my suspicions are proved correct. I can't work within MLI. I have no idea who of my colleagues are involved. And I am closely watched—"

Nohar stood up. "I don't deal with anything involving murder. I have to walk from this one—find an out-of-towner."

"I have a five thousand retainer, and I will pay five times your usual rate, another five thousand when you complete the job successfully."

Nohar froze, his usual rate was five hundred a day. *No,* he told himself, *it's a bad job all over. You don't get involved with killings. You don't get involved with pinks. You don't get involved with things bigger than you are.* Against his will, he found himself saying, "Double the retainer."

It was a ludicrous request. The frank would never go for it. He'd be able to walk away clean.

"Agreed."

Damn it. "Plus expenses."

"Of course."

Nohar had trapped himself.

"Time closes in on us." The frank handed him an envelope. Ten thousand. He'd been anticipated. "Start with Johnson, work back. Do not contact anyone at MLI. I'll contact you every few days. Get any information about MLI through me. We have few minutes. Any immediate questions?"

Nohar was still looking at the cash. "Why is a bunch of franks backing a reactionary right-winger like Binder?"

"*Quid-pro-quo,* Mr. Rajasthan. The corporate entity will see its interests served in the Senate. The fact that we're of a background Binder despises is of little consequence. Binder doesn't know who runs MLI. Anything else?''

''What's your name?''

Nohar heard the engine start up again. As the door closed with its pneumatic hiss, Nohar heard the frank say, ''You can call me John Smith.''

The ugly green van drove away, leaving a pair of divots in the grass. The ghost of the frank's smell remained, emanating from the money Nohar still held in his hand.

Once he took the money, he did the job. No matter what.

No matter what, damn it.

Nohar put the money in one of the cavernous pockets of his trenchcoat. Now that he was on the job, he pulled out his camera, slipped in a ramcard, and started recording the funeral.

CHAPTER 3

The ATM was half a block from Nohar's place. To his relief, it appeared to be working. At least the lights were on. He stopped in front of the armored door, and, under the blank stare of the disabled external camera, he pulled his card and slipped it into the slot. The mechanism gave an arthritic wheeze and he feared it was going to eat his card again. Fortunately, the keypad flashed green at him. He punched in his ID number while the servos on the lensless camera followed his every move.

The door slid aside with a grinding noise and he ducked into the too-small room. When the door shut behind him, he finally felt comfortable with all that money on him.

The chair the bank provided was too small to sit on. The best he could do was to lean against it and hunch over, hanging his tail over the back of the seat. Besides, somebody had pissed all over the damn thing.

There was a short burst of static, and a voice came through one of the intact speakers. "Welcome to Society Bank's Green Machine—bzt—Mr. Noharajasthan. Please state clearly what transaction you wish—"

The voice was supposed to be female human, but it was tinny and muffled. Nohar interrupted. "Deposit. Card Account. Ten-Thousand-Dollars."

"Please repeat clearly."

"Deposit. Card Account. Ten-Thousand-Dollars."

"Please type in request."

Great, the damn thing couldn't hear him. He typed in the transaction on the terminal.

"Is this a cash transaction?"

It didn't believe him. "Yes," he said and typed at the same time.

A drawer opened under the terminal. Unlike most of the ATM, it seemed to be in perfect working order. "—bzt—please place paper currency in the drawer. There will be a slight pause while the bills are screened."

Nohar placed the two packets of bills in the drawer. Nohar knew that the note of surprise he heard in the ATM's voice was in his own head more than anywhere else. "Your currency checks as valid. Thank you for banking with Society, Mr. Noharajasthan. The current balance on your card account is—bzt—ten-thousand-one-hundred-ninety-three-dollars and sixty-five cents. You may pick up your card and receipt at the door. Have a nice day."

Nohar left the ATM and turned up the collar of his coat against a sudden burst of more intense rain. He typed in his ID again at the keypad, blinking twice as water got in his eyes. The ATM released his card and the receipt. As he pocketed the items, he noticed a couple of ratboys hanging around across the street.

An ATM in use attracted vermin.

The two ratboys were crossing the street. Nohar had hoped that his appearance would have put them off. Apparently, they were too zoned or too stupid, perhaps both. As they closed he could smell that they were probably on something. Itching for a fight. both of them.

"Kitty."

"*Pretty* kitty."

Nohar decided to ignore them. All he wanted was to get home and shuck his wet coat. He walked down the road, past them.

The damn rodents didn't seem to know any better. They cut around in front of him, blocking his path.

"No, no, *wrong*, kitty." This rat was a dirty brown, shiny black in the rain. His nose seemed to twitch in time to his spastic tail. He wore an abbreviated leather vest and denim cutoffs. He was taking the lead in this idiotic display. "Doncha know who we are?"

This was more than enough for Nohar. "You're two rodent wetbacks too stoned for your own good. You're future road kill if you keep this up."

The big one—well, the relatively big one, maybe 70 kilos, mostly fat—didn't like that. "We the Ziphead, man, and you better up some bucks for that. We rule here . . ."

This was nuts. These guys were Latin American cannon fodder. Honduras, Nicaragua, Cuba, Panama, all the Central American countries went for quantity and quick reproduction. Huge standing armies from zero—most of the rats were never even trained to use their weapons.

Two of those, those jokes, were trying to face down someone whose genes had gone through a multibillion dollar evolution simulation to produce the elite troops of the Indian Special Forces. Nohar had no special training, but it was still ludicrous.

He smiled, teeth and all. He couldn't take this seriously. "Ever occur to you I just made a *deposit?*"

Fearless Leader was put out. "You don't fuck with us—stray—we'll *shave* you."

"We vanish what don't give us respect—"

"*Stigmata de nada.*"

Stupid and stoned. That last line only made sense to them, and they found it uproariously funny. Nohar stepped to the side and left them to their inside joke.

"Fucking stray." Snick. Bigboy had pulled a weapon, sounded like a knife. Nohar slowly turned around. Bigboy had a switchblade out and was showing the world that he couldn't use it. It was long, pointed, and had no edge to speak of. Bigboy was swishing the thing like a baton. Wide slicing arcs that, had they connected with anything solid, might raise a welt and would probably sprain Bigboy's wrist all to hell. "Teach you some respect. I'll have your tail for a belt."

Nohar stowed the comments. He spread his legs apart and bent down, lowering his center of gravity. He thrust his left arm, claws forward, in a defensive posture, while his right arm hung back behind him, hand cupped to slice at any opening Bigboy gave him. He growled, deep in his diaphragm. The sound didn't make it out of his throat.

Bigboy was oblivious in his advance. Fearless Leader had a little more brains and hung back. Bigboy was reeking of excitement and adrenaline. Fearless was almost as jacked, but he was beginning to realize he might have bitten off more than he could chew.

Bigboy swung one of his wide, predictable arcs. Nohar caught Bigboy's wrist with his left hand, remembering Nugoya, and smiled at the rat. Nohar's right hand swung forward in a well aimed sweep that left four light trails of blood on Bigboy's overlarge gut.

"Listen, ratboy, I *could* have pulled you into that sweep. We'd have a nice view of your intestines— Drop the knife."

The knife clattered to the ground. Nohar stepped on it and let Bigboy go. Fearless was still backpedaling. Fearless didn't seem to get the point, he was still on his line of bullshit. "Your pussy bastard ass is mine."

Fearless was reaching behind, into the waistband of his cutoffs. Nohar knew instinctively that the rat was going for a gun. Nohar was about to jump Fearless— he could clear the distance easily before the rat got his hand untangled from his pants—but the action was broken by a burst of high-pitched rapid-fire Spanish from down the street, by the old bus.

They all turned that way to face a snow-white female rodent. She wore the same abbreviated leather vest and denim cutoffs. Her naked tail was writhing, and she sounded pissed. Nohar immediately pegged

her as a superior. Bigboy and Fearless seemed to forget about him and began talking back to her in Spanish
as well. All babble to him, he just hoped she was cussing the fools out.

Cat-and-mouse is not a smart game to play when
you are the mouse.

The three rodents were talking among themselves,
and Nohar began to slowly withdraw from the rodent
fiasco.

Nohar had nearly gotten to the door to his apartment. Bigboy and Fearless had slunk away, but the
white one stayed.

"Rajasthan!"

The white rat was addressing him directly. She wasn't
making any threatening moves, so Nohar stopped and
waited.

"You are a lucky cat, son of Rajasthan—"

How did she know, how could she—"What do
you—"

"I speak! You listen." The force of the rat's voice
actually made Nohar stop his question in mid-breath.
The tiny rat's body could produce a voice that would
intimidate a rabid ursine. "The finger of God has just
touched your brow, son of Rajasthan. Those that control want your life for their reasons. They buy you
much tolerance."

The rat paused, and for once Nohar had nothing to
say. She just stood there, staring at him with eyes that
looked like high-carbon steel. Nohar turned toward his
door—

"Pray you that God doesn't forget you, Nohar. If
the blessing is lifted, Zipperhead will have you."

Nohar punched the combination on his door. He had
given the rats enough of his time.

"*I'll* have you, Nohar."

As Nohar ducked inside, the white rat added, "You,
or someone you love."

He slammed the door shut. It was a shame. She
hadn't been bad-looking. Her triangular face ended in

a delicate nose—but she was a die-hard creep just like her idiot subordinates.

She also wore cheap pink perfume. Why would a morey wear that kind of crap?

Nohar had hurried away from the smell as much as the spiel. He took a few deep breaths of relatively clean air before he started up the stairwell.

The humidity was making his door stick again, and it took him a few seconds to unwedge it. The damn thing was heavier than it should have been because it had a steel plate in it, a relic of the previous tenant. Nohar would have questioned the wisdom of sticking an armored door in a wooden door frame.

Cat ran up to the door and immediately began rubbing against his foot. "So you hungry or lonely?" Nohar asked the yellow tomcat as he picked it up. A loud purr from under his hand told him to figure it out for himself. Nohar pushed the door shut with his foot and ducked into the living room. Cat started butting his head into Nohar's chin, and, after glancing into the kitchen to check Cat's dishes, Nohar decided Cat wasn't hungry.

"Sorry I took so long, I got distracted by the local color." Cat closed his eyes as Nohar scratched him behind the ears. "But, lucky us, I got one hell of an advance from a client before the first of the month."

Cat started grooming Nohar's thumb.

"Yeah, right. Look, you little missing link, I have to put you down so I can get this damn pink clothing off. So don't start mewing at me—"

Nohar put him down and Cat started mewing.

He undressed and looked at the comm. Two messages waiting now.

"Comm on," he said to the machine as he started peeling clothing off of his damp fur.

"comm on."

Nohar reclined on the couch. Cat took up a perch on his chest and purred.

"Classify. Phone messages."

"two messages. july twenty-ninth, three-oh-five p.m. from detective irwin harsk, calling from—"

"Play."

Static, then Harsk's bald black head appeared on the screen.

"Sorry I didn't catch you, Nohar." There was a smile on Harsk's face and Nohar couldn't decide if it was ironic or sarcastic. "I thought I'd tell you that another little red light is flashing by your name. The DEA computer has this 'thing' about large cash transactions. Ten thousand dollars? The Fed is curious, and so am I. We're watching you, so—on the off-chance the cash is legit—remember to withhold your income tax."

That was damn quick, even for the Fed. The DEA must have a tap on the ATM down the street. It was irritating, but not that surprising. Harsk knew he was clean, but he'd let the Fed wonder just out of a sense of perversity. The comm was asking if he had a reply.

"Yes. Record," Nohar cleared his throat, "Harsk, don't call back until you have a warrant. End. Mail. Reply."

Nohar closed his eyes and clawed the back of the couch. He told the comm to play the earlier message without really paying attention to it. He wasn't looking directly at the screen when he heard a husky female voice.

"Raj?"

"Pause!" His eyes shot open and he turned to look at Maria Limon. The call had come in close to two in the morning, during his meet with Nugoya. In the pressure of the moment, Nohar had forgotten to call Maria and cancel their date—

This wasn't the first time either. Nohar had a sinking feeling.

She was at a public phone. He could see the streetlights behind her. There was a frozen shimmer on the screen where the lights were reflecting off the black fur under her whiskers. Apparently the Brazilians had been more creative with their moreaus. She'd been crying. Nohar doubted his tear ducts could be triggered emotionally.

Maria's golden eyes, her pupils almost round, seemed to level an accusation at him.

Cat tilted his head and gave Nohar a curious look.

"Replay."

Static, then Maria's face reappeared on the screen. Nohar watched as one delicate black hand wiped away the moisture on her cheek. The hand fell and she looked directly at Nohar.

"Raj? I'm sorry about this. I should have the guts to face you, but I can't. You'd say something and we'd end up shouting at each other, or fucking each other— or, God help me, both—I can't do this anymore. I still care for you, but if we keep seeing each other, I won't—" Maria's voice broke, and more tears came. Maria was a strong person. Nohar had never seen her cry before. "Good-bye, Raj, I have to leave while the memories are still worth something to me."

Maria's face vanished as she broke the connection.

Nohar felt like someone had just kneed him in the balls, and he was feeling his stomach drop out just before the pain came.

They had known each other for only two months. It shouldn't have been a surprise. He had been expecting something like this all along. She was right.

Cat must have sensed some of his agitation, because he started butting his head against Nohar's face and licking his cheek. Cat stopped after a few seconds and regarded Nohar with his head cocked to one side. Cat's expression seemed to be asking him what was wrong.

Nohar stayed quiet for a long while before he told the computer to put the message into permanent storage. He tried to call Maria, but her comm was locking out his calls. Maria would want a clean break. He could probably talk her out of it once, maybe twice, more. She didn't want him to.

He spent a few moments in relative silence, stroking Cat and listening to the high-frequency hum of the comm.

Instead of turning the comm off, he called up Maria's message, and paused it. He paused it where the claw on the index finger of her right hand had caught a tear. The small sphere of liquid was nestled between the hook in her claw and the pad on her finger. It refracted the unnatural white of the streetlight behind her, causing arcs of light to emerge from one golden half-lidded eye. It was the kind of image that made Nohar wish he had a scrap of romance in his soul.

CHAPTER 4

After a while, Nohar decided he had better things to do than stare at Maria.

"Load program. Label, 'Log-on library.' "

"searching . . . found."

"Run program."

Maria's face disappeared as the computer started the access sequence. It showed the blue-and-white AT&T test pattern as it repeatedly buzzed the public library database, waiting for an open data channel. It was close to prime time for library access. It took nearly fifteen minutes for the comm to lock onto the library's mainframe.

Even when the Cleveland Public Library logo came up, there were a few minutes of waiting. The screen scrolled messages about fighting illiteracy, and how he should spend his summer reading a book. Nohar knew that a few thousand users on a clunky time-sharing system at the same time tended to slow things down, but it still seemed the delay was directed at him.

He shifted on the couch, trying to become more comfortable. Waiting always made him aware of his tail.

Two minutes passed. Then, with a little electronic fanfare, the menu came up—though you couldn't quite call the animated figure a "menu." The library system called their animated characters "guides." The software was trying too hard to be friendly. It verged on the cute.

The "guide" facing him on the screen wore a sword

strapped to his side, and was in the process of contemplating a human skull when he seemed to notice Nohar's intrusion. The effect was spoiled by a glitch in the animation. A rolling blue line scrolled up and down the screen, shifting everything above it a pixel to the left. Nohar sighed. He had no desire to spend his time with a manic-depressive Dane. Especially after that call from Maria.

He spoke before the prince had time to object. "Text menu."

The only library "guide" he liked was the little blonde human girl, Alice.

The text menu came up and the first thing he did, despite Smith's admonition to start with Johnson, was to conduct a global search for information on Midwest Lapidary Imports. He wanted some sort of handle on his client's employer, which was also the home of the alleged suspects.

There was only a fifteen second pause.

The computer came back with the report, "Three items found."

Nohar shook his head. Only three? With a *global* search? That meant there were only three items in the entire library data base that even mentioned MLI.

Nohar played the first item and got a newsfax about diamond imports, legal and illegal. The focus on the article was how hard it was to keep track of the gems. It had a graph that dramatized the divergence between the gems known to have come into the country, and those known to be in circulation. In the last fifteen years, a hell of a lot more gems had been in circulation than could be accounted for. It was, in fact, causing a depression in the diamond market. The article blamed the Fed and new smuggling techniques. The least likely smuggling method Nohar read about was casting the diamonds in the heat-tiles on the exterior of a ballistic shuttle. Midwest Lapidary was only mentioned peripherally in a list of domestic diamond-related companies at the end of the article.

The second article was actually *about* MLI, but it was only barely informative. It was from some subscriber service and was just a sparse paragraph of electronic text. MLI, a new company, incorporated in 2038. Wholesale diamond sales. Headquartered in Cleveland. Privately owned. Address. That was it. Smith was right about these guys keeping a low profile. Nohar pictured most new corporate enterprises announcing themselves with trumpets and splashy media campaigns. It looked like MLI was trying to hide the fact it even existed.

The third item was a vid broadcast from December 2, 2043. The broadcast was dated. The guy with the news was still following journalistic fashion from the riots. Grimy safari jacket, urban camo pants, three-day-old stubble, sunglasses. The outfit had nothing to do with the story. The guy was standing in a snowdrift outside a pair of low office buildings faced in blue tile. Nohar recognized a stretch of Mayfield Road behind the buildings. The guy was only a few miles to the east of Moreytown.

Hmm, Nohar thought there was a prison there.

The guy was trying very hard to have the voice of authority. "I am standing outside the offices and the laboratory of NuFood Incorporated. Today, came the surprising announcement that NuFood had been bought by a local diamond wholesaler, Midwest Lapidary. There had been speculation that NuFood had been on the verge of bankruptcy when it sold its assets and patents to Midwest Lapidary for an undisclosed amount. Shortly after the sale, NuFood's two hundred employees were laid off in what Midwest Lapidary called in a press release, 'a streamlining measure.'

"NuFood, you may recall from a Special Health Report earlier this year, is the company with patents on the dietary supplement, MirrorProtein. While NuFood has had success creating synthetic food-products resembling natural items, which the human body cannot process, it has had continuing problems with the FDA

in getting its products approved. Sources say this created the financial difficulty that led directly to the sale
of the company. No one from Midwest Lapidary could
be reached for comment.''

That was a big help.

So Smith was right. He needed to start with Johnson
and work back. Johnson was Binder's campaign manager, so Nohar did a global search using both his name
and Binder's.

The pause was closer to a full minute this time. His
tail fell asleep. Nohar stood up to massage the base of
his tail. Cat took the opportunity to jump up on the
couch and snuggle into the warm dent in the cushions.

The screen flashed the results of the search. Over
six thousand items, more like it. No way he could
peruse all of it on-line, so he slipped in a ramcard and
downloaded the whole mess of data. He leeched nearly
fifteen megs in half that many minutes.

He now had his own little database on Binder and
his campaign.

By five, his examination of the public information
on Binder gave him no reason to alter his first impression of the guy as a right-wing reactionary bastard. It
seemed Binder had something bad to say about every
group or organization that didn't count him as a member; women, foreigners, liberals, intellectuals, blacks
and hispanics, Catholics, the poor, the homeless, por-
nographers, the news media—the list was endless. Despite the vitriol that coated every word the man uttered,
three groups in particular gained his very special attention. In order of the invective he threw upon them,
they were: moreaus, franks, and all their genetically-
engineered ilk, whose rights he was actively involved
in trying to repeal; homosexuals, whose sexual pref-
erence Binder seemed to rank primary in his personal
list of mortal sins; and the U.S. federal government—
the only place Binder and Nohar seemed to touch common ground—whose propensity for spending money

was only equaled by Binder's impulse to slash any spending program he could lay his hands on.

Nohar found it hard to believe he was investigating the murder of this guy's campaign manager.

The data on Daryl Johnson was more scattered. Nohar couldn't get a fix on his beliefs. All he got was the fact that Johnson was loyal to Binder and had been with the congressman since the state legislature. He had been recruited out of Bowling Green in the autumn of 2040. The same time as most of Binder's inner circle. Johnson's three classmates were: Edwin Harrison, the campaign's legal counsel; Philip Young, the campaign finance chairman; and Desmond Thomson, the campaign press secretary. Johnson graduated at the age of twenty-three, late. Apparently because of a shift in his major, from chemistry to political science. A bit of a jump. That would make him the ripe old age of thirty-nine when he died.

Not so ripe, Nohar corrected himself. This guy was human, so thirty-nine was barely on the threshold of middle age. Thirty-nine was better than the life expectancy of some moreys.

He was a little more familiar with the situation he was dealing with. That was all. His client wanted to find out if MLI was behind the Johnson killing. So far, he didn't have any connection between the two, other than Smith's assertion that the missing three megabucks came from MLI.

Time to start making some calls. Thomson looked like a good choice. The press secretary would be used to talking to people, if not actually to saying anything.

If he was going to talk to a pink, he'd better put some clothes on. He snorted. Clothes were a needless irritation that wouldn't have been necessary on a morey case. Getting dressed, just to make a phone call, was just plain silly.

He pulled a button-down shirt from a small pile in the corner of his bedroom. The storm had reduced the light in the apartment, so Nohar couldn't quite make out the color of the shirt. It was either a very light blue, or a very off white. Nohar put it on, claws catching on the buttons, and decided to forgo the pants. The comm was only going to show him from the waist up, as long as he didn't stand up.

He ducked into the bathroom and looked in the mirror. Pointless, really. What did a pink know about grooming anyway? Still, Nohar licked the back of his hand and ran it over his head a few times, smoothing things out.

After that, he sat on the couch, shooing Cat away. He set the comm to record and told it to call Desmond Thomson at Binder campaign headquarters. He routed the call through the comm at his office so his credentials would be shown up front.

Oddly enough, though it was only a little after five, no one at Binder headquarters seemed to be answering. After nearly a minute of displaying the Binder Senate campaign logo, the comm at Binder headquarters forwarded his call to Thomson's home. Nohar shrugged. It didn't matter as long as he got through to Thomson.

Thomson surprised the hell out of him by being black. In fact, Thomson had been the bearded pink that had tricked Nohar's eyes into seeing a morey in the crowd at the funeral. Thomson's hair and beard were shot with gray. He had the bearing of a pro wrestler and the voice of a vid anchorman. "Mister," Thomson's gaze flicked to the text on his monitor, "Rajasthan?" Thomson's voice had begun on a high note, indicating some surprise at Nohar's appearance. However, by the end of Nohar's name, the tone of Thomson's voice had become smooth, friendly, and utterly phony.

"Yes. Mr. Thomson?"

"I am. I see your call has been forwarded from our campaign headquarters. I presume you wish to talk to me in my capacity as Congressman Binder's press secretary?"

The man talked like a press release, and Nohar couldn't get over the fact that Thomson was black. It made about as much sense as having a Jewish spokesman for the Islamic Axis. Nohar nodded.

"I would like to ask about your late campaign manager—"

"Of course. I'll help as much as possible. We've been quite free with what we know about the tragedy. However, things are quite chaotic in the organization with the loss of Mr. Johnson. We've had to give the whole campaign the week off so we can sort out the mess. So my time is limited. I'm sure what you need has already been told to the police or the press."

Nohar could smell a brush-off coming from a mile away. "I only have a few questions. They won't take long."

"Would you mind transmitting your credentials?"

Either Thomson didn't trust the label from Nohar's office comm, or he was politely looking for an excuse to hang up. Fortunately, Nohar's wallet with his PI licence was sitting on top of the comm and he didn't have to stand up to get it. He slid his license into the fax slot on his comm and hit the send button. Thomson nodded when he saw the results. "I can give you ten minutes."

At the length this guy spoke, that wouldn't give Nohar much. "When did Johnson die?"

"I am given to understand the time of death was placed sometime in the middle of the week of the twentieth—"

"July twentieth?"

"Of course."

"When was the last official contact with Johnson?"

"As we have informed the police, he attended a political fund-raiser Saturday the nineteenth. He didn't come in to work the following week—"

"Didn't this strike anyone as odd?"

Thomson was undoubtedly irritated by Nohar's interruptions, but he hid it well. "No, it is an election year. It's common for executive officers to be pulled away from the desk for trips, speeches, press, and so on. Johnson was the chief executive under Binder, he often did such things on his own initiative—''

''Do you know what he was doing?''

''No. If it wasn't dealing with the media, it was not my department. Now, if you don't mind, the time—''

It didn't feel like ten minutes to Nohar. ''One more thing.''

Nohar thought he heard Thomson sigh. ''What?''

''About the three million dollars the police believe was stolen from the campaign—''

Thomson interrupted this time. ''I am sorry, but I do not have the authority to discuss the financial details of the campaign.''

Ah, Nohar had finally run into the brick wall. ''I am sorry to hear that. You see, I have conflicting information. I simply want to know if the three million was physically in Johnson's possession, in cash—''

''I said, I can't discuss it.''

Try another tack. ''Who has access to the campaign's financial records?''

Thomson was shaking his head. He even grinned a bit, showing a gold tooth that had to be decorative. ''Me, the legal counsel, the campaign manager and his executive assistant, and the finance chairman, of course.''

''Thank you.''

Thomson chuckled. ''I'm afraid they can't help you. No one but Binder has the authority to release confidential financial data. Except, of course, disclosures required by law.''

''Or a subpoena,'' Nohar muttered.

''I would call that a disclosure required by law. Now, as I said before, my time is limited. I really must go.''

''Thanks for your help,'' Nohar said, nearly choking on the insincerity.

''You're welcome. It's my job,'' Thomson replied, just as insincere, but much more professional.

The line was cut and Nohar was left staring at a test pattern.

Nohar ran through the record of the conversation a few times. It irritated him that Thomson was right. Nothing was in the conversation he wouldn't be able to get from the police record or the news. Reviewing the tape didn't tell Nohar anything more, other than the fact Thomson lived in a ritzy penthouse overlooking downtown—Thomson's home comm faced a window.

The comm told him it was fifteen after. It was time to call Manny down at the pathologist's office. Nohar wanted to set up a meeting for tonight. One he hoped would be more fruitful.

CHAPTER 5

During the night, the rain turned into a deluge. Nohar didn't feel half as uncomfortable under the sudden thunderstorm as he had in the misting drizzle in the cemetery. The dark violence of it suited him.

Coventry suited him.

The three block area was a ragged collection of bars close to the East Cleveland border. It was far enough away from the heart of Moreytown to see the occasional pink in the area. As always, there were two patrol cars, the riot watch, one on either end of the strip. Nohar passed one of them at the intersection of Coventry and Mayfield, and, while it was too far for him to see it, he knew its twin was parked in the old school parking lot, three blocks away.

Like Nohar's neighborhood, Coventry was blocked off from car traffic by three-meter-tall concrete pylons left over from the riots. Graffiti wrapped around the rectangular blocks, as if the strip were trying to escape its arbitrary confines by oozing through the gaps.

The rain hadn't slowed things down. Ten-thirty at night and the street was packed with the backwash of Moreytown. The downpour couldn't remove the omnipresent smell of damp fur.

Nohar made his way down the center of the old asphalt strip. He passed canines, felines, a knot of rodents in leather vests and denim briefs—he avoided the slight scent of familiar perfume—an unfamiliar ursine, a loud lepus shouting at a rapt vulpine congregation. The people around him only made the briefest impression. A few shouted greetings. Nohar waved without quite noticing who they had been.

His destination, *Watership Down,* was one of the few bars on the Coventry strip that was actually owned and operated by a morey proprietor—Gerard Lopez, a lepus. The reason Nohar chose to frequent this particular bar, out of the two dozen on the strip, was the high ceiling. This was one of the few places he could get fully toasted and not end up bashing his head into a ceiling fan or a light fixture.

Nohar entered the bar, shook some of the rain out of his coat, and took his regular seat, a booth in the back that had the seats moved back for people his size. The table was directly underneath a garish framed picture someone had once told him was an original Warner Brothers' animation cell. It was a hand drawn cartoon of a gray bipedal rabbit in the process of blowing up a bald, round-headed, human. Lopez had mounted a little brass plaque under the picture. It said, "1946—Off the Pink." Even if it was a joke, Nohar was glad that most humans didn't come down to Coventry.

Manny was waiting at the bar. He bore down on Nohar's booth carrying two pitchers of beer. Alert black eyes glanced over Nohar as the quick little mongoose put the pitcher on the table. "Nohar, you look like hell."

Nohar's mind had drifted off the case and on to Maria. He was at once irritated and defensive. Manny was the only real family Nohar had. The mongoose had come to America with Nohar's parents, and had been there when Nohar's mother had died. When he was younger, Nohar had resented him. It was still hard for Nohar to accept Manny's concern with good grace.

It had taken finding his real father to allow Nohar to appreciate Manny.

"Maria dumped me." Nohar poured himself a beer and downed it.

Manny slid into the opposite side of the booth and

chittered a little in sympathy. "That's hard to believe. After the last time I saw you two together, it looked like you finally found the right one."

"I thought so myself. Always do."

"Do you want to talk about it?"

"I want to talk to an M.E., not a psychiatrist."

Manny gave his head a shake and poured himself a beer. "Are you sure you want to talk business right now?"

Nohar glared down at Manny. "I didn't ask you to meet me for a counseling session." Nohar reined in the outburst. "Sorry. Been a tough day. Did you bring the database?"

Unlike Nohar, Manny couldn't form a smile, but between them a nose-twitch on Manny's part served the same purpose. Manny took a notebook-sized case and put it on the table and flipped up the cover. There was a pause as it warmed up.

"What happened to your wallet computer?"

Manny gave a brief shrug. His voice held a tone of resignation. "The Jap chip blew. It was a prewar model, so the county couldn't replace it. So, I got this new bug-ridden Tunja 1200. Soon we're going to be back to manual typewriters and paper records . . ."

Manny's head shook, accompanied by a high-pitched sigh. In a few seconds, the screen began to glow faintly and the keypad became visible. "I updated it from the mainframe after you called. Do you have a name for the stiff you're looking for?"

Nohar poured himself another beer. "Yes, but this isn't a normal case—"

"But you want records for a stiff, right?"

"The name's Daryl Johnson."

Manny's whole upper body undulated with a momentary shrug. "Off hand, I don't remember that name. What species?"

"Human."

Manny froze; the sudden absence of motion was eerie on the mongoose. "What?"

"I need the complete forensic record on the murder of a man named Daryl Johnson."

"What the *hell?*"

Nohar could see him tense up. He could almost see the vibration in Manny's small frame. Nohar could smell Manny's nervousness even over the smell of the beer. "You *can* access those records?"

"Nohar, you said *human*, you said *murder*."

"I said it wasn't a normal case."

Manny was silent. His black eyes darted from Nohar to his little portable computer and back. Nohar was a little surprised at his reaction. They'd worked together and had shared information ever since Nohar had gotten his license.

But then, until now, it had simply consisted of Nohar making sure the moreys he'd been hired to find hadn't ended up in the morgue.

After nearly a full minute of silence, Manny finally spoke. "Nohar, I've known you all your life. You don't ask for trouble anymore. You've never interfered with a police investigation. You've *never* messed with pink business."

"You slipped, you said the 'p' word." Nohar regretted it the instant he said it. Manny had to work with humans. He was one of perhaps a half-dozen moreaus in the city with medical training, and they would only let him cut up corpses. Only morey corpses at that. Manny was always open to the accusation of selling out, being pink under his fur. Nohar just rubbed Manny's nose in it.

"Forgive me if I don't want to see you mixed up in something that might hurt you."

"Sorry. It's just a case. An important one. I'm trying to find out who killed him."

Manny closed his eyes. His voice picked up speed. "You are trying to find out who murdered a human? You know what'd happen if word got on the street? You know what happens to moreys that get too close to humans—"

"I still need your help."

Manny made an effort to slow down. "I'm not going to change your mind, am I? I'll call up the file, but first—" One of Manny's too-long hands clasped Nohar's wrist. "Remember, my place is as far from Moreytown as you can get."

Nohar nodded.

Manny held Nohar's gaze for a brief moment. Then Manny looked down at his computer and started rapid-fire tapping on the screen. For a terminal with no audio, Manny handled it very efficiently. His hands were engineered for surgery, and their gracefulness permeated every gesture.

He did, however, have to hit the thing a few times to get it to work right.

Manny's nose twitched. "I don't believe it. The file's inactive. It's barely a week old."

"The police are under pressure to drop the investigation."

Manny looked like he was about to say something, but apparently thought better of it. "Fine, well, we have the autopsy report, list of the forensic evidence, abstract of the scene of the crime, a few preliminary statements from the neighbors, as well as the witness who found the body, etcetera. Pretty complete record. Compared to most I've seen."

One of Manny's lithe hands dove into a breast pocket and pulled out a ramcard and slid it into the side of the computer. Nohar briefly saw the rainbow sheen of the card reflected in a small puddle of beer on the table. "I'm running off a copy. Do me a favor and make a backup. Occasionally they *do* monitor access to the database."

Nohar nodded when Manny handed him the card. Nohar slipped it into his wallet, next to the as yet unexamined card from his camera, the pictures from Johnson's funeral. "Could you tell me how Johnson died?"

"It's all on the card I gave you. He was shot in the

head. Through his picture window. Splattered his brains all over his comm—oh, *that's* interesting . . .''

"What?"

There was the hint of what might have been admiration in Manny's voice. "Are you familiar with Israeli weaponry? Thought not. The forensics team found the remains of two bullets, from a Levitt Mark II, fifty-caliber." A slight whistle of air came from between Manny's front teeth.

"So?"

"Came out of Mossad during the Third Gulf War. It was designed for a single sniper, and, like most designs they came up with, it's made to keep the sniper alive. The bullets are propelled by compressed carbon dioxide. It can't be heard firing by anyone farther away than fifteen meters or so. The ammunition is made from an impact-sensitive plastic explosive impregnated with shrapnel. It's intended as an antipersonnel weapon. I haven't seen an impact wound from one of these since the war. The Afghanis favored them for night raids—Nohar, what the hell have you gotten yourself into?"

"I don't know."

Nohar knew Manny was tempted to try and talk him out of it. However, Manny wouldn't try. Nohar hated when Manny got into surrogate-father mode, and Manny was too aware of that fact.

Such meetings usually ended with them spending a few hours discussing innocent bullshit over too many beers. This time they finished the pitchers in relative silence. Nohar wanted to reassure Manny he wasn't in over his head. But it would have been a lie. Nohar had trouble with lies, especially with Manny.

So, at eleven-fifteen—an early night for them—they walked to the south end of the strip, and the lot where Manny had parked. The rain had intensified, finally chasing the moreys inside. The abandoned trash-strewn asphalt reminded Nohar of pictures of the Pan-Asian war. It was the view of a city waiting for a biological warhead.

They rounded the pylons on Euclid Heights Boulevard and Nohar caught sight of the other cop on the riot-watch. Nohar wondered what it would be like, to come to work each day, to sit and wait for something to explode. The cops would have to be on rotation. Someone on permanent assignment would go nuts.

The cop looked at them as they passed, two unequal-sized moreys huddling through the rain. There was a flash of lightning, and Nohar saw the cop's face. The pink looked scared. In that instant he saw a man, a kid really, no more than twenty-two—young for a human that was, most moreys who made it into their twenties were well into middle age. The pink kid would have no idea what he would do if Nohar and Manny decided to do something illegal. He could imagine he sensed the smell of fear off of the kid, even with the car and the rain between them.

They passed the police car and walked into the parking lot of the old school. Nohar couldn't help but feel sorry for the cop. No one deserved to be placed in that kind of situation unprepared.

They stopped at the van and Manny spoke for the first time since they'd left the bar. "I can't talk you out of this, but my door's open if you need it."

"I know." Nohar was uncomfortably reminded of last night.

Nohar told himself that there was no reason to except things on this case to go bad like that. Hell, he'd been paid a hell of a lot up front, things *couldn't* go that badly this time.

At least it didn't look like he was going to be stiffed again.

Manny got into his van, another Electroline. In the dark of the storm, away from the streetlights, the van reminded Nohar of the frank in the graveyard. Both vans were the same industrial-green, the same boxy make, and had the same pneumatic doors on the back.

The only difference—Manny's van had a driver's cab and "Cuyahoga County Medical Examiner" painted on all the doors.

As Manny drove back toward downtown, Nohar supposed the van's markings had a deterrent effect on car thieves.

"I said, a *fifteen* by *fifteen* grid with times *three* magnification!"

"instructions unclear."

Nohar almost shouted something back at the comm. Instead, he took a deep breath and stroked Cat a few times. *There are few things,* he thought, *more fruitless than getting angry at a machine.* Shouting at it was just going to overtax the translation software.

"Display. Photo thirty-five. Grid. Fifteen by fifteen. Magnification. Times three."

This time the comm did as it was told.

Photo number thirty-five was a good, panoramic shot of the seated parties at Johnson's funeral. It was the one picture that had a full facial on everybody. The haze had helped by diffusing the July sun. The indirect lighting eliminated stark shadows, and would help in making the attendees, especially those to the rear, under the tent.

He had enlarged it enough. Most of the faces were clear, which was good. Nohar did not want to wait half an hour while his cheap software enhanced the picture.

Now for the grunt work. "Move. Grid. Left five percent."

One box on the grid now enclosed a face.

He told the program to print it and a portrait of a funeral attendee started sliding out of the comm's fax slot. One down, forty-nine to go.

Nohar spent two hours getting identifiable portraits from the one picture. Most of them, he knew, would offer no useful information. However, the procedure calmed him. It was something he had done hundreds of times before.

The routine was so automatic that his mind kept traveling back to Johnson's murder.

According to the autopsy, the time of death was somewhere between 9:30 p.m. on Tuesday the twenty-second, and 10:30 a.m. on Wednesday the twenty-third. The body was discovered by a jogger who noticed the broken window around noon on the twenty-fifth. There was a violent thunderstorm Thursday night, washing away a good deal of evidence. Presumably, this was why no evidence was found of the party or parties who allegedly stole the three million the campaign finance records said should have been there. Well, that wasn't quite right. The police *thought* the finance records said the three million was there. However, before the cops folded, they only had a brief perusal of the campaign finances over the weekend. Apparently the records never left Binder's headquarters.

The autopsy also said Daryl had been having a good time before someone slammed a mini-grenade into the back of his head. Nohar read at the time of death Daryl had a good point-oh-two blood alcohol, traces of weasel-dust in his nose, as well as a few 'dorphs lying undigested in his stomach. To top it off, he'd shot his wad into somebody in the twelve hours previous.

Seems he died happy.

Nohar pictured him at the comm, riding his buzz, watching some party film or other, air-conditioning going full blast. Daryl might be giggling a bit. Then the sniper takes up his position. The sniper is hiding somewhere. The ballistic evidence gave an approximate trajectory giving a field of fire at the back of Johnson's head. Five houses across the street fit the bill, all occupied, no witnesses. Perhaps the sniper uses a driveway between those houses across the street.

It's night, to give the sniper cover. Night makes sense. Daryl's been partying. The sniper knows the alarm is off because Daryl is home. He can see Daryl through the sight. The sniper aims at Daryl's head, which might be bobbing to the beat from the comm. The sniper squeezes off a shot. The shot explodes, vaporizing the picture window.

The sniper squeezes off shot number two.

Daryl is sitting in the study, facing his comm, when his head gets blown away by the second exploding projectile belonging to the sniper's Levitt Mark II. It hits six centimeters from the base of the skull—dead center, according to the autopsy.

It hits from behind him, through the picture window in the living room, through the dining room, and through the open door to the study.

The cops found remains of two Levitt bullets. One set in Daryl's head. The other set by the picture window.

There was a problem with this sequence of events.

It was those two words, "dead center."

Daryl Johnson should have turned to see what the noise was.

For Nohar, that was a big problem. Daryl was shot in the back of the head. Nohar couldn't see someone so jazzed-up he'd be oblivious to twenty square meters of glass *exploding* directly behind him—now that he thought about it, the whole damn neighborhood was oblivious. What the autopsy listed shouldn't have zoned Daryl out that bad. Even a reflexive jerk toward the noise, no matter how fast the sniper got the second round off, would have put the shell toward one side of the head or the other.

Also, what was a nine-to-five working stiff doing that jazzed in the middle of the week? Given the time of death, Daryl was doing some heavy partying for a Tuesday.

Finally, even in Shaker Heights, a house standing open like that, two or three days without the alarm or a window, and nothing *else* was ripped off? That didn't ring true.

The final portrait ejected from the printer.

Nohar stretched and got to his feet. His throat hurt from all the commands. Someday he was going to have to fix the keyboard. Despite the overstuffed cushions on the couch, his tail had fallen asleep again.

Nohar rubbed his throat and decided he needed a beer. He ducked into the kitchen. As he ripped the last bulb of beer from its envelope, he realized how hungry he was. The only food in the fridge was a plate of bones, and the last kilo of hamburger. Nohar only briefly considered the beef bones, even though a few looked fairly meaty. He grabbed the lump of hamburger and tossed it into the micro as he snapped the top off his bulb.

The cold brew soothed the raw feeling at the back of his throat, leaving a yeasty taste in his mouth. One of the few decent things the pinks did with grain was turn it into booze.

Outside the dirty little kitchen window, the storm was worsening. The thunder rattled the glass in its loose molding.

Nohar drank as he watched the lightning through hazy glass and rippling sheets of water. If Smith was right, and there never was any three million, why was Johnson killed? What was Johnson doing Tuesday night? Why didn't Johnson, or anyone else, respond to the shattering picture window—

Ding, the burger was warm. Nohar dropped the empty bulb into the disposal and washed his hands in the sink. He pulled the meat out of the micro, and spent a few seconds finding a clean plate. The hamburger leaked all over the plate as soon as he began unwrapping it. The blood-smell of the warm meat wafted to Nohar and *really* reminded him of how hungry he was. He ripped out a red, golfball-sized chunk from the heart of the burger and popped it into his mouth, licking the ferric taste from his claws.

Another thing the pinks did well, picking their domestic prey animals.

Cat was suddenly wide awake, mewing, and rubbing against Nohar's leg. Nohar flicked a small gobbet of hamburger toward the other end of the kitchen. Cat went after it.

Nohar ate, standing at the counter by the sink, looking out the window, thinking about Daryl Johnson. Occasionally he flung another chunk of meat away, to keep Cat from distracting him.

CHAPTER 6

The rain broke Thursday morning and the sun came out.

Nohar barely noticed. He spent a few hours attaching names to the faces he had excised from the funeral picture. The only real interesting aspect of that drudgery was the fact that Philip Young, the finance chairman, had not attended the funeral.

He spent wasted effort trying to get a hold of Young. He tracked down an address and a comm number, but Young wasn't answering his comm. Neither was his computer, which was irritating. He called Harrison, but the legal counsel's comm was actually locking out Nohar's calls.

Nohar had never talked to the lawyer before.

Thomson's comm was also locking out Nohar's calls.

That left Binder. Nohar knew *that* would be hopeless. He tried anyway, going as far as calling Washington long-distance. The guy manning the phones was polite, condescending, and totally useless. Binder was somewhere in Columbus, raising money and campaigning, and the only way to talk to him would be to have a press pass or a large check.

Nohar didn't know if it was because he was a morey, a PI, or because they were hiding something. Nohar would lay odds on all three.

No need to be frustrated yet, Nohar told himself. There were a lot more people employed by Binder than the executive officers. Someone out there knew Johnson, and would hand him a lead.

He scanned through the items he had downloaded from the library yesterday. He was looking for a likely subject to hit. Predictably, the picture that caught his eye was a photo-op at a fund-raiser.

Behind Binder, with the upper crust of his campaign machine, there was an extra player.

Nohar leaned forward on the couch. "Magnification. Times five."

The picture zoomed at him. The resolution was excessively grainy, but he could see the extra person in the gang of four. To Binder's right were Thomson and Harrison, to his left were Young and Johnson—and Johnson's executive assistant. Johnson's assistant happened to be a woman. The picture implied a lot about them.

Nohar ran a search through his Binder data base with her name, Stephanie Weir. Every time the software found something with Weir in it, there was Johnson. They seemed inseparable.

Now, here was someone who'd know about Johnson. But would she talk to him?

He almost called her. However, when he thought it through, he realized this wasn't going to be one of those cases he could run from the comm. He had already seen how easy it was for the pinks to shut him out over the phone. He was at enough of a disadvantage as it was. He'd do this in person.

He should wear his suit for this. He hated it with a passion, but he was going out to the pinks' own territory. They had their own rules. He opened the one closet and took out the huge black jacket and the matching pants. He hesitated for a moment.

Maria wasn't here, but he could smell her tangy musk.

Nohar snatched shirt, tie, and shoes, and slammed the door shut. The memories didn't stay in the closet. He did his best to ignore them as he dressed. The relationship was over. It was only going to be a matter of time before he found one of her tops. She always left them here in hot weather.

He was still thinking about her by the time he got to the tie. The difficult ritual of getting the black strip of cloth properly wrapped around his neck was a welcome distraction. While he did so, he tried to force his mind off of Maria and on to Weir.

Nohar left the apartment comparing Maria's black jaguar fur to the long raven hair Stephanie Weir had in her pictures.

He had to walk three blocks to his car, because of the traffic restrictions. It was parked outside his office—actually a glorified mail drop—on the city end of Mayfield Road. It was a dusty-yellow Ford Jerboa convertible. Nohar wished someone would steal it. It was too old, too cheap, and for Nohar, too small. He could fit in the little thing, but the '28 Jerboa had a power plant that could barely push around its own two tons with Nohar on board.

He unplugged the car from the curb feed and tapped the combination on the passenger-side door, the one that worked. With the door open and the top down, he stepped over the passenger seat. Nohar eased himself behind the wheel, slipped some morey reggae into the cardplayer, and pulled away from the curb.

Shaker Heights was a different world. It was only separated from Moreytown by a sparse strip of middle-class pink suburbia. It could have been on the other side of the city. Driving into Shaker required some effort, since most of the direct routes were blocked off by familiar concrete pylons. In keeping with the neighborhood, these barriers were faced with brick and sat amidst vines, bushes, and tiny well-kept lawns. Nohar actually had to drive into Cleveland proper before he could weave his way into Shaker.

He expected to be stopped by the cops at least once, but he wasn't. Could be the suit. It didn't lessen the tension he felt. The roads were smooth and lined with trees. Not a morey in sight. The cozy one-family dwellings stared at him from behind manicured lawns.

Stephanie Weir lived in one of those intimidating brick houses.

Nohar pulled the Jerboa up to the curb in front of her house. Brick, one family, seven rooms, a century old or so. It was the kind of building that reminded Nohar how young his species was.

Come on, he told himself, *a few questions, nothing major.*

After saying that to himself a few times, he climbed out of the car and stretched. Before he realized what he was doing, he had reached up and started clawing the bark from the tree next to his car. No matter how good it felt, when he noticed himself doing it, he stopped. He hoped the Weir woman hadn't seen. It was embarrassing.

He shook loose bark from his fingers and walked up to the house. He pushed the call button next to the door and waited for an answer.

A speaker near his hand buzzed briefly, then spoke. "Damn, just a minute."

There was a very long pause. "Who do we have here?"

Nohar tried to find the camera. "My name's Nohar Rajasthan. I'm a private investigator. I'd like to talk to a Ms. Stephanie Weir."

Another long pause. "Well, you got her. You have any ID?"

Nohar fished into his wallet and held up his PI license.

"Stick that into the slot."

A small panel under the call button slid aside. Nohar tossed it in.

Nohar stood and waited. He was tempted to push the call button again. But, without warning, the door was thrust open. Nohar had to suppress an urge to leap back. Weir offered his license back. "What can I help you with, Mr. Rajasthan?"

Pronounced it right her first try. Nohar was relieved, and a little puzzled, not to smell any fear. He was also grateful Weir didn't wear any strong perfume. She had an odd smile on her face and he wished he was better at reading human expressions. "I'd like to talk about Daryl Johnson."

Weir bit her lip. "Complicated subject. You better come in."

Nohar watched her walk away from the door before ducking in and closing it behind him. He could stand in the living room and not feel cramped. He wondered what she did with all the space. A comm was playing in the background. He recognized the voice from his research, ex-mayor Russell Gardner, Binder's opponent.

". . . is in a crisis. Our technological infrastructure was fatally wounded when Japan was invaded, as surely as if the Chinese had landed in California. For nearly a decade my opponent has been leading a policy of government inaction. For twenty years our quality of living has been degrading. There are fewer engineers in the United States now than there were at the turn of the century—"

"Sit down." She motioned toward a beige love seat that looked like it could hold him. "I was just about to fix myself a drink. Want one?"

Nohar sat on the love seat and wriggled to get his tail into a comfortable position. "Anything cold, please."

Gardner went on as if he had found a new issue. ". . . space program as an example. It's been four decades since a government program—a program since disbanded for lack of funding—discovered signals that are still widely believed, in the scientific community, to be an artifact of extraterrestrial intelligence. NASA's nuclear rockets have been sitting on the moon ten years, waiting for the launch and we are losing the ability to maintain them. We've lost the ability to maintain cutting edge tech . . ."

Nohar wasn't interested in the political tirade. Instead of listening, he wondered why the pink female was acting so—relaxed wasn't quite the word he was looking for.

Weir walked into the kitchen and Nohar's gaze followed her. He enjoyed the way she moved. No abrupt motions, every move flowed into every other seamlessly. He watched as she stretched to get a glass from a cabinet. The smooth line of muscle in her arm melded into a gentle ripple down her back, became a descending curve toward the back of her knee, and ended in the abrupt bump of her calf.

She said something, and Nohar asked himself what he'd been thinking about.

"What did you say?"

Weir apparently assumed the comm was too loud. She called out, "Pause." Gardner shut up. "I said I've been waiting for you to mention it."

Nohar felt lost. "Mention what?"

She returned with two tumblers and handed one to him. He couldn't read the half-smile on her face. "Well, I'd picture a detective jumping all over me for not being more broken up about Derry."

"I was just trying to be tactful." That was a lie. The fact was, Nohar had been so nervous he hadn't even noticed. He took a drink, hoping it was something strong. It turned out to be some soft drink whose carbonation overwhelmed any taste it might have had. At least it was cold.

"I guess I'm not used to tact." She sat down in an easy chair across from him. He could identify her natural smell now, somewhere between rose and wood smoke. He liked it. "So, let's talk about Derry."

Nohar took another long pull from the glass. It did little for him but give him a chance to think. "Could you describe your relationship with him?"

"We weren't that close. At least, not as close as it was supposed to look. I suppose you've gotten the intended message from all the photo-ops and the social events. All window dressing, really.''

''Meaning?''

''Just what I said. It was supposed to look like Derry was hot for me when he could really care less about women. It was all an elaborate game. I was supposed to cover up one of Binder's political liabilities.'' *Now* Nohar could read her expression. The hard edge in her voice helped.

''Daryl Johnson was gay?''

She nodded. ''I got recruited by the Binder campaign right out of Case. Major in statistics, minor in political science. So I can go to parties and look cute. All because Binder is too loyal to fire his chosen, and is too right-wing to accept a homosexual on his staff. Publicly anyway.''

That was amazing, even though he had some idea how extreme Binder was. ''That attitude's bizarre.'' He had to restrain himself from adding, ''Even for a pink.''

''You don't know the man.''

''You put up with that?''

That brought a weak smile. ''Selling out your principles pays a great deal of money, Mr. Rajasthan. Until he died, anyway.''

She noticed they both had empty glasses. She got up. ''Can I get you a refill? Something a little stronger this time?''

Nohar nodded. ''Please—''

He didn't like questioning good fortune, but he was beginning to wonder why she was so open with him. ''What was playing on the comm?''

''One of Gardner's speeches. Sort of self-flagellation.''

Odd way to put it. ''Are you still *with* the Binder organization?''

She stopped on the way to the kitchen and shook her head. ''Binder's legendary loyalty doesn't apply to the window dressing. After all I put up with—you know, someone even started a rumor I was a lesbian.''

"Are you?"

Weir's knuckles whitened on her glass. Nohar thought she might throw it at him. The smell Nohar was sensing was powerful now, but it was more akin to fear and confusion than anger. The episode was brief. She quickly composed herself. "I'd really rather not talk about that right now."

Nohar wondered what he'd stepped in with that question. Pinks tended to lay social minefields around themselves. Nohar wished he had a map. "Sorry."

She managed a forced smile. "Don't apologize. I shouldn't have snapped at you. I've never been very good around people . . ." She sighed.

Nohar tried to get the conversation back on track. "I'm supposed to be here about Johnson. Not you. What *do* you know about Johnson? What kind of enemies did he have?"

Nohar watched covertly as she walked to the kitchen and went from cabinet to cabinet. "I suppose his only enemies would have been Binder's enemies. He had been with Binder since the state legislature. Straight from college. Loyal to a fault. A big fault considering Binder's attitude toward homosexuals. I never understood it, but I wasn't paid to understand. Young and Johnson were already an organizational fixture when I came on the scene."

"Were they—"

She came back with the drinks. "I really shouldn't talk about it. It's Phil's business. But he shouldn't have snubbed the funeral. After fifteen years, Derry deserved more than Phil worrying about someone figuring out the obvious."

"Could you tell me about what Johnson was doing the week he died?"

"I didn't see him the week he died. I think Young mentioned him seeing some bigwig contributor."

"When was the last time you *did* see him alive?"

"A fund-raiser the previous Saturday. On the end of

his arm as usual. He left early, around nine-thirty.''
She lowered her eyes. ''You know what the last thing
he said to me was?''

''What?''

''He apologized for consistently ruining all the dates
'an attractive girl' should have had.'' She lifted her
glass. ''To the relationships I should have had.'' She
drained it.

The way she was shaking her head made Nohar
change the subject. ''Can you tell me why Johnson
would have three million dollars of campaign funds in
his house when he was killed?''

Weir looked back up, her mouth open, and her eyes
a little wider. ''Oh, Christ, in cash?''

''According to the police report's interpretation of
the finance records, yes.''

Weir got up from her chair and started pacing. ''Now
I'm *glad* they let me go. There's no legitimate reason
for having that kind of money in a lump sum—''

''Why would he?''

''Could be anything. Avoiding disclosure, a secret
slush fund, illegal contributions, embezzlement—''

''Could this have to do with Binder pressuring the
police to stop the investigation?''

''I heard that, too. Sure. That's as good a reason to
pressure his old cronies in the council and the police
department as any.''

Nohar stood up and, after a short debate within himself, held out his hand. ''Thank you for your help, Ms.
Weir.''

Her hand clasped his. It was tiny, naked, and warm,
but it gave a strong squeeze. ''My pleasure. I needed
to talk to someone. And please don't call me Miz
Weir.''

''Stephanie?''

''I prefer Stephie.'' Nohar caught a look of what
could have been uncertainty cross her face. ''Will I
see you again?''

Nohar had no idea. "I'm sure we'll need to go over some things later."

She led him to the door and he ducked out into the darkening night. Before the door was completely shut, Nohar turned around. "Can I ask you something?"

"Why stop now?"

"Why are you so relaxed around me?"

She laughed, an innocent little sound. "Should I be nervous?"

"I'm a moreau—"

"Well, Mr. Rajasthan, maybe I'll do better next time." She shut the door before Nohar could answer. After a slight hesitation, he pressed the call button.

"Yes?" said the speaker.

"Call me Nohar."

Nohar sat in the Jerboa and watched the night darken around him. He was parked in front of Daryl Johnson's house, a low-slung ranch, and wondering exactly why he'd acted the way he did with Weir—with Stephie. He really couldn't isolate anything he'd done or said that could be called unprofessional, but he felt like he'd bumbled through the whole interview. Especially the lesbian comment—"I don't want to talk about that right now." Nohar wondered why. She was willing to talk about anything but, even seemed reluctant to let him leave.

The night had faded to monochrome when Nohar climbed out of the convertible. He decided the problem had been Maria. Thinking about that was beginning to affect his work.

Nohar watched a reflection of the full moon ripple in the polymer sheathing that now covered the picture window. The scene was too stark for Shaker Heights. The moon had turned the world black and white, and even the night air tried to convey a chill, more psychic than actual. From somewhere the breeze carried the taint of a sewer.

The police tags were gone. The investigation had

stopped, here at least. Nohar approached the building, trying to resolve in his mind the contradictions the police report had raised.

He stood in front of the picture window and looked across the street. Five houses stood in line with the window and Daryl Johnson's head. Similar ranch houses, all in well-manicured plots, all well lit. The specs for the sniper's weapon said it weighed 15 kilos unloaded, and it was over two meters long. None of the possible sniper positions offered a bit of cover that would have satisfied Nohar.

CHAPTER 7

It didn't rain on Friday.

Philip Young still refused to answer his comm, so Nohar donned his suit and went to see the finance chairman in person. Philip Young's address was in the midst of the strip of suburbia between Moreytown and Shaker. It was close enough to home that Nohar decided to walk. By the time he was halfway there, his itching fur made him regret the decision. When he had reached Young's neighborhood, Nohar had his jacket flung over his shoulder, his shirt unbuttoned to his waist, and his tie hung in a loose circle around his neck.

Young's neighborhood was a netherworld of ancient duplexes and brick four-story apartments. The lawns were overgrown. The trees bore the scars of traffic accidents and leaned at odd angles. Less intimidating than Shaker Heights—Moreytown, only with humans. He still received the occasional stare, but he wasn't far enough off the beaten path for the pinks to see him as unusual. Only a few crossed the street to avoid him.

Nohar felt less of the nervousness that made his interview with Stephie Weir such an embarrassment. Nohar was well on his way to convincing himself he might just be able to get Young to give him some insight on that three million dollars. His major worry was exactly how to approach Young about homosexuality. Pinks could be tender on that subject.

Nohar stopped and faced Young's house with the noontime sun burning the back of his neck. Young

should be home. The staff had the week off because
of Johnson's death.

Gnats were clouding around his head, making his
whiskers twitch.

He wondered why the finance chairman—who presumably guided those large sums under the table—lived
here. This was a bad neighborhood, and the house
wasn't any better off than its neighbors. The second
floor windows were sealed behind white plastic
sheathing. The siding was gray and pockmarked with
dents and scratches. The porch was warped and suc-
cumbing to dry rot. It was as much a hellhole as Nohar's apartment.

And the place *smelled* to high heaven. He snorted
and rubbed the skin of his broad nose. It was a sour,
tinny odor he couldn't place. It irritated his sinuses
and prodded him with a nagging familiarity.

Why did Young live here?

Young was an accountant. Perhaps there was a con-
voluted tax reason behind it.

Nohar walked up to the porch with some trepida-
tion. It didn't look like it could hold him. He walked
cautiously, the boards groaning under his weight, and
nearly fell through a rotten section when his tail was
caught in the crumbling joinery overhanging the front
steps. Nohar had to back up and thrash his tail a few
times to loosen it. It came free, less a tuft of fur the
size of a large marble.

After that, he walked to the door holding his tail so
high his lower back ached.

The door possessed a single key lock, and one call
button with no sign of an intercom. Both had been
painted over a dozen times. Nohar pressed the button
until he heard the paint crack, but nothing happened.
He knocked loudly, but no one seemed to be around
to answer. He had the feeling Young's directory listing
was a sham, and Young lived about as much at his
"home" as Nohar worked at his "office." He carefully walked across the porch to peer into what he

assumed was a living room window. The furnishings consisted of a mattress and a card table.

So much for the straightforward approach.

Nohar undid his tie and wrapped it around his right hand. He cocked back and was about to smash in the window, when he identified the smell.

The tinny smell had been getting worse ever since he had first noticed it. Nohar had assumed it was because he was approaching the source, which was true. However, he had been on the porch a few minutes and the smell kept increasing. What had been a minor annoyance on the sidewalk was now making his eyes water.

The smell was strong enough now for him to identify it. He remembered where he had smelled it before. It had been a long time since he'd watched the demolition of the abandoned gas stations at the corner of Mayfield and Coventry, since he had watched them dig up the rusted storage tanks, since he had smelled gasoline.

Instinct made him back away from the window and try to identify where the smell was coming from. His tie slipped from his claws and fell to the porch.

The smell was strongest to the left of the porch. It came from behind the house, up the weed-shot driveway.

The garage—

Carefully, he descended the steps and rounded the porch. He walked up the driveway toward the two-car garage and the smell permeated everything. His eyes watered. His sinuses hurt. The smell was making him dizzy.

The doors on the garage were closed, but he could hear activity within—splashing, a metal can banging, someone breathing heavily. He slowed his approach and was within five meters of the garage when the noise stopped.

Nohar wished he was carrying a gun.

The door shot up and chunked into place. Fumes

washed over Nohar and nearly made him pass out. Philip Young faced him, framed by the garage door. Nohar knew, from the statistics he had read, Young was only in his mid-thirties. The articles had portrayed him as a *Wunderkind* who had engineered the financing of Binder's first congressional upset.

The man that was looking at Nohar wasn't a young genius. He was an emaciated wild man. Young was stripped to the waist, and drenched with sweat and gasoline. Behind him were stacks of wet cardboard boxes, file folders, papers, suitcases. Some still dripped amber fluid. Young's red-shot eyes darted to Nohar and his right hand shook a black snub-nosed thirty-eight at the moreau.

"You're not going to do me like you did Derry."

Nohar hoped his voice sounded calm. "You don't want to fire that gun."

The gun shook as Young's head darted left and right. "You're with them, aren't you? You're *all* with them."

Young was freaked, and he was going to blow himself, the garage, and Nohar all over the East Side. "Calm down. I'm trying to *find out* who killed Derry."

"Liar!" Nohar's mouth dried up when he heard the hammer cock. "You're all with them. I watched one of you kill him."

Young was off his nut, but at least Nohar realized what he must be talking about. "A moreau could have killed Derry and I never would have heard about it. Why don't you put down the gun and we can talk."

Young looked back at the boxes he'd been dousing. "You understand, I can't let anyone find out."

Nohar was lost again. "Sure, I understand."

"Derry didn't know he was helping them—what they were. When he found out, he was going to stop. You realize that."

Young was still looking into the garage, Nohar took the opportunity to take a few steps toward him. "Of course, no one could hold that against him."

Young whipped around, waving the gun. "That's

just it! They'll *blame* Derry. People would say he was *working for them—*"

Young rambled, paying little attention to Nohar. Nohar worked his way a little closer. He could see into the garage better now. His eyes watered and it was hard to read, but he could see some of the boxes of paper were filled with printouts. They looked like payroll records. One suitcase was filled with ramcards.

Young suddenly became aware of him again. "Stop right there."

Young's finger tightened and Nohar froze. "Why did 'they' kill Derry?"

The gun was pointed straight at Nohar as Young spoke. "He found out about them. He went over the finance records and figured it out."

"You're the finance chairman. Why didn't you figure it out first?"

Mistake. Young started shaking and yelling something inarticulate. Nohar turned and dived at the ground.

Young fired.

Young screamed.

Nohar was looking away from the garage when the gun went off. He heard the crack of the revolver, immediately followed by a whoosh that made his eardrums pop. The bullet felt like a hammer blow in his left shoulder. The explosion followed, a burning hand that slammed him into the ground. The acrid smoke made his nose burn. The odor of his own burning fur made him gag.

Young was still screaming.

The explosion gave way to the crackling fire and the rustle of raining debris. Nohar rolled on to his back to put out his burning fur. When he did so, he wrenched his shoulder, sending a dagger of pain straight through his neck.

He blacked out.

* * *

The absolute worst smell Nohar could imagine was the smell of hospital disinfectant. As soon as he had gained a slight awareness of his surroundings, that chemical odor awakened him the rest of the way. Before he had even opened his eyes, he could feel his stomach tightening.

"Someone, open a window!" It came out in barely a whisper.

Someone was there and Nohar could hear the window whoosh open. The stale city air let him breathe again. Nohar opened his eyes.

It was what he'd been afraid of. He was in a hospital. It was in the cheap adjustable bed, the awful disinfectant smell, the thin sheets, and the linoleum tile. It was in the odor of blood and shit the chemicals tried to hide. It was in the plastic curtains that pretended to give some privacy to the naked moreys lined up, in their beds, like cattle in a slaughterhouse.

Nohar hated hospitals.

Nohar turned his head and saw, standing next to the window, Detective Irwin Harsk. The pink was as stone-faced as ever.

"Am I under arrest?"

Harsk looked annoyed. "You *are* a paranoid bastard. Young blew up, you're allegedly an innocent bystander. Believe it or not, we found two witnesses that agree on two things in ten. Give me some credit for brains."

"Why *are* you here?"

"I'm here because you're giving me problems downtown. I'm supposed to be some morey expert. They expect me to exercise some control over you. I don't like jurisdictional problems. I don't like the DEA staking out half of my territory. I don't like the Fed. And I don't like outsiders pressuring me to bottle something up. I don't like Binder. I don't like Binder's friends—"

Nohar struggled to get into a sitting position and his shoulder didn't seem to object. "What?"

"A bunch of people who think they're cops are trying to dick me around. They want me to keep you away from Binder's people, or bad things will happen. Like what, I don't know. I'm already as low as you get in this town." Harsk slammed his fist into the side of the window frame. "Hell, Shaker's screwing around the Johnson killing for Binder. They *deserve* you."

Harsk looked like he needed to strangle someone. For once, Nohar was speechless.

"Look," Harsk said, "I'm not going to do their shit-work for them. But you're on your own lookout. I just want to avoid the bullshit and do what someone once laughingly described as my job." Harsk walked to the door and paused. "One more thing. The DEA has a serious red flag on your ass."

With that, Harsk left.

Nohar watched Harsk weave his way between the moreys, and didn't know what to think. He'd always pictured Harsk as constantly dreaming up new ways to screw him over. Maybe Harsk was right, he *was* paranoid.

He felt his shoulder. The wound didn't seem to be major. The dressing extended to the back of his neck, which felt tender when Nohar pressed it. He pulled back the sheet. There were five or six dressings on his tail. That, and a transparent support bandage on his slightly swollen right knee, was the only visible damage.

Considering how close he was to Young when the nut blew himself up, he'd gotten off light.

"Damn it." Nohar suddenly remembered Cat. He didn't know how long he'd been out, and Cat only had half a day's food in his bowl when Nohar left.

He looked up and down the ward. No doctors, no nurses, not even a janitor. Harsk had been the only pink down here and he had already left. Nohar knew when, or if, hospital administration finally got to him, there would be a few hours of forms to fill out. Just to keep the bureaucracy happy.

To hell with that.

He swung his legs over the edge of the bed and gently started putting pressure on his right leg. It wasn't a bad sprain. It held his weight. He stood up slowly and felt slightly dizzy. He was alarmed until he realized it was still from that damn disinfectant smell. Breathing through his mouth helped.

There was a window between his bed and the next one. The fuzzy nocturnal view—Nohar wished he could kill the lights in the ward so he could see better—of the skyline told him he wasn't far enough down the Midtown Corridor to be at the Clinic. That meant he was at University Hospitals and only a few blocks from Moreytown. He was probably in the new veterinary building.

Lightning flashed on the horizon.

Nohar looked at the bed on the other side of the window. In it was a canine who had an arm shaved naked inside a transparent cast. He—like Nohar, the canine was naked and not covered by a sheet— was watching Nohar's activity with some interest. The canine spoke when he saw he'd caught Nohar's attention.

"You blow up?"

It was hard placing the accent, but defiantly first generation. Probably Southeast Asian. Nohar began looking for exit signs as he answered.

"Yes."

"Pink law's bad news. Best eye yourself, tiger-man—"

Nohar was barely listening. He'd located the exit. "Sure. You have the date?"

"Fade side of August two. Saturday is five minutes from nirvana."

Thirty-six hours. He must have been drugged.

That was it. He was leaving.

The canine was still nattering. Nohar thanked him and started toward the exit. Most of the moreys here were asleep, but a few watched him leave. There were a few comments, mostly of the "Skip on the pinks" variety. He did get one sexual proposition, but he didn't pause enough to register the species or the sex the offer came from.

He slipped out of the wardroom, the glass doors sliding aside as he passed, and found himself in a carpeted reception area. There was a waiting room, and a nurse's station across from it. No one in sight. The elevators and the stairs were directly across from the doors to the ward. All he needed to do was cross between the station and the waiting room. Once in the stairwell he could make it to the parking garage.

He limped across no-man's-land and nearly made it to the stairwell.

The elevator doors opened without any warning. He was caught right in front of the elevator. If it hadn't been so damn silent, he might have had a chance to duck to the side.

The last person he expected to see in the elevator was Stephie Weir.

As the doors opened, she took a step forward and her motion ceased. Nohar thought he must have looked as surprised as she did. Neither of them moved. They stood there, staring at each other, until the doors started closing again.

Realizing he was about to blow his escape, Nohar jumped into the elevator. He called out, "Down. Garage level," and pressed the button for the garage level just in case the thing didn't have a voice pickup. Nohar hoped no one else in the building would want to use this particular elevator in the next half-minute.

Stephie was staring at him. Nohar waited until he felt the car moving downward, then he asked, "What are *you* doing here?"

The question seemed to break her out of shock. She lifted her gaze. "I want to know what happened to Phil. I was waiting down there two hours until Detective Harsk—Christ, what are you doing with no clothes on?"

That damned pink fetish. "Avoiding bureaucracy."

"What the hell are you talking about? *You're na-ked!*"

"Not until they shave me."

The doors on the elevator opened and Nohar held his breath. They had made it all the way to the garage. Again, no one in sight.

Nohar turned to Stephie who looked and smelled of confusion. "If you want to talk about what happened, you better come with me."

He stepped out on to the cold concrete. He finally felt comfortable breathing through his nose. The only strong smells down here were the slight ozone smell from the cars, and Stephie's smoky-rose scent.

She choked back a few monosyllables and started walking after him. "Just tell me why, please."

He almost gave her a curt answer, but he decided she deserved something of an explanation. "I need to get back home. Checking out and getting whatever the explosion left of my clothes could take a long while, and they might just decide they want to keep me for a day or two. Besides, I hate filling out forms. They can bill me."

"What's so important?"

"I don't have anyone to feed my cat."

That got her. "You're not kidding, are you?"

Nohar shrugged and started toward the entrance of the parking garage. His claws clicked on the concrete.

She called after him. "Where's your car?"

"I suppose it's still parked outside my office."

"You're going to—" She paused. "Of course you intend to walk home like that. Come back here. At least let me give you a lift so you won't get arrested."

Nohar turned around. He didn't know what to make of the offer. "Can I fit in your car?"

"A Plymouth Antaeus? What it cost, you better fit."

"Sure you want to do this? My neighborhood—"

"Screw your neighborhood. We need to talk about Phil."

Nohar silently agreed they needed to talk about Phil. He allowed himself to be led to the brand-new Antaeus.

CHAPTER 8

The Antaeus pulled up behind the Jerboa, splashing a deep puddle by the curb. The barriers prevented Stephie from driving any closer to Nohar's apartment.

When Stephie parked, she turned to face Nohar. She seemed to be making an effort to keep her gaze fixed on his face. "It doesn't sound like Phil."

"It's what happened."

"The cops called it a suicide. Detective Harsk said Phil *shot* you."

Nohar reached up and rubbed his left shoulder. "Can *you* explain what happened?"

Stephie turned toward the windshield, shaking her head. She was silent for a few seconds. Finally she said, "He bought that house so he could have a separate address."

So, it *was* a sham. "He lived with Johnson?"

"Five years now." She still looked out the window. A street lamp shone through the cascading rain and carved rippling shadows on her face. She spoke slowly and deliberately. "I can't believe Phil would kill himself."

Nevertheless, that's what Young had done, as surely as if he had pointed the gun at his own head. Nohar could still picture Young saying they all—Nohar presumed Young meant moreys—were with *them*. Nohar suspected *they* were in MLI.

"How'd he feel about moreys?"

"I don't know—" *Very few people do*, thought Nohar. "I didn't talk to him much. I knew him mostly through talking to Derry.'' She sighed. The sound seemed to catch in her throat.

After an uncomfortably long pause, she changed the subject. ''I don't think Derry's death *would* make him . . .''

''What would it take?''

''More, just . . . *more*.'' Stephie turned and looked Nohar in the eyes. Her expression seemed to show bewilderment and she smelled of fear, nerves, and confusion. ''Do you think I'm a bad person?''

What the hell brought that on? ''Of course not, why?''

''I feel terrible about what I said about Phil snubbing the funeral—''

Nohar restrained the immediate impulse to ask her why she was telling him that. Instead, he tried a close-lipped smile. ''We all say things we end up regretting. It doesn't mean we're thoughtless.''

''It's not just that. My whole life has been a hypocrisy—''

''You don't mean—''

''I know exactly what I mean. I never even was a Binder supporter—I despise the man.'' She sucked in a shuddering breath. ''Me, Phil, and Derry—we were all playing the twisted charade. All of us hiding because Binder was signing our paychecks.''

''What were you hiding?''

The look in her eyes changed for a moment. Nohar felt like he had let his mouth make a major mistake again. Instead, she smiled, even let out a little laugh.

''I was hiding myself, I guess.''

Nohar realized he was only going to get that cryptic comment. He nodded and opened the rear door to let himself out into the rain. The damp soaked into his fur in a matter of seconds.

''Thanks for the ride.'' Nohar didn't know why he felt obliged, but he added, ''I'll give you a call later on, if I find out anything.''

Nohar shut the door and she looked like she still

couldn't quite believe he was going to walk home without any clothes. "Nohar?"

He paused and looked back into the Antaeus. "Yes?"

"Forget it, never mind. . . ."

She shook her head and drove the Antaeus into the darkness without an explanation.

Nohar stood and watched it go for a while, wondering.

Moreytown pressed around him. He had three blocks to go, so he started walking. He was safe from the cops here. Moreys were so casual about clothing that trying to enforce pink exposure laws in Moreytown would be impossible. His lack of attire would only be noted because of the rain, and the time of night. Now all he had to worry about were how many eyes had seen him with the pink female.

He nearly made it home—

A ratboy bumped into him.

No, they wouldn't be that stupid.

He was on the wrong side of the street. He was between the abandoned bus and a boarded-up pizzeria. His usual alertness had failed him, and he realized the hospital smell was still clogging his nose.

The familiar-looking ratboy, brown fur and denim cutoffs, rebounded from Nohar's side. "Lookee—"

Now Nohar could catch the rat's musk. The ratboy was flying a wave of excitement, reeked of it. It was Fearless Leader, and he was jacked about as far as a rat could go.

"The stray just ruffed my fur!"

Footsteps, two sets at one end of the bus, two at the other. Subordinates. From the look and smell of it, Fearless' boys were jacked worse than he was. Bigboy was there, and he snicked a blade. Nohar should have taken the knife when he had the chance.

Bigboy made a few ineffective waves with his switchblade. "Let's shave the kitty pink."

A chain rattled from the other end of the bus. "Teach some respect for the coat."

Great, they *were* that stupid.

So much for the Finger of God.

Fearless Leader pulled a gun, a twenty-two. Fortunately, he wasn't doused in gasoline. "We don't like pink moreys. We goina mark you. You move and we veto your pretty kitty ass."

Nohar always held his fighting instinct under iron control. Both nature and the Indian gene-techs had designed his strain for combat, for hunting, for the spilling of blood. Almost always, that part of his soul was at odds with his conscious mind. Nohar thought of it as The Beast.

When Fearless pulled the gun, Nohar felt a shock of adrenaline. His heart began to pound and he felt the rush in his ears and his temples. There was the anticipatory taste of copper in his mouth. His breath like a blast furnace in the back of his throat.

The Beast wanted out. It was scratching at the mental door Nohar always kept locked.

Nohar opened the door and let The Beast take over.

The night snapped into razor-sharp monochrome. The smells erupted into a vivid melange. He could hear the ratboy's heartbeat as well as his own. Time crawled.

The Beast roared.

Nohar roared. The sound bore no trace of his speaking voice. It was a scream of rage that tore the skin from his throat. The ratboys hesitated at the sound. Fearless smelled of fear now, fear that told Nohar he had never seen a morey turn wild before.

Nohar's left arm, the one with restricted mobility, shot out toward Fearless' gun hand. Nohar grabbed the weapon and turned it toward the ground. There was a snap of bone before the gun blew a hole in the side of the bus. Fearless Leader had some control. No scream.

Not until Nohar's right hand, sweeping upward with

the claws fully extended, caught Fearless between the legs. Nohar didn't simply rake his claws across Fearless' body. His claws came up, point first, and when they bit flesh, jerked up, hooked forward, and partially retracted. Fearless Leader screamed when Nohar lifted him up. Nohar's claws were hooked into the flesh of his groin.

Nohar was jacked higher than the rats now. Fearless Leader's 50 kilos weighed nothing. Fearless slammed into the bus through a broken window. The gun was still in Nohar's left hand. Fearless' hand was still holding it, reaching through the bus window. Nohar yanked the gun away. There was another crack.

Bigboy was now within reach, swinging his knife. Nohar pivoted and the knife missed. Nohar's cupped right hand aimed for the eyes as Bigboy passed. Bigboy slipped in the rain before the claws hit him. Lucky. The claws sank in behind the ear and tore off a flap of skin down the left side of Bigboy's face.

Nohar's left arm blocked a chain coming at his head. It wrapped around his forearm. He pulled that rat toward him and upward. He sank his teeth into the weapon arm. A toss of Nohar's head disarmed his attacker and dropped the rat off to his right. Into the same puddle that had saved Bigboy's eye.

Two others. They spooked.

Leader in bus. Bigboy huddled in doorway to pizzeria, trying to hold half his face on. Chain trying to stop the bleeding, hand limp, muscle severed. Fight over.

Slowly, Nohar shut the door on The Beast.

The comedown was hard. He began shaking. The rats didn't notice. They had their own problems. That fifteen seconds of savagery had jacked him higher and faster than these ratboys had ever thought of going. The crash would've killed them.

Nohar stumbled across the street and to the door of his building.

When he staggered into his living room, Cat hissed

at him. Nohar was covered in rat blood. He wobbled into the kitchen, opened a cabinet, and spilled Cat's food all over the counter.

It would have to do, for now.

Nohar dragged himself into the bathroom and slumped into the shower. He turned on a blast of cold water.

Dipping into his reserve as a bioengineered weapon had its price.

When Nohar woke up, the shower was still going full blast. Cat was asleep on the lid of the john, and the only remains of the night's activity was the taste of blood in his mouth. The bandage on his shoulder fell off the moment he moved. It revealed a puckered red wound where they had dug out Young's bullet. There was a shaved area around it the size of his hand. The flesh was a pale white, contrasting with Nohar's russet-and-black fur. Nohar quickly looked away from it. The skin made him uncomfortable.

The support bandage was still there. At least he hadn't aggravated the injury to his knee. That was good because there was no way he was going to end up in a hospital again.

He stood up, killed the cold water, and hit the dryer. He barely noticed when Cat spooked. Nohar stood under the dryer and shook. He tried to tell himself it was his unsteady knee, but he was too adept at spotting bullshit. He knew it was a reaction to loosing The Beast.

All moreys dealt with The Beast in one form or another. Some, like Manny, lived with it without it making so much as a ripple in their psyche, the techs had let a basically human brain mute the instincts they weren't particularly interested in. Then there were moreys like Nohar, who bore the legacy of techs playing hob with what nature gave them. This was only the second time he had let out The Beast with no restraint. Nohar was grateful nobody had died.

He had enjoyed it too much.

He saw in himself the potential for becoming another type of morey. The one who gave himself over to The Beast and reveled in the bloodlust. The one like his father—

"No," he said to his reflection as he left the bathroom. To his practiced ears, it sounded like a lie.

Forget the rats, he told himself. He still had a job to do. Even if it cost him two days, his run-in with Young had given him something besides a gunshot wound and a sprained knee. If Young was not totally out of touch with reality—no mean assumption—Nohar now had some idea of how Daryl Johnson was killed, if not why.

First things first—he went to the comm and turned it on. "Load program. Label, 'I lost my damn wallet!' Run program."

"searching . . . found. program uses half processing capacity and all outside lines for approximately fifteen minutes, continue?"

"Yes." It was going to take him that long just to run through his messages. While his cards and IDs were being canceled and reordered by the computer, he perused the backlog.

There were no phone messages on the comm, but a pile of mail was waiting in memory for him.

It was early in the morning on Sunday the third. Predictably, bills predominated in the mail. He'd have the comm pay them off as soon as it was done with his lost wallet program. There was the usual collection of junk mail. However, for once, there was something more than those two categories in his mail file.

"John Smith," his client, had been true to his word to keep in touch. Two days after their meeting, he had left a voice message for Nohar to meet him in Lakeview Cemetery, for noon on Saturday—when Nohar had been zoned in a ward at University Hospitals. About twelve hours after that little bit of mail, Smith apparently found out what had happened. The slimy voice carried little emotion. "Mr. Rajasthan, I regret this incident with Binder's finance chairman. I am unable to meet with you personally, but I finance your medical expenses when I hear what happens to you—''

''Pause.'' Nohar was having trouble following the frank's heavy accent. Nohar, living in the middle of Moreytown, had to deal with, and understand, an incredible variety of unusual accents. A Vietnamese dog not only had an Asian accent, but a definite canid pronunciation. The problem with the frank was more subtle. Nohar didn't think it was a South African accent—even if that *was* one of the few countries to have defied the long-standing United Nations ban on engineering humans. Nohar promised himself he'd press the frank a little more closely about his origins next time they met.

''Continue.''

''—I hope this does not prevent you from the discovery of Daryl Johnson's murderer. I increase your fee to reflect your current difficulties. I call to set up meeting when you are released from hospital. There you tell me what you discover.''

It took Nohar a few seconds to figure out exactly what the frank meant.

The next item in the mail file was from Maria. Nohar was afraid to play it. Then he cursed himself and told the comm to play the damn thing. It was the same husky voice, much calmer this time. Nohar wished he could see her face. ''Raj, I thought you deserved a more civilized good-bye. I still can't meet you face-to-face, and for that I apologize. I just want you to know it isn't your fault. We're incompatible. Maybe it would be easier for me to deal with your wholesale contempt for everything if you weren't such a decent and honorable person.''

There was a pause as Maria took a long breath. ''I am going through with it. You were right about the money—you always are about things like that—but I'm going anyway. California is a lot more tolerant, and the few communities there aren't just glorified slums the humans abandoned. I know you can't appreciate this, but God bless you.''

Nohar sat, her voice still ringing in his ears, remembering. He had the comm store the message and sighed.

''instructions unclear.''

He had sighed too loudly. ''Store mail. Comm. Off.''

She had been wrong about one thing. He *could* appreciate the blessing. Especially after their last argument, the night before he had stood her up for that fiasco with Nugoya—

It had started when she suggested they both move to California. Of course, there was no way they could afford it. She brought up God, and Nohar went off. That damned little bit of pink brainwashing infuriated him. Especially when a moreau spouted it. Religion, pink religion, wasn't just a form of mind control, but the primary justification for people like Joseph Binder to consider moreys worse than garbage. Why should a morey believe in God, when people like Binder said they were an abomination in His eyes?

Maria was a devout Catholic and Nohar had been drunk enough to think he might be able to talk her out of such stupidity. How could she be secure in her belief when she only had a *soul* by dispensation of some sexagenarian pink in a pointed hat? A decision that had more to do with politics than divine inspiration.

Why couldn't he keep his damn mouth shut?

Worse, all his money problems had evaporated with the ten thousand Smith gave him. Maria's message had come in yesterday. Knowing her, she had left town by now.

CHAPTER 9

Nohar parked the Jerboa in front of Daryl Johnson's ranch. He stayed in the car. Shaker Heights still made him paranoid about cops. It was early Sunday morning and he suspected the slow-moving bureaucracy at University Hospital was just now discovering him missing. Shortly afterward, the cops would be notified. Nohar didn't know exactly what would happen then. He was a witness to Young's explosion—they *should* want a statement from him. But Binder was pressuring the cops. Binder probably wouldn't want any real close investigation of Young's empty house, or the records Young had destroyed.

At least Nohar's investigation, such as it was, was progressing. He had checked the police records again. The air-conditioning *had* been going full blast when Johnson was blown away.

Nohar yawned and raked his claws across the upholstery of the passenger seat. He spent a few minutes picking foam rubber as he looked at the sheathing covering the picture window. His watch beeped. It was eight, Manny would be answering his comm.

Nohar took the voice phone out of the glove compartment and called him.

"Dr. Gujerat here. Who—" There was a pause as Manny must have read the text on the incoming call. "Nohar? Where in the hell are you? I got to the hospital during nocturnal visiting hours. You were gone—"

Fine, his disappearance had been discovered that

much earlier. "Manny, I'm fine. I need to ask you something—"

"Like the percentage of untreated bullet wounds that become gangrenous? Damnit, you weren't in the hospital just to be inconvenienced."

Nohar shook his head. At least Manny wasn't saying, "I told you so." Even though he'd been right about getting involved with pink business.

"I needed to feed Cat."

"Great, just great. I won't even tell you how silly that sounds. You couldn't have gotten me to do that?"

Nohar thought of the ratboys. "No, I couldn't."

Manny sighed and slowed his chittering voice. "I know how you feel about hospitals, but you can't avoid them forever. Things have gotten a lot better. They don't make mistakes like that anymore—" Nohar knew Manny stopped because of the ground he was treading. *Thanks for reminding me,* Nohar thought. He was about to say it, but, for once, he managed to keep his mouth shut.

"You better promise to come over and let me look at that wound. There are a lot more appropriate things to die of."

"Promise."

"I know you didn't just call to say hi. What do you want?"

Nohar caught the dig at him. It was unlike Manny. Manny really was worried about him. "Before I ask you, promise *me* something."

"What?"

"When this is over, we get out together. No business, no corpses."

There was a distinct change in the quality of Manny's voice that made Nohar feel better. "Sure . . ."

Damn, Manny was almost speechless. "I wanted to ask you about the time of death. How accurate can that be?"

Manny found his professional voice. "Depends on a lot of things. The older the corpse, the less accurate.

Need a good idea of the ambient temperature and the humidity—''

That's what Nohar wanted to hear. ''What if they were wrong about the temperature? Fifteen degrees too high.''

''Definitely throw the estimate off.''

''How much?''

''Depends on what they thought the temperature was to begin with.''

''Thirty-two at least.''

Nohar could hear the whistle of air between Manny's front teeth. ''Nohar, the time of death could be put back by up to a factor of two. If the humidity was off, maybe more.''

''Thanks, Manny.''

''You're welcome, I think.''

Nohar hung up the phone and looked at the ranch. All the little nagging problems with Johnson's death— And it was so damn simple.

Problem—it took much too long for the local population to notice the gaping hole if it had been shot when Johnson was shot. Solution—the window was shot out long after Johnson was dead. Probably during the thunderstorm that Thursday, so few people would have heard the glass—real glass, expensive—exploding and none would recognize its significance.

It had taken Young to make Nohar think of that. Young said he had seen a morey kill Johnson. ''One of you,'' he said. The only way Young could have seen the killer shoot Johnson was if he, the killer, and Johnson were all more or less in the same place when Johnson died. If the assassin was in the house, he could have offed Johnson with one shot—no need for a shattering window to draw Johnson's attention. Johnson could have remained facing the comm, oblivious enough to be shot dead center in the back of the head.

Because no alarm, no break-in. That meant Johnson let him in.

With a Levitt Mark II? Not likely.

Johnson let in someone else—one of *them*—and that person let in the assassin. Yes, Johnson let in someone. Perhaps to confront the person with whatever he had found in the financial records. Young lived in the ranch with Johnson, but no one was supposed to know that. So Young would be hidden from the guest. Maybe in a darkened bedroom, looking out a crack in the door.

The guest—maybe one of the franks from MLI—talks to Johnson in the study. The frank leaves the door open, so the assassin can sneak into the living room and set up the Levitt. The door to the study must remain closed except for the last minute, to give the assassin a chance to prepare. Young would only see the gun when the frank opens the study door to give the morey killer a field of fire.

The one shot gets Derry Johnson in the back of the head. Young is in shock. The frank and the morey clean up a little and leave.

It must have been Saturday night, after that fundraiser Young and Johnson had departed early. That would explain Johnson's state, and why no one could finger Johnson's location during the week. Young wasn't thinking right. He freaked, packed his stuff, and ran out to his empty house.

The corpse was left in an air-conditioned, climate-controlled environment, until the morey with the Levitt blew away the picture window on Thursday. The storm ruined the traces of the assassin in the living room. The killing became an anonymous sniping. The time of death shifted to Wednesday and nobody got the chance to plumb the inconsistencies because Binder clamped down immediately.

Neat.

But why didn't Young call the cops?

Something had freaked Young. If Stephie was right, something beyond Johnson's death. From the way Young acted, it was something linked to the financial records. Something Johnson saw and Young didn't.

Nohar looked back at the broken window. The police ballistics report was based entirely on the assumption that both shots came from the same place. Now the second shot, the one that blew the window out, no longer had to be in line with Johnson's head. The field of fire at the picture window was *much* wider. The sniper no longer had to be crouching in one of the security-conscious driveways across the street.

Nohar stood up on the passenger seat of the Jerboa and looked for good fire positions. He scanned the horizon—lots of trees. The Levitt needed a clear field of fire; crashing through a tree could set off the charge in the bullet. Nohar kept turning, looking for a high point, above the houses, behind them, without a tree in the way.

Feeling a growing sense of disillusionment, Nohar parked the Jerboa next to the barrier at the end of the street. He had been pounding pavement and checking buildings for most of the day. Evening was approaching and, while he had found a number of buildings both likely and unlikely to hold a sniper, he was little closer to discovering where the sniper had shot from. He was afraid he might actually cross the path of the gunman and not recognize it.

Fire position number ten was inside Moreytown, which was a plus as far as likelihood was concerned. Nohar figured you could drive a fully loaded surplus tank inside Moreytown and the pink law would give it just a wink and a nod.

The name of the building was Musician's Towers. It was a twenty-story, L-shaped building, supposedly abandoned since the riots. Good spot for a sniper. Hundreds of squatters in the place, but there weren't likely to be any *witnesses*.

There had been a halfhearted effort to seal it up. It'd been condemned ever since a fire took out one wing— as well as the synagogue across the street. Most of the plastic covering the doors and windows had been torn off ages ago.

He slowly approached the doorway, on guard even though it was still daylight. The entrance hall was in the burned-out wing. The hall went through to the other side, looking like someone had fired an artillery round all the way through the base of the building. He had to climb over the pile of crumbled concrete in front of the entrance, debris that came mostly from the facade on the top five floors.

White sky burned through the empty, black-rimmed windows at the top of the building. That was the place for a sniper.

Above the gaping hole that led into the building someone had spray-painted, ''Welcome to Morey Hilton.''

Inside, the heat became oppressive. Nohar was nearly used to the itch under his shirt, but in the sweltering lobby—it might have been because of the still lingering smell of fire—he had to take it off. He leaned against the hulk of a station wagon someone had driven into the lobby, waiting to become acclimated to the heat.

No sign of the squatters yet, but Nohar doubted any lived near the first floor. That would be a little too close to the action. The empty beer bulbs scattered across the floor, the occasional cartridge from an air-hypo, the fresh bullet pockmarks, marked the lobby as a party spot for the gangs. Not to mention ''Zipperhead'' painted on the side of the station wagon. Hmm, Nohar corrected himself. *Gang*—singular. Lately, the one gang seemed to be it. He didn't know exactly what to make of that. There had been at least five gangs around when he had been running with the Hellcats. But that was a long time ago—the years before this building burned up—and Nohar really didn't want to think about it.

He decided he had waited long enough and went straight for one of the open stairwells. The winding concrete stairs were swathed in darkness, and Nohar's view became colorless and nocturnal. Here, the heat was even worse, and the smell of fire was overwhelmed by the aromas of rust, mold, and rotting garbage. The stairs were concrete, but every other footstep fell on something soft.

Nohar tried to ignore the garbage and think like a sniper. The face of the burned-out wing was pointed at the target, so the assassin would take a point amidst the wreckage. Few squatters in the remains of the fire—

Nohar hit floor ten and had to pause because he thought he'd come across a corpse. A lepus was curled in a fetal position in the corner of the tenth-floor landing. An acrid odor announced the fact the rabbit had soiled—him, her? Nohar couldn't tell in the dark—itself. As he approached, the rabbit's twitching showed it was still among the living. An air-hypo cartridge lay on the ground.

A jacked rabbit—might have even been funny if it hadn't been so obvious the rabbit was on flush, and having a bad reaction. Nohar knelt next to the rabbit. She—Nohar could tell now—wasn't wearing anything. Filth covered her dark fur. He felt a wave of anger when he didn't see the hypo. That meant one of two things. Either someone had done her, or had stolen the hypo. In both cases they'd left her on her own like this. Scenes like this made Nohar think the fundamentalists might be right and moreys were an abomination in the eyes of whatever deity.

It was flush, all the classic symptoms. Near catatonia, chills, dehydration, voiding the bowels, rolling up of the eyes, shallow breathing, slight nosebleed. She was lucky. In truly severe reactions, the nervous system went. Then he *would* have found a corpse. She'd been through the worst of it, though. What she needed now was light and water. The darkness tended to perpetuate the hallucinogenic effects of flush. She could be psychologically unable to move long after the physical effects had worn off.

Nohar picked her up. She weighed nothing. She was a small morey to begin with, and she was skinny as well. He hoped the squatters still kept those rain barrels up topside.

On the burned-out wing, with the exception of the concrete facade, the top three floors were gone. Nohar carried the rabbit out of the stairwell and into the open air of the seventeenth floor. Nohar saw the orange plastic barrels immediately. Good, the occupants still collected rainwater. He looked at the shivering rabbit, silently asked himself what he was doing, and lowered her face gently into one of the cleaner barrels.

The moment the water brushed the side of her face, her ears picked up. Good sign. They stayed like that, Nohar holding her face just above the water, the rabbit curled up with her neck resting on the edge of the barrel, for close to fifteen minutes. The only thing keeping Nohar from giving up on her brain-lock was the gradual improvement, and the fact she did seem to be drinking a little.

There had to be a better way to deal with this, Nohar thought. He wasn't a trained medic. He was following the home procedure for a bad flush trip. It was a lot easier with a toilet handy—the running joke was, the comedown in the head was the way the drug got its street name.

A sputtering came from the barrel. Nohar hoped she wouldn't vomit. "Listen to my voice." Nohar tried to sound reassuring. "It was a bad trip, but you're coming back. It wasn't real. You can relax now. It's important to untense your muscles, slowly—"

After a decade plus, the lines came back with surprising ease. She didn't say anything as he talked her down, and Nohar counted himself lucky she wasn't a screamer.

"Let go, damnit!"

A wide foot made a hollow slap on Nohar's chest,

announcing the fact she had regained some contact with reality. Nohar didn't think letting go of her was a good idea, but the rabbit had suddenly erupted into thrashing motion from near paralysis. She was saying something in Spanish, and from the tone of her voice, it wasn't very pleasant. Good intentions only went so far. He set her down next to the barrel. She was panting, and a little unsteady on her feet.

Nohar rubbed his shoulder. It was tightening up after the stress of holding the rabbit above the barrel. He knew he was asking for it, but he said it anyway. "Are you all right?"

She looked up. She had a scar on one cheek that turned up her mouth in a quirky smile, as if she enjoyed some private joke at his expense. "Don't do no favors, Kit."

"Name's Nohar." He shrugged and started walking toward the windows on the south wall.

He got to the windows, began looking for Johnson's house, and immediately realized the limitations of his vision. The houses were mere blobs.

Nohar turned back to the rain barrel and saw the rabbit, apparently recovering out of sheer cussedness, doing her best to clean herself off with a rag. Oops, not a rag, he had left his shirt over there. Oh, well, the shirt was too hot anyway.

"Hey, Fluffy—"

She glared at him.

"Better at giving favors than receiving them?"

"Name's Angel. Fuck you."

"You owe me something for that shirt you just wasted."

She looked at the dripping cloth she'd been wiping herself with. "Yeah, you and every Ziphead this side of nirvana."

"Your trip an old debt coming home?"

"Wow, Kit, you have a grasp of the obvious that's worthy of a cop." She stood up—most of the filth was out of her spotted brown fur—walked over to the window and slapped the wet shirt across his midsection.

"Your shirt."

Nohar wrung out the shirt and tied it around his waist. "Thanks, Angel— Can you help? I need someone with better vision than I have."

Angel sighed. "What you want?"

"I need to find a window overlooking a ranch house with a shot-out picture window."

"You say shot?" A real smile overcame the ghost of the scar.

"Yes. I can't pick it out—"

She shook her head. "Kit, I didn't know the cops were hiring—"

"I am not a cop!"

Angel stepped back, still smiling, showing a pair of prominent front teeth. "Sore point? What are you, then? What you looking for?"

"I'm a private detective. I'm trying to find a sniper."

She laughed and said, "I can tell you who. What I get?"

It took Nohar half a second to realize she was serious. He closed the distance between them in an instant and grabbed her shoulders. There was a brief adrenaline rush, but he contained it.

"Tell me."

"Not for nothing."

"What do you want?"

"You played the savior, play it all the way. I want protection. You're a big one, Kit. Keep Zipheads from expressing me to nowhere again."

She had him. He'd gone to the trouble of saving her life. Now, he had to make it worth something.

Nohar looked into her eyes and she stopped smiling. "I will, if you tell me two things. First, why are they after you?"

She shrugged. "Made stupid mistake. I tried to keep Stigmata, my gang, going after the Zips moved in.

Didn't know then that they were backed from downtown. My clutch didn't fall off the map, so got erased.''

Nohar could live with that. ''You on flush—or anything else?''

''Do I look stupid?''

He told himself not to answer that.

He might as well play the samaritan while he could. ''You get the couch.''

CHAPTER 10

Nohar didn't see any rats when he parked the Jerboa across from his office. He hoped that meant Fearless Leader and his cronies were laying low. Even so, he was nervous, and Angel was more so. He gave her his shirt—it dragged on the ground when she wore it—and had her hold her ears down.

With ears down and her body covered, she could pass for a deformed rat.

It was the longest three blocks Nohar had ever walked.

They got to his apartment, and no ambush was waiting for them. Nohar breathed easier once he managed to unwedge the warped door and close it behind them.

Cat ran up, as usual, and seemed puzzled to find one of Nohar's shirts moving under its own power. When Angel lowered a hand, Cat shied away and hissed, but the moment she stopped paying attention to him, Cat attacked the end of her foot that stuck out from under the edge of the shirt.

"Ouch! Shit, Kit, put a leash on it."

"*His* name is Cat. If you have an argument with his behavior, you have to take it up with him. He doesn't listen to me."

Cat backed up, crouched, shook his ass back and forth, and pounced on Angel's exposed toes.

Angel jerked her foot up and Cat tumbled back into the living room. She twitched her nose and snorted. "You think that name up by yourself?"

Angel unbuttoned the shirt and took it off. She

tossed it so it landed on Cat. Cat found the shirt more absorbing than Angel's toes, and he started rolling across the living room floor buried inside it. Occasionally a paw would come out and swipe at the air. Angel made for the couch. Nohar went into the kitchen and filled a bottle of water. When he returned with it, she took the bottle and started drinking greedily.

By the time she'd finished her first bottle, Nohar had already made the trip for the second one. She drank this one more leisurely, and her story came out.

Angel had seen the sniper on the twenty-fourth, the stormy Thursday. "Ancient history now," she said. Stigmata still had a few loyal holdouts at the time. By then, though, the Zips had confined Stigmata's turf to the tower. War was about to break out all over. Everyone knew that. The Zips were going to vanish the remaining gangs. Only three were left—Babylon, Vixen, and Stigmata. According to Angel, Vixen's last shred of territory was the strip of Mayfield Road between Kenelworth and the concrete barrier, and Babylon was hunkered down in an enclave somewhere on Morey Hill.

Everyone was edgy. There was always someone watching, hidden behind a wall of rubble in the lobby. Angel, and the rest of them, wanted the chance to take some ratboys down with them. The twenty-fourth was her watch and Thursday was the night all hell broke loose. Angel thought Stigmata must've been the first of the mopup because the Zips must've realized there were only six members left.

The Zips weren't subtle about it. They announced their presence by having a burning station wagon rocket into the building. She told him car wrecks were a territorial symbol for the Zips. The wagon was loaded with explosives and went off in the lobby. Not enough to do any major damage, but enough to spook the whole building and knock Angel out before she could get warning upstairs.

She was only out a few minutes, just long enough

for her and the ratboys to miss each other. The rats
had made their way upstairs and she could hear gunfire
and fighting above her. The Zips had left three as rearguard to catch stragglers. Two brown males and a white
female hung around the open stairwell. Angel said she
wanted to be sure of taking down one particular rodent. They didn't know she was there, the fighting
covered her noise and the garbage covered her smell.
She aimed her Nicaraguan ten-millimeter at the white
one's head. Their leader, Angel said.

She was about to lay a slug right between the white
rat's eyes when the canine showed.

"This guy was a chiller, Kit. Should've seen that
righteous weapon."

From Angel's description, that "righteous weapon"
had to be a Levitt. It was two meters long, with a
scope the length and twice the diameter of Angel's
forearm. The canine was carrying the weapon in one
hand, a tripod in the other.

The newcomer was out of place at the scene of a
gang war. The way Angel described him, the gene-
techs that designed him were at least as advanced as
the ones who produced Nohar's stock. That made the
canine Pakistani or Afghan.

Nohar had a bad feeling that he had met this canine
before.

Angel described a dog with the domestic veneer removed. The canine was lean and had a shaggy gray
coat, prominent snout, green eyes. He stood about two
meters and massed about 100 kilos. Angel said he
looked mean enough to take a bite out of a manhole
cover.

"He had a raghead accent. Walked right to Terin—
the white one—and asked, 'Is the roof cleared?' Ain't
going to forget him. You could smell my people getting whacked up topside, and I smell *him* when he
passes me. He was getting off. The blood was turning
him on something fierce.

"She calls him Hassan, Hazed, Hazy—something like that."

Damn it, it *was* Hassan. The same morey who offed Nugoya. Nohar shook his head. What the *hell* did a small-time pimp and a gang war have to do with Daryl Johnson and the franks running MLI?

"There's this mother of arguments between Terin and the pooch. The raghead is blowing my shot, standing right in front of me—"

"What were they arguing about?"

"Fuck if I know, Kit. Terin's pissed for some reason, like the dog is treading on her territory. She also rants about her best people being dragged off to the four corners of the country—hell and gone, she said. Dog's frosty, though—think he's got the handle on the Zip's supplier, guns and drugs. Terin can mouth off, but not do much. Pissed her good.

"After blowing off steam, she leads him up. There goes my shot. I might've written myself off to get Terin, but I wasn't about to give it up for two goons. I laid it low. Not that I wasn't tempted when they tossed Hernandez out a window, but not much I could do. I waited them out, hoping for another shot at Terin. Didn't happen."

Nohar was sitting on the floor across from Angel. Cat, half wrapped in the shirt, had tired of his game and had come to rest by Nohar. Angel was chugging her third liter of water.

"They caught up with you."

"Inevitable. They knew all of us. Snatched me by surprise—five to one, they like that kind of odds—up the Midtown Corridor. Wasn't in Moreytown so my guard was off. Was last Thursday—end of the month— the day after Vixen bought it."

Nohar remembered the burning Subaru and the dead foxes, both Wednesday.

Angel was still talking. "Surprised they didn't vanish me then and there. Upset I'd survived, more upset I had been at the tower when the raghead dog showed—

someone saw me book outta there an' told the Zips. Terin wanted to know if I had told people, told her to fuck off. Pissed her good. Took me back to the tower an' pumped me with flush. Someone calling the shots said look like an O.D. That really pissed Terin. I could tell she wanted to off me painful. Must've been Friday when they left me. What day is it?''

''Sunday.''

Angel yawned and stretched out on the couch. She barely filled a third of it. ''Well, I'm getting some real sleep.''

She fell asleep instantly.

They should have pumped another into her—but that would have looked like murder—and they were trying to make it look like an O.D.

Why? Because she'd seen the canine?

Again, what the hell did Zipperhead have to do with Daryl Johnson?

Nohar had a nasty thought—another morey uprising?

He shuddered at the idea. He'd been through that once already, when he was in the Hellcats. His own father had been shot, deservedly, by the National Guard.

''Don't let it be a political killing,'' Nohar whispered to Cat.

The express mail people had left a message for him. He'd have to come pick up his package of ID replacements, they didn't deliver to his neighborhood.

Nohar let Angel sleep when he went out. Once he got most of his wallet replaced, Nohar realized there was nothing for his guest to eat. Nohar did some hasty shopping down by the city end of Mayfield Road, around University Circle.

Then, now that he had a card-key replacement, he stopped at his office.

The Triangle office building was a crumbling brick structure that was still trying to fight off the advancing

decay from Moreytown. The brick looked like a patch-
work from the many attempts to remove graffiti. It was
getting dark, and the timers had yet to turn on the
lights inside. There was just enough light to give Nohar a slight purple tint to his vision. He climbed the
stairs in the empty darkness. Nobody else was around
this late on a Sunday.

His office lived in the darkness at the end of a second floor hallway. It didn't even have a number to dis-
tinguish it. The door was simply a fogged-glass
rectangle with a basic card-key lock. Nohar ran his
key through the lock and the door slid aside with a
slight puff of air.

The room was barely big enough to hold Nohar,
even though it only contained two items of furniture—
a comm that was a few generations out of date, and a
file cabinet that was older than the building it lived in.
Nohar knelt down and punched the combination on the
padlock that held the bottom drawer shut.

"Comm on."

There was a slight change in the quality of light in
the room as the screen activated. This comm was mute,
the synth chip had burned out a decade ago. He made
sure the forwarding list was up to date, and got a bit
of a surprise in the mail—a note from Stephie Weir.
She'd found his listed number. It had been forwarded
to his home comm while he was out. He played her
message.

"Nohar, I need to talk to you. Can we meet for
lunch tomorrow at noon? I'll be at the *Arabica* down
at University Circle."

That was it. At least the joint she picked for the
meet wasn't adverse to moreys. Although Nohar wasn't
a great fan of coffee or coffeehouses, the college crowd
seemed a little more tolerant.

He wondered what she wanted.

Nothing more interesting on the comm, so he
opened the file drawer. It was nearly filled by a dented
aluminum case, about a meter long by a half wide.

The electronic lock on the case had long been broken, and there were scorch marks on that side. There was a painstaking cursive inscription on the lid that contrasted with the ugly functionalism of the box itself. The inscription read, "Datia Rajasthan: Off the Pink."

He pulled his father's case out of the drawer. The lock had been broken for nearly a decade, ever since Datia Rajasthan had been gunned down by a squad of National Guardsmen. Nohar'd gotten it a few weeks later when he split the Hellcats.

Nohar opened it. The seal was still good. The lid opened with a tearing sound as the case sucked in air and released the smell of oil. Nohar looked at the gun. The Indian military had manufactured the Vindhya 12-millimeter especially for their morey infantry. A pink's wrist couldn't handle the recoil. It was made of gray metal and ceramics, surprisingly light for its size—the barrel alone was 70 centimeters long. The magazine held twelve rounds. There were three magazines in the case, all full. A dozen notches marred the composite handgrip.

He held up the gun and cleared it, checked the safety, and slid a full magazine in. The magazine slid home with a satisfying solidity. The Vindhya was in perfect condition, even after ten years of neglect. The weight was seductive in his hand.

Nohar had practice with guns before it was a felony for a morey to own a firearm, but he had never even taken this one out of its case.

There were two holsters in the drawer. He left the combat webbing and removed the worn-leather shoulder holster. Nohar had never worn it, but he tried it on now. It fit well, comfortably, and that disturbed him.

One final item—a file folder containing a sheet of paper and a card for his wallet. Both items were pristine, the card still in its cellophane wrapper. It was the gun's registration and his license to use it. They were still valid, despite the ban on morey firearms. He'd gotten them a year prior to the ban.

He put the card in his wallet, holstered the loaded gun, and, hot as it was, put on his trench. Nohar had brought the trench coat despite the fact there had been little threat of rain. He had brought it to hide the gun. He pocketed the two extra magazines and put the case back in the drawer. As he locked the drawer up again, he told himself he was never going to fire the thing, but he knew, if he'd really believed that, he would have never opened that drawer.

Nohar left the office, the gun an oppressive weight under his shoulder.

Angel was awake again when Nohar returned with the groceries. She began cursing in Spanish the second he opened the door. Nohar had thought he'd get back before she woke up. After an experience like she'd been through, she should have slept like the dead.

"We had a fucking deal, Kit—" More Spanish. "You don't leave me alone like that."

He ducked through the living room and into the kitchen, shucking the trench as he went. Cat followed Nohar, and the food, into the kitchen.

"You listening to me, Kit?"

The dry cat food was still covering the counter where he had spilled it last night. Nohar had forgotten the mess. He set down his bag and picked up Cat's dish. After rinsing it off, he swept about half the spilled food off the counter and into the dish. When he put it down, Cat pounced on the bowl, oblivious to the fact that it was filled with the same stuff that was on the counter.

Nohar decided he could afford the waste and brushed the rest of the spill into the sink and turned on the disposal.

Angel was leaning against the door frame. She looked a lot better. She had taken a shower, returning her dirty brown coat to its original light tan. Her ears had perked up, though even with them she was still over a meter shorter than Nohar.

She was jabbering in Spanish, and Nohar knew she wasn't saying anything nice.

He asked her what she wanted to eat.

She walked into the kitchen and looked into the bag. She was still angry, Nohar could smell it, but her tone was softening. "And I thought you *weren't* a cop."

"I'm not."

She squatted next to Cat. She was calming down, and Nohar began to realize exactly how scared she must have been when she woke up here alone. Angel was someone who wouldn't like being scared. It would screw with her self-image.

Angel was looking at Nohar's left armpit. "What about the sudden artillery?"

Nohar had forgotten the Vindhya. "Just because I have a gun—"

"That righteous? That fine? Something that worthy goes for 5K at least. Tell me you bought it."

She tried to pet Cat, but Cat was eating and couldn't be bothered. When Cat hissed at her, she stopped.

Nohar began putting away the stuff he'd bought, tossing a half-kilo of burger into the micro for himself. "I didn't *buy* it. My father brought it over from the war. Got it when he died."

She stood up. She wasn't argumentive anymore. She seemed to have gotten it out of her system. "Knew your sire?"

"It's not unheard of."

"Only morey *I* heard of with a set." She intercepted a bag of tomatoes he was putting in the fridge. "Even the rats make kids with a needle, and they're as common as fleas on a Ziphead. How'd two modified *panthera tigris* ever get together to make you?"

The micro dinged at him and he pulled out the burger. Angel's nose wrinkled. She was vegetarian.

"Mother and Father were in the same platoon. He led a mass defection. The entire company of tigers, even the medic. Of all the cubs he must've made, I was the only one to track him down afterward."

From her expression he could tell he'd talked too much. "Hot shit, that *is* a Vind twelve. You're talking about the Rajasthan Airlift. You *knew* Datia—"

"Yes, I knew him. I don't want to talk about it."

Nohar took his food and ducked into the living room.

Angel followed, with her tomato. "Datia's a legend, the first real morey leader—"

Oh, that was great. A true leader. Nohar whipped around to face Angel. Cat was there to pounce on a spilled hunk of burger. "Datia Rajasthan was a psychopath. He needed to be gunned down, and if you so much as mention him one more time I am going to hand-feed you to the Zips one piece at a time."

Angel just stared at him.

Nohar sat on the couch, ate a handful of hamburger, and turned on his comm to the news.

CHAPTER 11

Monday morning was breaking into a steel-gray dawn when the Jerboa pulled up in front of Young's shadow house.

"Wake up, Angel. We're here."

The rabbit, who'd looked like an inanimate pile of clothes until Nohar spoke, stirred. "Kit? Time is it?"

"Five after." Nohar stood up and stepped over the nonworking driver's side door. Young's house was the worse for wear. The garage had gone up like a bomb. The only remains of it was a black pile of charred debris at the end of the driveway. The house itself had caught. Nohar supposed some burning debris had landed on the roof.

There was a yawn from behind him that seemed much too large for the rabbit. "Five after what?"

"Six." The fire had gutted the house to the basement. The windows looked in on one large, black, empty, roofless space. The two neighboring buildings—Nohar hoped they had been unoccupied—had caught, too, but had escaped with relatively light damage.

"Six, Kit, this is no sane time to be awake—"

"You said that when I woke you up."

"Could have let me sleep—"

Nohar shook his head. "Not after that tirade yesterday."

Angel hopped over the door. She was dressed in an avalanche of black webbing and terry cloth that used to belong to Maria. The only clothing Nohar had for her. Somehow Angel had gotten the castoffs to fit her with a shoelace and a few strategic knots. The problem was, she smelled like Maria. "Couldn't wait till a decent hour?"

"Quit complaining. If I had a safe place to file you, I'd do it. For now, you're along for the ride."

Angel yawned again. Her mouth opened so wide it seemed to add twenty centimeters to her height. She shook her head and her ears flopped back and forth.

"So, what we doing here?"

Nohar started walking down the driveway. He could smell the gasoline. Even now, after at least one night of rain, there was still no question of arson. "I want to see if anything made it through the fire."

They passed the rear of the house, and the damage was much worse. The entire rear wall of Young's house had collapsed. The siding was sagging and puckered and bowed in the middle. Angel was only a few steps behind him. "Hope you're not talking architecture. This place is worse than the tower."

Nohar wasn't talking about architecture.

There's a difference between a supervised, methodical destruction of a body of records—Nohar was pretty sure Young was trying to torch, judging by the volume, close to everything in the Binder campaign finance records—and the accidental combustion Young had initiated. Something would have survived.

Apparently he hadn't been the only one to think so. He walked up to the spot where the garage used to be. The charred remains were in piles that were much too neat, and it looked like someone had gone through the ashes with a rake. "Damn it."

"What's the prob?"

Nohar waved at the garage, and expanded the gesture to take in the entire backyard. The rear lawn had been turfed by truck tires to the point that no grass was left. "Someone beat me here. Whoever it was, shoveled up everything Young didn't torch."

Nohar wasn't expecting to find *the* piece of evidence, but it would have been nice to find *something*. Angel was walking around the backyard, wide feet slapping in the mud. When he had looked for clothing for her, Nohar couldn't find a damn thing that even resembled a shoe for a rabbit.

"What am I looking for?"

Nohar was surprised Angel wanted to help. He supposed she was bored. "It was mostly paper. Some might have blown to the edges of the property where our trash-pickers missed it."

That was a bit of wishful thinking. The plot was bare of even normal garbage. Nohar supposed the people with the truck had grabbed everything that had even a slight chance of having been part of the records. They had a full weekend to work in. They were very thorough. Nohar wondered if they'd been the cops, or Binder's people, or MLI, or—

Nohar looked up from the edge of the driveway he was examining. "Angel? Do the Zips have any workings with a congressman named Binder?"

Angel's laugh was somewhat condescending. "Must be kidding. Zips and politics? Me becoming president'd happen sooner. All Zips want is a free hand to deal their flush."

Nohar shrugged. A connection seemed unlikely, but he couldn't deny the fact that there was a connection— somewhere. Hassan was involved with the Zips, and it looked like Hassan killed Johnson. But Hassan wasn't working for the Zips. If anything, it looked like the other way around.

"Were the run-ins with the other gangs because of the drugs?"

"Don't know about other folks, but my clutch was into protection— When you do, you have to protect people you charge. Both Zips and flush were pretty dangerous." She sighed. Her ears drooped. "Too dangerous for us."

She turned to face him. Her scar was fighting the

frown she wore. "Could've used someone like you back then, Kit."

Nohar didn't have a response for that. So he went back to his fruitless search.

By nine they had combed every inch of the property at least twice. The only result was part of a letter-fax Angel had found halfway across the street. It had been written by a gentleman named Wilson Scott, presumably to Binder or someone in the campaign. They only had the bottom half, so Nohar didn't know. It could be totally unrelated.

The letter went into detail on "the late morey violence." It got pretty down on the moreys, talking about moreys offing pinks, moreys taking hostages, morey air terrorism, and other generally alarmist topics.

Sounded like something somebody wrote during the riots. It was dated the tenth of August. Nohar wished he had a year to go with it. He also wished Scott didn't have a habit of writing in sweeping generalities.

With just half a hysterical polemic, the morning seemed to have been a waste of time. They didn't even have an address for Scott.

Nohar took Angel to his office with him. He wanted to make a few phone calls, now that people in the Binder campaign weren't on vacation. He would have liked the less-cramped atmosphere of his apartment. However, he figured the more he kept Angel away from Moreytown, the better off they both would be.

Even with Angel, the office wasn't any more cramped. He lifted her up, and she fit on top of the filing cabinet, out of the way—and out of view of the comm. . . .

Not that he intended to use the video pickup. He was going to try and bull through to the one living member of the Bowling Green gang of four he had yet to talk to. Edwin Harrison, the legal counsel.

Nohar's funeral picture had him sitting right next to Binder, front row, center. With Daryl Johnson's death,

Harrison would be the most powerful man in the Binder organization, after Binder himself. In fact, Nohar remembered news off the comm had him as the current acting campaign manager.

The top, or close to it.

He killed the video pickup and hoped he could reach Harrison before anyone realized who was calling. Nohar also engaged in a slight electronic legerdemain. The outgoing calls he had been placing from his apartment had all been piped through his comm in his office. This was the listed one, his professional voice, so to speak. This was the comm everyone was locking out.

However, the process worked in reverse. He could pipe calls from the office through the unlisted comm at his home. They wouldn't be locking that out—yet.

It turned out to be easier than Nohar had expected. The strained voice and the strained expression on the secretary—from the obvious makeup, and the hair perfect as injection-molded plastic, she would fall into Stephie's category of window dressing—made it obvious she'd been operating the phones too long. Nohar could see lights blinking on the periphery of the screen. She had at least a dozen calls coming in. The way her eyes darted, she had at least four on the screen.

Nohar asked for Harrison. Her only response was, "Hold on, I'll transfer you."

The screen fed him the Binder campaign logo and dry synth music as he waited for Harrison's secretary to pick up the phone. It was a long wait and Nohar had to restrain the urge to claw something.

The call was finally answered, not by a secretary, but by Harrison himself.

Edwin Harrison had to be the same age as Young and Johnson. They had all been contemporaries out of college about the same time. But Nohar knew pink markings well enough to see the graying at the temples and the receding hair as some indication of premature aging. Harrison bore the slight scars of corrective optical surgery—Nohar had a brief wish his rotten day-vision could be corrected as easily—distorting his eyes. Under a nose that had been broken at least once, he had a salt-and-pepper brush of a mustache. There was no real way to estimate height over the comm, but Harrison looked small.

Harrison's shirt was unbuttoned and his face looked damp. The man was rubbing his cheek with one hand. Nohar figured he'd been shaving, a pink concept the moreau didn't understand.

Nohar found his polite voice. "Mr. Harrison—"

Harrison sat down in front of his comm. "Whoever you are, if you want to talk to me, you better turn on your video pickup. I can tell the difference between a voice-only phone and someone with a full comm who just doesn't want to be seen. I have no desire to spend a conversation with a test pattern when you can see me perfectly well."

So much for polite.

Nohar just hoped the guy was too long-winded to hang up immediately. He did as requested.

Harrison's reaction was immediate. In the same, level, conversational tone of voice, he said, "Holy mother of God, it's a hair-job."

Hair-job?

Nohar hadn't heard moreys referred to as hair-jobs in nearly a decade. "Can we talk?"

"Mr. Raghastan, correct?"

Nohar hated it when people mispronounced his name, even if it was only a generic label for that particular generation of tigers. Nohar nodded.

"I am sorry, but I have a very busy schedule. If you could make an appointment—"

So you can ignore me at your leisure, Nohar thought. *Not without a fight.* "I only have a few questions about Johnson and the campaign's financial records."

Harrison seemed to be indecisive about whether he wanted to be evasive or simply hang up. "I am sure you know any financial information that isn't a matter of public record is confidential. I can refer you to our press secretary. I am sure he can—"

—*brush me off as well as anyone in the campaign,* Nohar thought. "No, you don't understand. I don't want specifics." *A lie,* Nohar thought, *but there's little chance of getting specifics out of you, right? Right.* "I was just wondering how thorough Young was in torching the records."

Harrison looked pained. "I am afraid I can't discuss Young. We are still dealing with the police on that matter."

Probably true. Trying to cover things up, no doubt. "Your headquarters was closed down last week. I suppose Young just waltzed in and took what he wanted?"

From Harrison's expression, Young *had* just walked in. It also looked like Young had done a lot of damage. "How many years back, five? Ten? Fifteen?"

From Harrison's face, fifteen.

"How much were you able to salvage?"

Harrison looked puzzled. "Salvage?"

Binder wasn't the one with the trucks. Nohar supposed there was little harm in telling the lawyer, and it might jar something loose. "I was under the impression you were in charge of the trucks that carted away the remains of the fire."

That got Harrison. "I am sorry. I really must go—"

I bet you must, Nohar thought to himself. He wondered exactly what kind of illegal crap was in those records that could turn Harrison that white.

Harrison regained his composure. "I should tell you. Stay out of this—it doesn't involve you, or your kind."

As the connection broke, Nohar said, "But it does. More than you know, you little pink bottom feeder."

If *he* could pick up that much from Harrison's face, Nohar decided the lawyer would never win a jury trial.

There was a snore, and Nohar saw that Angel had fallen asleep on top of the filing cabinet. Instead of waking her up and leaving, he leaned against the wall and thought.

All that talk—well, all *his* talk—about Young had shaken loose a doubt. He was missing something, a big something.

Young's motivation.

It just wasn't your standard grief reaction to torch the finance records of your employer. Nohar could, even with Stephie's doubts, believe Young blew himself up over lost love. But why the records?

Slowly, it began to dawn on Nohar that he was missing the obvious.

True, Johnson and Young had been lovers, fifteen years, above average for any relationship, pink or otherwise. Young saw Johnson's killer—the morey canine Nugoya called Hassan—he probably saw Johnson get shot. *But Young never called the cops.*

Not only didn't he call the cops, but Young actually covered for the missing Johnson. Stephie said Young had mentioned Johnson was out with "some bigwig contributor."

Then, after a few weeks, he blows himself up.

Someone very purposefully removed almost every trace of the records Young had torched. If the motive for Johnson's assassination was in those records, the odds were they had been carted away by the people responsible for Johnson's death. There were four ways they could have known what Young had been trying to destroy. Binder's people, Young himself, or the cops could have told them. All unlikely.

Or, they *told Young to destroy the records.*

"You're not going to do me like you did Derry."

Fear. Young was scared when he said that. He was talking paranoid. "You're *all* with them." Moreys, he was talking moreys and—something else. Franks? MLI? Whoever *they* were, *they* were in charge of Johnson's death—and Young.

Young was afraid of *them.* Young was also pathological about Daryl Johnson taking the fall for something.

"Derry didn't know he was helping *them*—what *they* were. When he found out he was going to stop. . . . People will say he was working for *them*."

Why that fear for Johnson's rep? If Young cared that much, why wasn't he at the funeral?

Guilt.

Nohar triggered Young's suicide: "You're the finance chairman. Why didn't you figure it out first?"

Then, blam.

Of course Young knew what was in the finance records. Nohar felt like an idiot for not realizing sooner. *Young* was the one to let in the canine assassin with the Levitt Mark II. Young was in a conspiracy with *them*. Somewhere there was a trail in the records. Johnson had found it and had confronted *Young* with it.

The two of them were close, but Johnson was going to put a stop to it, whatever *it* was. Young couldn't let that happen—no, not quite right, *they* couldn't let that happen. *They* hired the morey. *They* killed Johnson. *They* probably just told Young to turn off the security and leave the door open so *they* could explain things to Johnson. When Young blew up, *they* made sure the records vanished.

No way Young could call the cops. Whoever was handling Young must have forced him to go on, business as usual. Go into work, go back to his shadow house. All the while, guilt ate Young up. He felt responsible for Johnson's death.

The whole charade of blowing out the picture window was to cover *Young's* tracks. To give *Young* an alibi.

It was working so well—up to the point Young torched the records.

That seemed an act of desperation, and not just Young's desperation—

Nohar had a bad thought.

Thomson had mentioned Johnson's executive assistant, Stephie, as having the same access to the financial records as the gang of four. That was obviously just the "official" slant on things. After all, Stephie described herself as window dressing. What if *they* didn't know that?

That worried Nohar.

What if *they* thought Johnson's executive assistant knew something, and just weren't sure enough to go to the lengths they went with Johnson?

What if she was being watched?

Could it be a coincidence Young went ballistic the day after Nohar talked to her?

Could it be a coincidence that the white rat's—Terin's—"Finger of God" seemed to have lifted?

He called Stephie. No answer.

It was ten-thirty, an hour and a half before he was to meet her. Damn. Nohar clutched the filing cabinet and started deep breathing exercises. His concern had triggered the fight-or-flight reflex, the adrenaline was pumping. He wanted to fight something. It was still too soon after those Ziphead rodents behind the bus. Something inside him was responding to the pulse, the adrenaline, the stress—

He fought it off.

Nohar couldn't let his control slip like that.

He had barely brought himself back under control, when the comm buzzed.

Nohar told the comm. "Got it."

The comm responded.

Smith had the video on. He was as eldritch as ever. The glassy eyes still stared out of a flat, expressionless face in the center of a pear-shaped head. Moisture glistened on the rubbery-white skin. On the monitor, Nohar got a chance to examine Smith from a closer perspective than he really wanted to. The pear shape of the frank's head, Nohar now saw, was caused by a massive roll of flesh that drooped over the frank's collar. The roll of fat obscured any neck or chin the frank might have had. The frank was totally hairless, too, no hair at all, anywhere. No pores Nohar could see.

The frank could have been a white polyethylene bag filled with silicone lubricant.

The reason the frank didn't blink was because he didn't have any eyelids.

Smith also didn't have any nostrils.

No ears either.

The frank was calling from an unlisted location, and the lighting only picked up the frank's white bulk, nothing of the background. "I am glad I see you mostly unhurt from when you go to Philip Young."

"Thanks." Nohar immediately noticed Smith's weird accent again. It was not Afrikaans. "Your message said you paid the hospital."

"It is a legitimate expense of the investigation."

"You want a progress report."

The frank attempted a nod, sending the flesh of his upper body into unnatural vibrations.

Nohar told the frank what he knew and what he thought he knew. How Johnson was killed, who was involved, and, of course, the as yet nebulous why. Nohar had convinced himself, despite Young's unreliability, that the reason lay in the now-destroyed-and-or-missing financial records of the Binder campaign.

"Excellent progress in such a short time."

"Now let me ask *you* a few things." Nohar knew he had jumped into the case prematurely, and what bothered him most wasn't his involvement in a pink murder, or even his involvement with a murder, period. What bothered him was the absence of information on his client and his client's company.

"I render what aid I can."

"First, you're worried about MLI being involved in the killing, and you told me you're an accountant— What's in the campaign records that could have connected back to MLI?"

"Only our heavy financing of the Binder campaign. A connection our board informs me will be severed as of our last payment—the three million Binder is missing and we are not. Our only contact with the Binder campaign is our money and suggestions on appropriate votes to take on the issues before him.''

Nohar snorted. Having a bunch of franks telling Binder what to do bordered on the absurd. ''You dictated the way he voted in the House?''

''He never votes against us. Our support is based on his closeness to our views.''

That *did not* ring true. A frank's views being close to Binder's? Binder was a little to the right of Attila, was for the sterilization of moreys and probably the outright extermination of franks.

However, the finance records *were* the only connection between MLI and Binder. That gave credence to Smith's suspicion someone in MLI was behind the killing. Since the money trail had been sitting tight that long—fifteen years back, the way Harrison acted— if the motive was in the records it was in some incredibly obscure financial tidbit where Johnson never would have seen it in the first place, or it was in those ''suggestions on appropriate votes.''

''Second, I want to know where you and the other franks at MLI *really* come from.''

For the first time Nohar saw what could be the remotest trace of expression on the frank's face. *Close to a nerve.* The bubbling voice seemed just a little strained when Smith responded. ''I told you. We come from South Africa—''

''South Africa never signed the U.N.'s human genome experiment ban—but it's just one non-signer of at least two dozen that have the technology. One of a half-dozen that uses it. That isn't an Afrikaans accent.''

Smith let out a sound that could have been a sigh. ''I do not know if I am glad or not I hire such a perceptive investigator.''

''Don't compliment me on noticing the obvious.''

''I am afraid this information I cannot give you.''

''Oh, great—''

The sigh, it *was* a sigh, came again. ''Please, I explain. Our origin must remain private. Just as we must remain unseen ourselves. It is for the company's survival. If MLI has a murderer, or murderers, in its midst, such secrets are public. But my loyalty will not permit such knowledge until I know if the guilt is there. If you can't pursue this without that information, I will let you go with the money you have earned.''

Good, you have an out. Nohar stood there, staring. He told himself he was going to say to hell with it. Drop the whole mess then and there. . . .

He thought of Stephie.

He couldn't.

He had never ditched anything in the middle.

''You know you're hobbling me when you withhold information.''

''I am sorry.''

''I need copies of those 'suggestions.' ''

''They're on file. I get them. At ten-thirty Wednesday night we meet in the cemetery.''

''Comm off.''

What in the hell did he think he was doing?

He should have dumped the case when he had the chance.

CHAPTER 12

The walk past the city end of Mayfield was nerve-racking for Nohar. His sudden concern for Stephie had hit a few buttons. He was passing Ziphead territory with Angel. He felt the gun was all too obvious under his green windbreaker, even though when he chose the jacket it had seemed up to the job of concealing the Vind.

It felt like there was a target strapped to his back and the weight under his arm didn't really help.

There were no rats around, hadn't been since yesterday. That was becoming suspicious. There were always rodents around in Moreytown, even in daylight.

The streets were bare of them.

There was new graffiti under the bridge that separated Moreytown from the Circle. It was under the sarcastic, "Welcome to Moreytown." It read, "The Zipperhead rules here." The Zip graffiti was becoming too ubiquitous.

Nohar remembered the too-common slogan, "Off the pink," from the riots. A decade later, that slogan—Datia's slogan—had passed into general usage as a stock antiauthoritarian comment.

Nohar wondered if the people who used it habitually were consciously aware it was a call for human genocide.

It felt like he was in the Hellcats again and everything was about to explode into brimstone and shitfire. The feeling didn't leave after they passed the concrete pylons demarking the end of Mayfield Road.

The pink universe of Case Western Reserve University was only a few blocks from the farthest extention of Moreytown. The border was marked by the sudden shift into decent landscaping.

Angel turned toward him. "You feel safe, Kit?"

"No."

"Feel the shit's about to go ballistic?"

"You, too?"

"When the players absent all of a sudden, you know the situation is going to ground zero on you."

Nohar shrugged. "I've got a meeting to go to."

"Right. Whatever it is, it ain't us."

Nohar let it go with an insincere nod. He knew Angel didn't believe that. Neither did he. He didn't believe in coincidence. He thought it pretty damn likely the absence of Zips had a hell of a lot to do with them.

They made the coffeehouse at a little after twelve. The aroma of exotic, rare, and engineered coffees overwhelmed Nohar's sense of smell—at least it removed Maria's ghost-odor from Angel's clothes.

It was a college lunchtime crowd, with only one other morey—at least he and Angel weren't the only ones—a graying red vulpine who was engaged in a chess game with a black pink. Some of the patrons gave the new pair a few stares. Nohar, being a rather singular morey, got more than his share. Nohar was relieved to see Stephie in the back. She had chosen a table with enough room for him to maneuver around.

Nohar walked straight to the table and sat down. Angel hovered a second at the counter, until she seemed to realize she didn't have any money. Stephie was looking at Angel, but she directed her question to Nohar. "Who's your friend?"

"She's a lead from the Johnson killing."

"She?"

Sometimes pinks weren't quick on the uptake when it came to morey gender. Nohar supposed it had to do with the lack of prominent breasts.

Angel turned a chair around and sat on it backward.

She rested her chin on the back, and scratched the base of her scar—her nose twitched. "Name's Angel, Pinky. Kit here's my bodyguard."

"Ah, hello. My name's Weir, Stephie Weir."

Odd, Nohar thought, now she *was* acting like he'd expect a pink to around morey. It was usually one of three things—fear, condescension, or this vague nervousness that was now spilling off of Stephie in waves.

"You wanted to talk. What about?"

She took her eyes off the rabbit and looked at Nohar. "I've been offered my job back—"

Nohar gave her a close-lipped smile. "Congratulations—"

Stephie interrupted him. "—aren't in order. It was conditional I didn't talk to you. That kind of job security I don't need. I've been let go once, like excess weight on a ballistic shuttle. I'm not going to be blackmailed into helping in a cover-up."

Angel chuckled. "Good for you, Pinky. Fuck the PTB."

Stephie looked confused. "PTB?"

Nohar felt his claws digging into the table. He untensed his hand and tried to stare Angel into shutting up as he explained. "P. T. B. Powers that be. Terminology from the riots—When did you get this offer?"

"After I gave you the lift from the hospital. It was waiting on my comm when I got back home. I never liked Harrison that much." She smiled now. "I called his house the minute I got the message. I got him out of bed at two in the morning to cuss him out and tell him what to do with his offer. He gave me a raise twice. I told him, at this point, not even if I supported Binder."

That nagged at something. The Binder campaign was riddled with that kind of inconsistency. "I want to know why the campaign has people like Thompson, Young, and Johnson in it."

"I never probed too deeply into that. I told you I

was just window dressing. It was a money thing. I admit it. I sold out. They needed me for Derry. Anyway, there are precious few women in my age-group that are for Binder. Those that were might have had some principles.''

He appreciated the fact she wanted to tell him about Harrison's offer. It also reminded him about his worries earlier today. "Who'd you tell about our meeting?''

Stephie shrugged. "No one, not even Harrison— though I was tempted to tell him he was too late with his little job offer. Just to make him stew.''

Angel beat Nohar to the next question. "Why not?''

Nohar glared at her as Stephie answered. "It's *my* business. Why should I have told him about it?''

There's the anger again, Nohar thought, *just like that lesbian comment.* It was laced with confusion, too, but less of it. It felt like she had come to some sort of decision.

Oh, well, let Stephie be pissed at the rabbit. "Stephie, you told no one?''

"Right.''

"Not boyfriend, girlfriend, family, your mother?''

"I said, no one—'' She gave a weak smile. "Not even my nonexistent boyfriend.''

Now Nohar had reason to worry. Young's self-destruction and the Zip attack on him had been just too well-timed.

"Someone found out. You're being watched.''

"What?''

Nohar glanced at Angel, and gave Stephie the story. Nohar briefly wondered if he should be doing all this exposition in front of Angel, but she *was* involved in this—however tangentially—and she was getting the short end of it as well.

After the brief rundown, Stephie looked thoughtful. "You might be right. I think Phil could handle the strain of losing Derry. But if he thought himself responsible. If he actually *was* responsible . . .''

Stephie shook her head. "But I *do not* understand why you think the black hats from Phil's conspiracy are watching *me*. Of all people, I am—was—the least significant person in the Binder organization."

Angel dived in again. "Pinky, do *they* know that? Overheard your story, and the whole point was to make you look like honcho's squeeze *and* his second. Like, this is what pissed you in the first place, right? You just *looked* high-mighty when your *real* job was to make mister rump-ranger look like an upstanding pink hetro."

Angel was crude, but right. Nohar jumped in before Stephie could say something to Angel. "As Johnson's 'executive assistant,' you 'officially' had access to all the finance records Young torched. *They* might not realize your only function was to cover for Johnson's homosexuality. Also, Young started destroying records, not right after the murder, not when the body was found, not even right after the funeral. Young waited till nearly two weeks after the killing—"

Nohar leaned in for emphasis and tapped the claw of his index finger on the table. "He waited until the day after I talked to you."

"I see what you mean—"

"Hey, Kit. You smell something?"

Nohar looked at Angel. He was finally about to tell her to shut up, when he smelled it too. If it wasn't for the coffee, he would have noticed it immediately. Someone was wearing a very distinctive perfume. Nohar remembered the first time he had smelled it—in front of the ATM in Moreytown. It belonged to a female white rat.

Terin.

The Zipheads were here.

Nohar looked to the front. The front door was closing. As it did, the waft of sickening perfume died out. The fox was still the only other morey in evidence inside the coffeehouse.

"Terin?" Nohar asked Angel.

"Terin," she agreed.

The only change in the street was the car parked in front. It was a black ailing Jerboa, like Nohar's. Older and not a convertible. The windows had been painted black on the inside. Nohar heard the door slam on the car, and saw a hunched form run away from the vehicle. Nohar couldn't tell if it was pink, morey, or one of the Ziphead rodents. But Nohar remembered the Zips' trademark.

The driver was running away—

"Stephie, get down!"

Angel had already dived under a table. Nohar didn't wait for Stephie to reach cover on her own. He circled his left arm around her chest and slammed her against the far wall behind the table, putting him between her and the windows. His right hand went for the Vind.

For three seconds, Nohar felt real stupid.

Then the car exploded.

The windows weren't glass. They were some engineered polymer. They didn't shatter so much as tear and disintegrate. Then the air blew in carrying the heat and smoke of the blast. The pinks were yelling and screaming. Thankfully, Stephie wasn't one of them. Her face was buried in the fur of his chest.

The sounds began to fade as Nohar became too aware of his own heartbeat in his ears. He felt his pulse behind his eyeballs and in his temple.

He tried to fight it.

Nohar turned as soon as he realized there wasn't going to be a secondary explosion. He wasn't surprised to see four rodents diving through the now-open windows. The pinks didn't know squat. They had all hit the ground. The members of the gang advanced on the patrons, jumping overturned tables, kicking aside chairs.

Nohar was back in the riots again, watching one of Datia Rajasthan's terror runs on the pinks.

He was breathing heavily. Against his will, he could feel his time sense telescoping. Things were slowing down. His head throbbed as the adrenaline started kicking in.

A black rodent with a sawed-off shotgun was diving straight for their table. The room was hazed with smoke, and his eyes stung and watered, but Nohar knew Blackie was aiming at them. Nohar jumped to the side, hoping to draw Blackie's fire.

Nohar assumed he was the target.

He was wrong.

Blackie kept going straight for Stephie and leveled the shotgun at her.

The Beast kicked the door wide open, roared, and pulled the gun.

The Vind 12 slid out of its holster like it was on greased bearings. His thumb had clicked the safety as it cleared his windbreaker. He leveled the Vind about twelve centimeters away from Blackie's head and pulled the trigger.

The report deafened Nohar.

It did worse to Blackie, who had started to turn when he realized Nohar was armed. The bullet caught Blackie in the face, under the right eye. Datia's bullets weren't the standard Indian military teflon-coated armor-piercers. They were twelve-millimeter dumdums, strictly antipersonnel. The bullet carried away half of Blackie's head out the back of his skull.

Time was moving incredibly slowly. It seemed there was a full second between each heartbeat, but Nohar knew his heart was running on overdrive and trying to jackhammer out of his rib cage. His nerves were humming like an overloaded high-tension wire.

He had whipped around to face the other Zipheads before Blackie hit the ground. The rodents, who had been about to lay waste to the pink population, were all looking in his direction. One of them had an Uzi nine-millimeter. The rat had been facing the wrong way, and was only now swinging the gun toward Nohar.

The Vind was already pointing in Uzi's direction.

Three shots in rapid succession. One for each heartbeat in the space of a second. Nohar's aim wasn't great. The first shot went high. Nohar corrected and the second went low, taking out Uzi's right knee and knocking the rodent sideways—sending the gun sailing over the counter. Third correction got Uzi right in the chest as the rat was spinning. The shot took Uzi off his feet and slammed him down nearly two meters back toward the smoking window.

There was a pop, it sounded like someone breaking a light bulb. Someone rammed what felt like a white-hot knife into Nohar's right hip. The warmth spread down his leg, soaking into his fur.

The rats were unfreezing.

One had a familiar-looking twenty-two revolver. Wasn't Fearless. As Nohar turned, the popgun fired again. Nohar felt a breeze on his cheek, brushing his whiskers as a supersonic insect grazed his neck. The Vind swung at the rat with the popgun and Nohar saw one of the Zipheads had a forty-four. Forty-four had a nice, expensive Automag. Problem was, the rat must have been used to revolvers. He seemed to have forgotten about the safety.

The Vind stopped on the dangerous one and unloaded four rounds as Twenty-two popped off another shot that missed.

Forty-four got it in the gut twice, once in the neck.

Twenty-two ditched his gun and ran for the window, diving.

Nohar had a perfect shot and three bullets left. He almost pulled the trigger.

The door creaked shut on The Beast. Reluctantly.

The front of the *Arabica* coffeehouse was now obscured by smoke from the burning car. Pinks were making for the exits. Nohar's hearing was coming back and he could hear the fire alarms wailing. The sprinklers came on.

Unlike most everyone in the room, with the exception of Angel, Nohar had been through shit like this before. It wasn't over.

"Angel, you still with us?"

A table turned over and Angel climbed out. "Yeah, Kit."

"Grab Blackie's shotgun, cover our rear."

"Gotcha."

Stephie, like most of the other pinks, had yet to react. She was still staring at the rodent whose head had done a halfways vanishing act in front of her. "Stephie, rear exit."

She turned toward Nohar with a blank expression. The crash was already hitting him. He didn't need to deal with this. He grabbed her and shook her a little too hard. "You know this place, where's the back door? They're only hesitating because they didn't expect a gun in the crowd!"

Angel had the shotgun. She was leveling it at the windows. "That Vind ain't a gun, it's a howitzer. Kit, I got two shots—and the way this shotgun's been treated, lucky if it don't blow up."

"Exit!"

Stephie was finally getting a grip on herself. She started back to the rear of the place. Nohar was grateful. She wasn't one of those pinks that suddenly collapse at the sight of blood and violence. And thank whatever deity, she didn't suggest waiting for the cops.

"Here."

The rear of the shop was, for the most part, covered with old sacks and bags that used to hold coffee. At this end of the store, the bean smell overrode even the smoke. Stephie pulled aside one of the bags. Behind it was a short hallway with a public comm and restrooms, terminating in a fire exit.

They piled in, Nohar first. For the first time since he had broken free from the adrenaline high, he realized the hole in his right hip was more than minor. The engineered endorphins were wearing off. Felt like someone was holding a hot iron on his leg. "Stephie, you drive here? Where'd you park?"

"Lot behind the building. Were they after *me*?"

Nohar pressed himself against the fire door and peered through the one small pane of cracked yellow glass. "Blackie went straight for you. The Zips are hooked into the Johnson killing."

"If they've been watching, they know my car."

"Pinky has a point. Zips are real fond of burning transport." Angel paused because the chaos in the front room had just upped a notch. Nohar thought he could hear the sound of distant sirens. "We best vanish ourselves, quick."

Nohar had been scanning the parking lot, looking for the Antaeus. The huge Plymouth was hard to miss. Especially with the rat fumbling over the open hood to the power plant. Nohar grunted. His temple was pounding and there were little flashes of color interfering with his peripheral vision. Keeping his concentration focused while he slid the downside ride from that violent high was giving him a migraine.

"Bad news, you're right. They're wiring the car. Angel, cover me and be quiet."

"Gotcha, Kit."

Lucky, lucky. They were lucky because the Mad Bomber didn't quite seem to have a handle on what he was doing. Lucky because there weren't any other rats in the back. Mad Bomber was supposed to be the rearguard. Apparently the Zips gave him too much to do.

Nohar didn't rely on stealth, but Bomber seemed oblivious. Nohar closed the space between him and the rat in five running steps—each lumbering step drove a spike into his hip—and leveled the gun at the back of Bomber's head. By then, the rat knew something was up.

Mad Bomber was in the process of turning around. Nohar cocked the Vind and and clucked his tongue at the rat. "Car has a wonderful finish, I wonder if you'll see the brains leave your head in the reflection?"

"Wha?" The wave of fear that floated off the rat was gratifying.

"Undo it, now. Or we're walking and you're on permanent vacation."

"Yeah . . ." The rat started taking things out of the power plant. Too slow, the sirens were getting louder.

"Remember, fifteen seconds and you're going to start the car."

Bomber hurried, ripping other things out of the power plant. Nohar hoped the rat knew the wires he was pulling.

Mad Bomber finally came out with what looked like an Afghani landmine. It had Arabic markings on it.

Bang from behind them.

Angel called back as the smell of cordite and blood drifted over. "Kit, that's one shot. Hurry up, pink law's coming!"

Nohar kept his eye on the rat. It was becoming hard to keep his vision focused. He had all his weight on his left leg. "You heard the rabbit, hurry up. That sound back there was your backup."

"Done, it's done . . ."

Mad Bomber was shaking now. Nohar could see why he didn't get the job of diving in on the pinks. The rat couldn't handle it. He was going to die. Not from the cops or another gang's guns. He was going to die from his own stupidity—or the gang would kill him itself. Nohar waved the two females over.

"Some advice. Quit the gang before you make a fatal screwup. Take the mine, stand over there."

Nohar motioned with the gun and Mad Bomber did meekly as told. Angel ran up, Stephie in tow, and leveled the shotgun at the rat. "Shell left, let me vanish the ratboy."

At least she asked. "Self-defense, no preemptive strikes." The migraine was getting worse.

"Fine with me, Kit. Saves the ammo."

Stephie eased behind the wheel and Nohar hustled Angel into the passenger side. Bomber was still blubbering under the stare of the Vindhya, but he managed to say something. "You said I would start the car . . ."

"I lied."

Nohar dived into the back seat. The fire in his hip totally blacked out his vision when he hit the seat. As Stephie floored the Antaeus, the door slammed shut. Nohar heard the cables tearing out of the metered feed. He hoped they had some jumpers in the trunk or they'd only have one full charge to go on. A car this size didn't go far on one charge.

They were topping sixty klicks per as they jumped the curb on to the Midtown Corridor. Nohar's sight came back a little as he watched the destruction from out the rear window. Smoke billowed out from the car in front of the *Arabica*. Black, brown, and white rodents were bugging out of the place, heading toward Moreytown. All attention was riveted on the coffee-house, or the flashers coming from the east. Except—

Two moreys in an off-road four-wheeler, the kind of thing you needed to drive into Moreytown past the barriers. With the speed the Antaeus was going and his pain-shot vision he could only make the types. White rodent, grayish canine. Terin and Hassan, had to be. Terin was aiming what had to be military binocs at them.

Nohar gave her the finger.

Stephie called back to him. "Where are we going?"

After telling Angel to make sure they weren't being followed, Nohar gave her an address on the West Side that, in Manny's words, was about as far from Moreytown as you could get.

With luck and a pink driving, they might not get stopped by the cops.

CHAPTER 13

Nohar woke up somewhere on the Main Avenue bridge. Someone had bandaged his hip. Maria's clothing was pulled tight on his leg and seemed to have stopped the bleeding.

The Antaeus was tailing a three-trailer cargo hauler out the other side of downtown Cleveland. The car was surrounded by the towering structures of the West-Side office complex. The sun glared off the acres of mirrored glass—it felt like they were traveling through a giant microwave. Nohar's eyes hurt. It felt like someone was squeezing them in time to his pulse. Nohar's blackout had lasted nearly fifteen minutes, and his migraine was still sending streaks of color across his field of vision. His hip still throbbed.

He tried to focus out the rear window, but his vision was too blurred to make out any details on the cars behind the Antaeus. He did a self-inventory and found himself in less than ideal shape. He had bled all over the back seat, despite Angel's—at least he hoped Angel had done it, Stephie shouldn't have stopped the car—field dressing. The twenty-two had only grazed his neck, opposite his bad shoulder, but the shot that clipped his right hip felt like it had ripped out a good chunk of meat. It felt like someone was running a drill bit in the joint. Between that and the sprained knee, his right leg was nearly immobile.

He didn't remember doing it, but somewhere along the line he had cleared, safetied, and holstered the Vind. Stephie was still driving. Angel still had the shotgun. Fortunately, Angel wasn't stupid and kept the gun down in the foot well out of sight of neighboring drivers. Armed moreys usually didn't even get a warning from the cops. . . .

Angel was the first to notice him revive. "Kit, how you doing back there?"

"I'll live." Nohar tried to get into a sitting position. His groan got Stephie's attention.

"Nohar, I've been trying to tell Angel here that we've got to get you to a hospital. She stopped the bleeding, but—"

"No pink hospitals."

"Pinky, Kit's in charge. He said West 58th, we do West 58th. You don't break command structure if you wanna live."

"Nohar, you're wounded."

He grunted and finally shoved himself up into a sitting position. He could feel the bones grinding together in his hip. "Don't worry about me. We're going to the house of the best combat medic that was ever in the Afghan theater. Be worried about someone following us."

Angel turned around and wrinkled her nose. "Moreys this far west shine, Kit. We've not been stopped only 'cause Pinky's driving. The off-roader with Terin in it paced us halfway up the Midtown Corridor. Quit when they figured we were headed downtown."

"Stop calling me Pinky."

"Hey, Kit, we got a sensitive one here—"

The byplay was getting on his nerves. "Angel, did anyone ever tell you you don't know when to shut up?" Nohar's vision was still blurred, but the colors weren't washing over as badly. He thought he caught a hint of a smile play around the edge of Stephie's mouth. He wondered exactly what kind of conversation the two of them had been having while he was blacked out.

"Sorry, Pin—I'll quit. What's your name again?"

Stephie made an abrupt lane change that shot them around the left of the cargo hauler. They rocked out in front of the truck to the blare of its horn. "The name is Stephanie Weir. I would like it if you call me Stephie."

"Sure, Stephie . . ."

The Antaeus pulled off the bridge and on to Detroit Avenue. In the space of one city block the glass monoliths gave over to old brick warehouses with dead windows. Even the few places that were in use were aged black. They passed the first Ohio City marker and they were in Manny's neighborhood.

Nohar pointed to the side of the road, next to a whitewashed building that held an unnamed bar that was just opening. "Pull over."

"What?"

"We pull over and wait for our shadows to catch up with us."

"Kit, I told you they pulled—"

"Angel, the Zips aren't the only ones in on this."

Stephie pulled over. "Now what?"

"We hunch down, out of sight."

"If you say so." Stephie crouched in the foot well with Angel. Nohar eased back into a prone position.

Nohar looked back the way they had come. At the height of lunch hour, in this part of town, traffic was dead.

It only took half a minute for their shadow to show up. An unmarked industrial-green Dodge Electroline, programmed or remote-driven, was moving down Detroit. It paused, hazards on, directly across from them and stayed there for nearly a full minute. Then it accelerated and took the next right. Nohar figured it was about to perform some sort of search pattern.

Angel shook her head. "What now? And where did that come from?"

"Now, we walk and avoid the pattern that remote is running."

Stephie was pulling herself out of the foot well. "What about your leg?"

"I'll manage—"

Nohar felt a little more warmth ooze down his leg. He pressed the bandage and tried to get adequate pressure on the wound. "Van's from Midwest Lapidary Imports, I think. The company involved in this mess."

He pulled the shirt tight and winced. "Ditch the shotgun, let's go."

He hobbled out and his leg nearly buckled. In the daylight, his leg was soaked from the hip down, and his denim pants were beginning to adhere to his fur. He could put weight on it, but the bloodstains could be seen from a block away. Nohar was getting the feeling any halfway decent search would turn them up. They were too damn conspicuous.

He just hoped nobody called the cops on them.

He led the way through a vacant lot across the street from the bar, down an alley between two warehouses, through someone's cracked-mud backyard, across a narrow brick dead-end street, through a gaping hole in a rusted chain link fence, over the rotting ties that were the only remains of the abandoned train tracks, and finally into an alley that led behind some residential garages.

When he stopped, he had to look down to make sure his leg didn't end in a ragged stump. Angel spoke.

"Lady above, Kit. You know this place better than my runners knew Moreytown. And this place is solid pink—"

Nohar paused a second to catch his breath. "Angel, the divisions aren't as clear as they seem to be when you're in Moreytown. I used to *live* up here."

Stephie asked, "Open housing policy?"

Nohar snorted and rubbed his leg. "Call it no housing policy and a relative absence of lethal anti-morey violence. By the way, we're here."

Nohar hooked a thumb at the rear wall of the garage they had stopped behind. Carved in the wall, amid a host of childish doodles and vertical claw marks, was some blocky lettering. "Nohar and Bobby, 2033." The threes were carved in backward.

Stephie was tracing the old carving. "Who was Bobby?"

"First and only pink friend— Let's get inside."

Nohar limped off around the garage. Manny's van was gone. Manny probably wouldn't be back until late afternoon or evening. When Nohar thought about it, he had probably contributed a lot to Manny's current caseload.

The side door was locked—in this neighborhood, predictable. Nohar rang the call button. He was right. Manny wasn't home. Angel and Stephie were rounding the side of the house. He called out to them. "This place has an old key lock, if you check the loose clapboard under the vehicle feed in the garage, you'll find a spare."

Nohar didn't add the "I hope" he felt. It had been nearly fifteen years since he'd had occasion to use the spare key. Luck was with them. Stephie came back with the key in hand.

Nohar let them in.

It was close to seven-thirty and they were all waiting for Manny in his living room. Nohar sat on his windbreaker to avoid leaking blood on the furniture, while Stephie and Angel watched the news off the comm. News wasn't great. The attack on the coffeehouse resulted in three dead—all rodents—and the local news called it a morey gang war. Great.

Even better were the reports of similar, and more deadly, incidents on the fringes of morey communities in New York, Los Angeles, and Houston. All had the car bomb tie-in. All Honduran rats.

Reports were still coming in, they said, about unconfirmed attacks in San Francisco, Denver, and Miami. Everyone made connections back to the "Dark August" of 2042. Eleven year anniversary of the first riots in Moreytown, also on a Monday, August 4. Nohar didn't need the reminder.

What really freaked the pinks was the obvious coordination between all the incidents. Same gang name. Same M.O. The Zips could have done no damage whatsoever, and the pinks would still freak.

The mall in New York was the worst. All four Zips there had automatic weapons, and the car bomb was a bit nastier than most. The vids had panned with loving attention to every body-bag.

Angel had overheard Terin complaining about her best people being dragged to the four corners of the country. While all the attacks were violent and bloody, the news never mentioned more than four rats involved in any one attack. Thirty rats, max. All heavily armed, supplied with explosives, and timed to the minute.

Terrorism staged to be a media event.

The whole situation made Nohar sick to his stomach. "A decade out of the hole, and a bunch of psychopaths push us back in."

Angel stared at the screen. For once, her wiseass attitude was gone. "Kit, hell the Zips trying to do? Why?"

"Wish I knew."

"Binder's moreau control bill is going to make it through the House."

Angel turned toward Stephie. "Huh?"

"The bill shuts down moreau immigration and starts mandatory sterilization."

Nohar shut off the bodies on the comm. "We're on the wrong side of another anti-morey wave. The riots all over again."

Angel let out a nervous laugh. "Come on, Kit. You were there, this ain't nothing like the riots."

Stephie responded for him. "All you need is some media terror and Congress will jump on the bandwagon. It seems almost engineered to push Binder's legislation."

The front door interrupted their conversation. A very tired-looking mongoose entered the living room. Manny glanced at Stephie, then Angel, and finally Nohar. He seemed beyond the ability to register surprise.

He was still wearing his lab coat, and a ghostly odor of blood, death, and hospital disinfectant was following him.

"You stupid bastard, why aren't you in a hospital?"

Nohar was still wearing the Vind, but from Manny's attitude, more concerned than angry, Nohar knew Manny hadn't connected him with the rodent attack yet. Guiltily, he didn't explain.

Manny released a whistling sigh from his front teeth. "I wonder what would happen to you if I wasn't a medic. Can you walk?"

"I got here, didn't I?"

"That's not what I asked. How long have you been sitting there?"

Manny had a point.

Nohar tried to get up, but a shivering wave of agony rippled up the entire right side of his body. He collapsed on to the floor, pulling the bloody windbreaker after him. Both girls underwent a brief panic, but Manny shooed them away as he pulled out a sheet and laid it on the floor. It took all three of them to help roll Nohar on it.

"I hope you've already written off the clothes . . ."

Manny walked out of the living room and in to the kitchen where he kept his medical equipment. Manny came back with a loaded air-hypo and a medical bag. He set the hypo down, next to the sheet.

"Introduce me to your friends." Manny started shredding Nohar's jeans with a pair of scissors.

Nohar tried to ignore the pain of the clotted blood tearing out his fur. "Angel, Stephanie Weir, the doctor doing violence to my pants is Manny, Mandvi Gujerat."

Manny nodded. "Pleased, I'm sure."

Angel twitched her facial scar. "You were really a combat medic?"

Manny had laid open Nohar's pants leg and was examining the remains of Maria's shirt that still bound the gunshot wound. "Five years in the Afghan frontier before New Delhi got nuked—You, Stephanie? Hand me those forceps.'' Stephie removed them from the bag. Manny took the forceps from her and used them to start peeling away the outer layer of the makeshift bandage. ''Nohar, if it wasn't for that engineered metabolism of yours—''

Manny shook his head at the mess of Nohar's hip. ''No, forget it, I'm not going to get through to you anyway.''

Manny stood up. ''I'm going to wash up. I've got to do some cutting and stitching on this obstinate lump of stupidity.'' He looked at Angel. ''You know, when this bastard was six, he broke his arm and forced me to set it myself? A compound fracture yet . . .''

Manny left the living room and soon there was the sound of running water from the kitchen. Stephie looked at Nohar. ''What is this with you and hospitals?''

Nohar looked down at the gory mess on his right hip and suppressed a shudder. ''I don't trust them—''

Manny came back, pulling on a pair of gloves. ''Yes, he'd rather trust himself to my floor. Who needs a sterile environment?''

Manny turned to Angel. ''Pick up that hypo I brought in here?''

Angel did as she was asked. Manny turned to Stephie. ''It's probably a futile gesture, but would you tie on my mask?''

Stephie tied the conical face mask around Manny's muzzle, muffling his voice. ''Angel, can you handle that thing?''

Angel nodded and there was a mumble behind Manny's mask that sounded like, ''Doesn't surprise me.''

In a louder voice trained to be heard from behind a jaw immobilized behind the restrictive mask, Manny told Angel to empty the cartridge into Nohar's arm. Angel rolled up Nohar's right sleeve, there was a slight sting, and the world floated away.

CHAPTER 14

Nohar had an intense fear he would wake up in a hospital.

However, no disinfectant assaulted him when he awoke. He could smell alcohol, a much sharper and cleaner scent. There was also the faint coppery rust smell of his own blood. There was the dry dusty smell of old cloth and paper.

And nearby was the smell of roses and wood smoke.

Nohar opened his eyes.

He was in the attic. His old room still had no air-conditioning, and should have been hotter than Hades—but the omnipresent rumble and the breeze through his whiskers told Nohar the old ventilation fan still worked, pulling a crosswind through this two-room insulated oven. His eyes quickly shifted into nocturnal monochrome.

Her scent had betrayed her presence. Stephie Weir was asleep in a claw-scarred recliner across from Nohar's bed.

He gave the room a brief scan and was thankful Manny wasn't overly sentimental. The chair and the bed were the only remains of his old furniture. The attic was now a haven for boxes, old luggage, and older clothes.

Nohar's gaze lit on the small end table that jutted out the side of the antique headboard. After a decade and a half, the table was still familiar. Nohar remembered the scratches that marked its surface. His name and idle crosshatches had clawed through five layers of paint to reveal the black finish underneath. The desk lamp was still clamped to it, still with three or four knots of electrical tape holding the cord together.

Orai's picture was still in its cheap gold-plated frame, cocked at an obsessively perfect forty-five degree angle toward the bed. Its lower edge rested in a groove worn in the last two layers of paint. The gold was flaking and rust spots dotted the gray metal beneath. The glass was hazy with dust and, in the dark, Nohar could barely make out the picture.

Nohar sat up on the edge of the bed—his hip objected, but only slightly—and turned on the desk lamp which, to his surprise, still worked. Now he could see the picture. In it, Orai was in her combat harness, but unarmed. She was center frame and holding up one end of an American flag. The other end was being held by some friend from her unit. In the background he could see the Statue of Liberty and part of the Manhattan skyline. Orai and her friend, both tigers, were smiling, totally oblivious to the show of teeth. Orai was already beginning to show her pregnancy. The writing on the old picture was faded a bit, though the picture itself was still in good shape. It read, "Rajasthan Airlift—March 2027."

Nohar sighed.

He realized Stephie was awake now. She was leaning forward in the recliner, probably trying to get a glimpse of the picture. Nohar didn't know what to feel about that. It was a personal part of his life. But Stephie was just sitting there. She seemed to know it was his decision to tell her. She didn't ask.

Nohar realized he liked this pink woman.

He handed her his childhood icon. "She's the one on the left."

Stephie took the picture. "Who is she?"

"My mother. She was already pregnant when the company defected. Her name was Orai."

Stephie's eyes raised from the picture. "You used the past tense."

Nohar was about to evade the question, but why shouldn't she know? He cleared his throat. "Died when I was five, just old enough to remember. She'd gotten inseminated, wanted to give me a little brother or sister. She'd saved for the procedure since getting to the States. Things went fine. Then, three months in, she went for a prenatal checkup—" Nohar sucked in a breath. "Those *damn* idiots at the Clinic—do you know what Pakistani gene-techs had done with feline leukemia?"

Stephie shook her head. The color drained from her face.

Nohar went on. "Those doctors didn't know either. They misdiagnosed a Jaguar, put him in with the other felines, including Orai." Nohar's voice cracked a bit. He brought it under control. "They *could've* quarantined the Jaguar. But they don't give moreys private rooms. Every feline in the ward started dying. *Then* they knew. She was near to term. She died miscarrying two cubs—"

Nohar fell silent. There wasn't much left to say. He closed his eyes and tried to remember when he had told anyone that story in full. No one came to mind. Not even Manny, though Manny knew the story well enough.

The smell of smoky rose was suddenly very close, and Nohar felt a tiny naked hand on his cheek, brushing his whiskers. He opened his eyes and saw Stephie's face, close to his own. Her breath was warm on the skin of his nose. Her eyes were a liquid green, nothing like the eyes of a cat—visible whites, tiny round pupils.

Nohar had never realized how alien human eyes were.

Her lips parted in a whisper. "Lord, how you must hate humans."

Nohar shook his head. "No, no hate. Not for people."

The hand left and Stephie replaced the picture, in

its groove and at its forty-five degree angle. She did it in one fluid motion, stretching across Nohar to replace the picture. Again Nohar found himself admiring her muscle tone and her economy of movement.

She sat down next to him on the bed. The springs barely noticed her weight. Her nervousness was back. Just like at the table at the *Arabica*. She shook her head and looked up at him. Nohar wished once again that he was better at reading human expression.

"Nohar, would you tell me, who's Angel?"

Back to business. "I told you, she's a lead. She saw the sniper—"

Stephie was shaking her head again. "Not what I meant. I want to know who she is *to you*."

Huh? Maybe not. "What? Only met her yesterday— We sure as *hell* aren't lovers. If that's what you mean."

Stephie turned a bright red. She clenched a fist that made her knuckles whiten. "I'm sorry, forgive me. I didn't mean to offend—"

Nohar got a sensation he often got when talking with humans. There were two different conversations here. Stephie was, he felt, about to bolt off somewhere and cry. He didn't want to be responsible for that, even if he didn't understand what was going on. He placed his hands on her shoulder. Nohar didn't know how to do this gracefully, so he just told her the truth. "I *wasn't* offended. But the idea of having relations with that little twitch is ludicrous."

Nohar could tell Stephie almost laughed. She was still flushed.

"Why ask?"

Nohar could sense a slight tensing of her muscles under his hand. "Angel was bragging all the time while you were unconscious. I just wondered, you're such different . . ."

Ah. "Different species? I'd admit, me and her, it would be unusual, but not unheard of."

"Isn't that bestiality? Would it be possible?"

"Some human taboos, like nudity, can't wash with moreys for practical reasons."

Stephie was still looking up at him, and Nohar realized he'd only answered half the question. "And, uh, some morey characteristics came out the other end of the labs remarkably similar. I think it might be linked to bipedal . . ." He trailed off.

Great, now *he* was getting embarrassed.

Stephie had a questioning look in her eyes. The flush was fading. "Who *do* you have, Nohar?"

Nohar thought of Maria. "No one, anymore."

"You're lonely, aren't you?"

He would have objected, but he had trouble lying to people he felt something for. He nodded. "You?"

They faced each other, on the bed. He was feeling her breath on his nose again. No longer warm, hot. Beads of perspiration were forming on her forehead. Her voice was a whisper. "My nonexistent boyfriend." She tried to laugh, but it died. "No girlfriend either."

"Why did you get so upset when I asked if you were a lesbian?"

"Too close to what I was feeling."

They were very close now. He could feel her pulse under the hand that still rested on her shoulder. It was incredibly rapid, like her heart belonged to a kitten or a small bird. His heartbeat was racing to catch up with hers. Her sweat was beginning to lend a tang to the air that was alien to him, one he liked. What was going on had dawned on him gradually, and a small part of his mind was screaming at him, asking him what the hell he was doing. It wasn't the time for that question.

Her alien—human—eyes were staring deep into his own. "You saved my life. Have you ever heard of Chinese obligation?"

Nohar had. "I'm responsible for you now."

She sucked in a shuddering breath, and her lips touched his. He had seen kisses in human videos—but

a feline skull and lips didn't move the right way for it.
Even so, he tried. He let her small lips part his mouth
and felt her amazingly smooth tongue alight on his
own, caress one of his canines, and withdraw, to be
felt, briefly, under his nose. When her eyes opened,
the nervousness was gone.

Nohar, what are you doing? He ignored the questioning voice because he needed her, human or not.
He moved his hand up from her shoulder and undid
the bonds that were keeping her hair in a ponytail. He
nuzzled the top of her head, thankful not to smell any
heavy chemicals, and began to groom her hair. The
taste and texture of her human hair was different from
Maria's fur. The ritual perhaps seemed as strange to
Stephie as kisses did to Nohar.

When Nohar had cleaned her hair, he began to move
to her ears and the back of her neck. He expected the
taste and feel of naked skin to repulse, but it was quite
the opposite. The sweet acidic taste of her sweat and
the smooth surface of her walnut-colored skin was beginning to excite him.

The questioning voice shut up.

By the time he had reached her shoulders, he realized she did have fur, of a sort. Tiny, downy hairs
were scattered over her arms and her back. Somewhere along the line, he didn't know where, her blouse
had disappeared.

They both reclined on the bed as Nohar worked his
way down her body. He groomed both her arms. Her
skin broke into a burning flush under his tongue. He
cleaned the small puddle of perspiration that pooled
between those odd human breasts. When he cleaned
her breasts, she began to moan loudly. Nohar thought
he was too rough, so he lightened the pressure. Stephie immediately responded by locking her hands in
the fur on either side of his head and pulling his face
back down.

He worked his way down her abdomen. She continued to urge him lower with her hands—

Humans kept their hair in the strangest places.

When Nohar could no longer restrain himself he rolled over on his back, ignoring the pain in his hip, and pulled her on top of him. She drew him in and shuddered, arching her back.

Nohar added his voice to hers.

It took them a long time to expend each other.

Nohar awoke.

He could still smell Stephie—between them they had drenched the bed with their scent—and he realized it wasn't a dream. Now was the time to ask the question. He opened his eyes and whispered, "Nohar, what the hell are you doing?"

The desk lamp was still on. The small fluorescent tube was now overwhelmed by the morning light. Stephie was curled up next to him. Her head rested on his chest, spilling her black hair across his upper body. It contrasted with the areas where his russet stripes faded to near-white. In the sunlight, where his color vision reached its optimum, he could appreciate the similarity of their coloring. Her black hair and golden-tan skin formed a near-perfect match to the shading of his stripes. They both had green eyes—

He had been perfectly prepared to blame last night on the emotional pit he had fallen into. But when he considered the way he was watching the light from the window curve its shadows around her tailless rear, he couldn't blame that night on any temporary condition.

Stephie stirred, and turned to face him. "Morning."

"Do you realize how much this complicates things?"

He could feel her twisting the tip of his tail between her toes as she spoke. "You're as romantic as five lanes of new blacktop."

"Please, I'm serious."

Her foot was going up and down the undamaged

length of his tail. "I know." She rolled over and sat up, looking down at him. "Is this going to be it?"

Nohar tried to answer the question, but his thinking process was a mess. "Damn, I don't know how I feel about it. What prompted you to—with a morey—why *me?*"

Nohar damned his mouth, it was still running away with him. At the worst times. He'd just parroted one of the five stupidest questions anyone had ever uttered in any situation.

Stephie closed her eyes. "Don't ask that. I don't know *why*. Until I met you, I didn't think I could care for anyone—male *or* female."

She exhaled. Nohar didn't interrupt her. She was quiet for a few seconds. Then she opened her eyes and looked at him. "You've asked me twice, I might as well tell you. I *was* a lesbian—for about four months at Case Western I was the most radical bull-dyke feminist lesbian you could want. It didn't do a damn thing about my inability to have a relationship with another human being. I was posing as much as Phil and Derry ever were."

She idly ran her fingers through the fur on his abdomen. "Then I met you. I was set to be lonely for the rest of my life, and you screw everything up. After I met you the first time, I couldn't wait to see you again. All during that drive from the hospital I desperately wished you were human. Last night I decided I didn't care."

Nohar knew the kind of repulsion most humans held for moreys. Stephie had to be feeling even more confused than he did. He didn't know what to say. "I *should* dump you. For your own good."

There was a hopeful note in her voice. "Why don't you?"

Nohar thought of Maria. "I may be stupid and self-destructive, but I'm *not* going to do that to you."

Stephie gave him a hug that made him forget moreys weren't supposed to get involved with pinks.

He left Stephie to clean herself up and hobbled down to breakfast. As loud as they had been with each other, there was no question Manny and Angel knew what had gone on with him and Stephie last night. They didn't mention it.

He walked into the kitchen and found Angel watching Manny with rapt attention. Manny was involved in one of his passions, cooking. Angel actually seemed interested in Manny's omelette-making procedure. She wasn't even wrinkling her nose as Manny started adding raw hamburger to the cooked sausage. They both seemed to avoid watching his entrance.

"Found a disciple, Manny?"

Manny added the sausage/hamburger mixture to the omelette in the large skillet and folded the eggs over perfectly. "Don't make fun of an appreciation of good food, even if she's never heard of olive oil."

Manny got out a platter and let the omelette slide out on to it. Angel was trying to act spellbound. "Doc, how you keep the eggs from sticking?"

"You just have to remember not to start with a cold pan—"

Stephie came down, interrupting what might have been an endless speech—Nohar had always seen Manny's cooking as obsessive. Nohar noticed, with some pleasure, Stephie wasn't put off by the lack of clothing on him and Angel. Stephie, however, was fully clothed, and she'd worn the outfit long enough that it was beginning to broadcast her scent on its own, even over the sausage.

Manny cut his omelette speech short. "What will you have? We have a vegetarian and a carnivorous version."

"Could you do both?"

"No problem—"

Nohar and Angel had the same reaction. "In the same omelette?"

CHAPTER 15

Stephie sat on the recliner as Nohar searched the boxes in the attic for something to wear. Nohar's mind had drifted back to MLI, Binder, Hassan, and the Zipheads. Somehow they were connected and he still had no easy way of fitting the pieces together.

"The answer has to be in those financial records."

Stephie sighed. "I know. That's the third time you said that."

Nohar pulled out a relic of his gang days, from before he'd left school—and Manny. It was an old denim Hellcats jacket. It still fit and it was big enough to hide the Vind when he wore it. "Are you sure that you never saw or heard anything that would help me?"

She shook her head. "I don't care what they wrote down on my job description. They never let anyone near those records. It was a tight little group, the five of them. Even though Derry trusted me, no one got into the inner circle who wasn't there back in '40."

"Trusted you?"

"Yes, not to screw up the campaign machine. He knew me from my radical phase at Case. It's a tight little community, even for the ones who are still in the closet. I managed to convince myself that I was helping him out. Found out it was Binder's idea much later. By then I was used to the life-style."

"Why didn't Binder just let Johnson go?" The potential for a media explosion was even worse with Johnson in the campaign, than if he left under a cloud.

"I don't know. Derry never expressed any great love

of Binder, but he also never gave any indication of ever being willing to resign. Believe me, I tried to talk to him about it. He was always evasive about why he stayed.''

''What about Young and Thomson?''

''Young was never willing to talk about anything but business. I think he resented me. Thomson, I don't know, he's slick and never says an ill word about Binder or the campaign—but he acts like he knows some joke the rest of the world doesn't.''

Still batting zero for hard information.

Nohar pulled out a T-shirt. It was the only black one, but it had a yellow smile-face on it. Stephie repressed a giggle.

Nohar frowned as he pulled out the most intact set of jeans. They'd still been using the human model for morey clothes when they'd made it. The seams on the legs were split so his legs could move, and there was a slit in the ass for his tail. He pulled them on. ''And nobody ever discussed Midwest Lapidary, or morey gangs?''

''You must be kidding.'' Stephie had reached over and pulled the Hellcats jacket off of the bed. The denim covered her legs like a blanket, and she ran her fingers over the embroidery. ''How come you get to ask all the questions?''

Nohar pulled the shirt over his head. It ended up twenty centimeters short of his waist. ''What do you want to know?''

Stephie looked up. Her fingers still traveled over the demonic feline form that graced the back of the jacket. ''Well, you called Bobby your first and only pink—''

Nohar felt like he'd gotten blindsided by a baseball bat. ''No. That's not—I mean . . .''

She laughed. ''I'm sorry. I didn't want to sound accusatory.'' Stephie stood up, leaving the jacket on the chair. ''I was just wondering who Bobby was.''

Nohar was still recovering. ''Bobby, Bobby Dittrich. I met him when I was trying to make it through high school. We were both sort of misfits— Though as we got older, he fit in more and more, and I fit in less and less . . .''

He lapsed into silence.

Stephie walked up and put her hand on his arm. ''Are you okay? Did I hit another bad memory?''

He shook his head. ''No, not at all.''

He grabbed the jacket and hobbled down the stairs. He was wondering why he hadn't thought of it sooner. Stephie was following. ''Where are you going?''

''I have to call Bobby.''

''Are you sure it's the time to look up old friends—''

Nohar didn't answer until he got down to the comm. ''I think he might be able to help me.''

He switched off the news. ''Move it, Angel—''

Angel said something unkind in Spanish as she moved off the couch. ''Damnit, Kit, you *could* ask.''

She stalked off to the kitchen, probably to take out her aggression on some poor vegetable. Nohar ignored her as he called the number for Robert Dittrich. It buzzed once, then he got a test pattern as the home comm forwarded the call.

''Budget Surplus, can I help—'' Bobby displayed a rapidly growing smile of recognition.

Nohar was happy to see a friendly face.

''Christ, what's going on with you? The Fed is looking for you—''

''I need your help as a prime hacker.''

''You *know* I *never* engage in illegal activity—'' Bobby winked.

''Can you help?''

''Come down, we'll talk.''

Stephie's car was out of the question. Everyone—the cops, the Zips, MLI—everyone would know it on sight. Nohar called a cab.

Angel didn't object when Nohar left. She seemed a

little resentful. Nohar supposed he'd been a little too curt with her, but he had other things on his mind.

The cab that showed up in front of Manny's house was an anachronism. It was a prewar Nissan Tory. The thing was almost as big as the Antaeus, but the huge hood covered batteries and a power plant that took up nearly half the car's volume. Nohar got into the back of the cab before he realized it had a driver.

A black human woman, her hair dyed red and strung into dreadlocks, was staring at Nohar with a wide-eyed expression. Nohar decided it had been too much to ask them to send a remote into this neighborhood.

"Shee-it." She was articulate, too.

"Don't tell me, you've never given a ride to a morey before."

"Dispatch didn't tell me no—"

Nohar slipped his bank card into the meter and tapped out his ID on the keypad. In addition, he typed in one hell of a tip. He could afford it. "Well, I didn't tell *them*. Is there a problem?"

She saw the numbers come up on her display. She spent a few seconds composing herself. "Sorry *Mr.* Rajasthan, didn't 'spect someone like you 'sall. Where you going?"

Money was a great equalizer.

Budget Surplus was a dirty little marble-fronted warehouse that hugged a nook between—really under—the Main Avenue bridge, and one of the more obnoxious mirror-fronted towers of the West Side office complex. It took more than a little creativity to find the grubby dead-end street that was the only access to the building.

The cab pulled up and Nohar typed in a hundred, on top of the tip. "Will waiting for me be a problem?"

The cabbie shook her head. "No problem at all. Take your time."

Nohar stepped out of the yellow Tory and felt like he'd been abandoned at the bottom of a well. One side was the warehouse, one side the black-dirt underside of the bridge, the other two sides flat sheets of concrete forming the foundation of the office building—whose doors would open on more wholesome scenery.

When Nohar entered the building, it no longer seemed small. The interior was one huge room. Windows made from dozens of little square panels let in shafts of bright sunlight. Despite the sun, the corners of the building were covered in darkness. Standing in the light, Nohar found the shadows impenetrable. Endless ranks of metal shelving dominated the space, tall enough to barely give clearance to the slowly rotating fans hanging from the corrugated ceiling.

Nohar heard the slight whine of an electric motor. Then Bobby's wheelchair made a sudden appearance through a gap in the shelving that was invisible from Nohar's vantage point. The shelf Bobby rounded held nothing but oscilloscopes ranging in age from the obsolete to the archaic. Bobby wheeled forward and thrust his hand in Nohar's direction. Nohar clasped it.

He released Nohar's hand and maneuvered the chair around. "Let's talk in my office."

Nohar followed the chair as it wove its way through the acres of shelving. He smelled the omnipresent odor of old electronics—a combination of static dust, ozone, transformers, and old insulation. Shelves held dead picture tubes, keyboards, voice telephones, spools of cable—optical and otherwise—and rows and rows of nothing but old circuit boards. Mainframes were stacked against the walls like old footlockers filled with chips and wire.

Bobby's office was defined by four shelves that met at right angles with a single gap in one corner that would have been difficult to detect if Nohar wasn't looking for it. The shelves of electronics tended to camouflage themselves, any open space looking over more of the same. The illusion was of endless parallel rows, when the reality—demonstrated by their erratic maneuvering—was anything but.

His suspicions of the eccentric layout were confirmed by a rank of four monitors behind Bobby's desk. The monitors were connected to security cameras looking down on the floor. The arrangement of shelves resembled nothing so much as a hedge maze.

Bobby whirred behind his desk—a rusty cabinet trailing optical cable, it had the Sony logo on it—and motioned to a chair that was another chunk of techno-flotsam. Nohar sat down. It was hard to get comfortable, buttons in the armrests dug into his elbows.

"We shouldn't be bothered here. Now you can tell me what's going on."

Nohar told Bobby what was going on.

An hour later, Bobby leaned back in his wheelchair and shook his head. "I thought the shit had hit the fan with Nugoya. I guess there's shit, and then there's *shit*."

Nohar had almost forgotten about his run-in with Nugoya.

"You picked the right politico to involve in this." Bobby whirred around the desk toward one of the shelves. The shelf he picked was dominated by a large bell jar-looking thing; it sat on a sleek black box. Nohar recognized the box as an industrial card-reader. "Even though all politicians are slime."

"Why the right one?"

Bobby parked himself next to the bell jar, and drew a metal cart from another invisible gap in the shelving. Three different processor boxes rested on the cart. There was an ancient Sony that was held together with duct tape. On top of it was a more compact Tunja 2000. On a shelf, by itself, was a huge homemade box. Frozen rainbows of ribbon-cable snaked from box to box.

"Can't get more right than Binder—" Bobby snickered. "Hate Binder. Wish you were investigating *his* absence from the mortal coil."

"Why?" Nohar could understand Bobby's dislike for Binder. But Nohar had never heard him express a political view on anything before. Legislation had always been irrelevant to Bobby.

"Need a license to hate a politician? Give you just an example—last session in the House, he led a vote to scuttle NASA's deep-probe project."

Ah, the space program.

Bobby pulled a small blue device from a shelf. Nohar got up and walked over. The device had AT&T markings on it, a pair of LCD displays, and a standard keypad. It could have been a voice phone, but there was no handset. Instead it had five or six different jacks for optical cable. "Those probes have been sitting on the moon—would you plug this in?"

Bobby handed him the end of a coil of optical cable and indicated a small plate on the floor. The plate had old East-Ohio Gas Company markings. Nohar reached down and lifted it. Under the plate was a ragged hole in the concrete. Half a meter down was a section of PVC pipe running under the concrete floor of the warehouse. A hacksaw had cut a diamond-shaped hole in the pipe, and a female jack had been planted amidst the snaking optical cable. Nohar knelt down and made the connection.

Something Bobby was working on, probably the blue AT&T box, made a satisfied beep.

"Thanks, I have trouble getting down there myself. Where was I? Oh, yeah, Binder's shortsightedness. His group of budget nimrods in the House have been stalling the launch for nine-ten years. Finally decided maintenance was too expensive, so they're going to dismantle the project. Forget the fact they would have *saved* money in the long run by launching on schedule, *and* we would be getting pictures back from Alpha Centauri by now, and the Sirius probe would have started transmitting already—"

Nohar shrugged. "My concerns lie closer to home."

"Yeah. My friend, the pragmatic tiger." Bobby snapped home a few more connections. "Worst bit is, he started as a liberal."

"You're kidding."

"Nope, kept running for the state legislature as a civil libertarian, government-for-the-people type guy. Lost. Kept losing until he shifted to the far right and got elected. Never looked back. Children—can we say 'hypocrite'?

"Enough of that—*The Digital Avenger* is now on-line."

Bobby flipped a switch and a new rank of monitors came to life with displays of scrolling text. Inside the bell jar, lasers were carving the air into a latticework of green, yellow, and red light. "Now what kind of system do we want to run our sticky little fingers through?"

First things first. "Any information on MLI you can dig up."

"As you wish—" Bobby pulled out a keyboard and rested it across the arms of his wheelchair.

He paused for a moment. "Another thing about Binder. With just a little tweak of government finances, we might have caught up to the technology that got wasted with the Japs—"

"I thought you were an anarchist."

"Don't throw my principles at me when I'm drooling over bio-interfaces nobody this side of the Pacific knows how to install. Besides, the engineering shortage is degrading the quality of my stock."

There was hypnotic movement in the bell jar as the holographic green web distorted and a blue trail started to snake through the mass. Bobby noted his interest. "Like the display? You ever hear a hacker refer to the net? That's it. My image of it, anyway. The green lines are optical data tracks, the yellow's a satellite uplink or an RF channel, red's a proprietary channel—government or commercial—the few white ones are what I and the software can't figure out—whoops, close there, someone's watching that one." The blue line took a right angle away from a sudden pixel glowing red. "Nodes are computers, junction and switch boxes, satellites, office buildings, etcetera. Jackpot!''

Bobby smiled. ''Anyone ever tell you credit records are the easiest things in the world to access?''

The blue line had stopped at a node, which was now glowing blue and pulsing lightly. Text was scrolling across three screens as Bobby's smile began leaving his face. ''You gave me the right name?''

''Midwest Lapidary Imports.''

Bobby sighed. ''Never as easy as it looks.'' He typed madly for a minute or so, then he typed a command that faded the blue line back to the neutral green. Bobby shook his head. ''MLI doesn't exist.''

''What are you talking about?''

''No credit records—''

''Check *my* credit. Someone is making deposits to my account.''

More mad typing and colored lights. Bobby ended with a whistle. ''You want to loan me some money?''

''Did you find anything?''

''Just daily cash deposits to your account, untraceable. Thirty kilobucks, plus . . .''

Nohar was speechless. He hadn't had the time, lately, to check the balance on his account. After a while, he said, ''Check somewhere else.''

''If you say so. I have an in at the County Auditor's mainframe.'' The blue trail snaked out again, and headed straight for a small nexus of red pixels and lines in a corner of the bell jar. Just before the blue line hit the nexus, it turned red itself. ''Isn't that neat? But I am telling you, you *can't* have a company without a credit record. Economically impossible. Even the most phony setup in the world is going to be in debt to someone, you can't—''

Bobby paused as the new red line pulsed and text scrolled across one of the screens. ''Okay, I'm wrong, you can.''

''What?''

"I just downloaded the tax info on MLI." The scrolling continued. "Shit."

Bobby remained silent and the scrolling eventually stopped. The new red line faded. Bobby hit the keyboard again and numbers scrolled across another screen, and stopped. Bobby was looking at the display with his jaw open. Nohar looked at the screen. No more than columns of numbers to him. "What're you looking at?"

"The third line. The net assets they reported to the County."

"Eighty thousand and change, what's so great about—"

"Those figures are in *millions*."

Time for Nohar's jaw to drop. Eight—no, *eighty*—billion dollars in assets. Bobby started scrolling through the information. "And forty thousand megabucks in sales and revenue— With no credit record? Someone is playing games here."

These guys were having billion-dollar turnovers from gemstones? Maybe he was in the wrong line of work. This was one set of rich franks.

"And Christ is alive and selling swampland in Florida—these guys have never been audited."

"So they play by the rules."

Bobby shook his head. "You dense furball. That has nothing to do with it. The Fed assigns auditors for anything approaching this size. And those auditors aren't paid to sit on their hands. They're paid to dig up dirt—"

"So why hasn't MLI been audited?"

"Beats me." Bobby studied the screen. "It ain't normal. For some reason, MLI hasn't raised a single flag in the IRS computers. They don't pay too little, or too much—and that is damn hard to do. They even have this little subsidiary, NuFood, to dump money into so they can smooth out their losses. Know what I think?"

"What?"

"It's all a fake and they have a contact in the Fed telling them what their tax returns should look like."

Nohar shrugged. "So what are they spending their money on?"

"I can give you a list of real estate from the property taxes." This was accompanied by a few keyboard clicks and scrolling text on one screen. "There's records of withholding, I can give you a list of employees and approximate salaries." More clicks, another scrolling list, "That and a few odd bits of equipment they depreciate. Not much else, sorry."

Nohar was looking at the names scrolling across one of the screens. He was hoping he might glimpse a name he'd know. No luck on that score.

"The main thing I want to know is how they were paying Binder—"

Bobby shrugged. "Public database at the Board of Elections, no sweat. But there's a solid limit on the amount of individual and corporate contributions, even for a Senate race. I can itemize the public record, but all the illegal shit ain't gonna be there."

The blue trail began snaking its way through the net.

Bobby had just raised another question in Nohar's mind. The cops had at least one look at the finance records that told them that the three million was in Johnson's possession. However, Smith said all the money was from MLI—and that wasn't legal. Nothing in the police report he'd read had mentioned it. From the campaign end of things, the money had to have looked legitimate—to the cops at least.

More names were scrolling past Nohar on the last screen. Again, Nohar watched it for names he knew— and, suddenly, he got lucky. Nohar stared in widening fascination at the scroll. It was almost too fast to read at all. He was only picking up about every tenth name, but that was enough.

Except for the label on it, he was looking at a copy of MLI's employee list.

Bobby stopped clicking and in the periphery of Nohar's vision, the blue line faded. The room was silent for a moment. The only noises were the slow creaking of the ceiling fans, the buzz from the holographic bell jar, and the high-frequency whine of the monitors.

"What do you see?"

Nohar was smiling. "Can you cross-reference the MLI employee list with the Binder contributors?"

"Sure thing, compare and hold the intersections." Tap, tap, tap.

"Why don't you have a voice interface on this thing?"

"Silly waste of memory. My terminal smokes about twenty megahertz faster than anything else because I don't bother with the voice. Besides, some of the shit I pull with this thing is best conducted in silence—Bingo!"

A third list was scrolling by on the last monitor. "Hell, I missed that. Good thing you were paying attention. The intersection set is the entire MLI payroll. Every single one of MLI's employees made a contribution close to the limit. . . ."

Bobby had stopped talking. Nohar was beginning to smell anger off his friend. "What is it?"

"The contributions from Midwest Lapidary cover sixty-five percent of Binder's treasury. These guys *own* Binder. I knew he was corrupt, but *this*—"

Now it made sense. Binder's finance records held the key—but it now made even less sense for MLI to be behind the killing. Their investment in Binder was incredible. MLI was probably going to lose all that hard-bought influence.

Then, Nohar remembered what Smith had said—MLI's connection with Binder was to be *severed*. That was right before the attempt on Stephie. He still didn't believe in coincidence, and sever was a sinister verb. Nohar wondered if the other people in the Binder campaign were all right.

"You've got a rat's nest of innuendo here."

Nohar looked at the three lists. Only the last portion

of each was shown on their screens. On the left was
the list from the public contribution records. In the
center was the withholding list from the County Auditor. To the right was the list of the names that intersected the two other lists. Something bothered him—

"How many people are on the withholding list?"

"Eight thousand, one hundred, and ninety-two."

The employee list had finished with an endless list
of T's—Tracy, Trapman, Trevor, Troy, Trumbull,
Trust, Tsoravitch . . .

"This alphabetical?"

"Yes, you seeing something?"

"There's something about this list of names. It
seems unnatural somehow. I can't put my finger on
it."

Bobby hit the keys again. "Perhaps if I ran some
pattern-analysis software on it—"

A brief summary replaced the list on the screen.
Bobby read a couple of times. "Blow my mind! There
are—get this—exactly 512 names for sixteen letters of
the alphabet. 512 starting with A, 512 starting with B,
same thing for C, D, E, F, but no G's, 512 H's, 512
I's, no J's or K's. There's L, M, N, O, P, no Q's, R
through T, then nothing till the end of the alphabet.
Talk abut unnatural patterns—"

"It's all fake."

CHAPTER 16

Nohar stayed with Bobby until it was nearly noon. After Bobby had found those unnatural patterns, he had started dumping tax and credit info on individual employees. All the employees they had checked had no credit record and overpaid their taxes. None of them took more than the standard deduction, no investments, no losses, no dependents. The credit record was an anomaly, since the employees they had checked had all been homeowners without a single mortgage among them.

One of MLI's employees was named Kathy Tsoravitch. She allegedly lived in Shaker Heights. Her address gave Nohar something to check, to see just how phony the MLI employee list was.

The Tory was still waiting for him when he left Budget Surplus. The cabby had been leaning back and listening to the news, looked like it was going to be a profitable day for her. Nohar got in the back.

'' 'Kay, where to now? Back to 'hio city?''

''No, Shaker—''

She shrugged and started off east. She was a talker, and started going off on recent news events. The Ziphead attacks, a bomb on the Shoreway, and so on. Nohar let her, all her passengers probably got the same treatment.

When they pulled up outside an empty-looking one-family brick house, there was still thirty dollars left on the meter. Nohar added another twenty and told her to wait.

Nohar got out and quickly walked up the driveway to get away from immediate observation. He wasn't dressed for the neighborhood. The clothes made him look like a hood.

The back of the house was as closed up as the front. Shades were pulled at every window. There wasn't the ubiquitous ozone smell by the empty garage. It hadn't been used in a while. The backyard had withered in the summer sun. It was too yellow for Shaker Heights.

Nohar stood in front of the back door of the house. The lock was a clunky one with a non-optical keypad. The door probably led to the kitchen, but he couldn't tell because a set of venetian blinds blocked his view. He tried the door. It was locked.

He stepped back and raised his foot to kick it in, and he had an inspiration. He lowered his foot and typed in zeros—five of them, enough to fill the display—and the enter key. The keys were full-traverse and a little reluctant to move, but Nohar managed to force them to register.

In response to the dipshit combination, the deadbolt chunked home.

It made a perverse sort of sense that someone on the MLI payroll never bothered to reprogram the deadbolt combination when it came from the factory.

He opened the door and went inside Kathy Tsoravitch's house.

The door *did* lead to the the kitchen—a pretty damn empty kitchen. He let the door close behind him as he surveyed the nearly empty room. No furniture except the counters, no stove, no micro, no fridge, not even light spots on the linoleum tile floor to show where they should be. The only appliance was a dishwasher built into the base cabinets. He turned on the lights and the overhead fluorescent pinged a dozen times before coming on full.

He walked over to the sink and his left foot slipped. He looked down and saw that one of the linoleum tiles—some faded abstract geometric pattern on it—

had come loose from the floor in a small cloud of dust. The adhesive was no more than crumbling yellow powder. He slid it across the floor with his foot and it hit in the corner of the room, shattering into a half-dozen brittle pieces.

He stopped at the sink. Its stainless steel was covered with a thin layer of dust. He turned on the water. There was a banshee scream from the plumbing, and a hard knocking shook the faucet. It sputtered twice, splattering rust-red water speckled with black muck, and settled into a shuddering stream. Nohar killed it.

He opened drawers, but there wasn't much to see. One drawer held a five-centimeter-long mummified body—a mouse or a bat.

The house was empty. The place had the same smell as the boxes in Manny's attic—dry and dusty. Any odor with texture to it had faded long ago to a nothing-smell. Even the little mouse corpse smelled only of dust.

There was a newspaper—a real newspaper, not a fax—lining a drawer. He pulled out the sheet. The date on the paper was January 12th, 2038, fifteen years ago. The headline was ironic, considering Bobby's view on recent events. According to the paper, NASA had just gotten appropriations to test the nuclear engines for its deep-probe project. The original plan was to have a dozen probes going to all the near star systems. Now, fifteen years later, Congress was going to scuttle the project before the first one was even launched.

The end of the Pan-Asian war was news, even two years after the fact. The paper had a rundown on the latest Chinese atrocities in occupied Japan. It also contained the latest 2038 reshuffling of the boundaries within a balkanized India. The Saudis had finally killed off their last oil fire, and found their market gone along with the internal-combustion engine. Even the sheikhs were driving electric. Israel hadn't yet been driven into the sea, but most of the occupied territory was now radioactive. Russia had signed peace treaties with

Turkmen and Azerbaidzhan—finally. And the INS released new figures on annual morey immigration. In 2037, it topped at one-point-eight million. Putting the new, 2038 moreau population at over ten million. The United States had the largest moreau population in the world—with the possible exception of China from which no figures were available.

A candidate for the state senate named Binder was adding his voice to the growing concern about moreau immigration. Bobby was right about Binder's radical shift. Binder spoke before the Cleveland City Club about the moral imperative to allow moreau refugees across the border. Poor tired huddled masses and all that. Five years later, Moreytown would explode into an orgy of violence, and Binder would be in the House as the congressman from the 12th district of Ohio with promises to ban moreau immigration altogether.

He balled up the depressing paper. It crinkled and disintegrated like an old brown leaf. He dropped the remains and kicked the pieces away as he entered the living room.

The living room had wall-to-wall carpeting, an old comm, nothing else. Nohar walked to the comm, kicking up dust and loose pieces of carpet. Worth a try. "Comm on."

It must have heard him. He could hear a click from inside the machine. Nohar looked over the relic as it began to warm up. It was a Sony, and that meant old, at least five years older than the paper. Probably came with the house.

The picture was wavy, and the "message waiting" signal had carved a ghost image into the phosphor. The voice the comm used was obviously synthetic. It tried to sound human, but it sounded more fake than Nohar's own comm. "Comm is on."

At least the commands were standardized. He asked it for messages, and there were one hundred and twenty-eight of them. The comm's memory was filled, and had been for quite some time. Each new message was erasing an older one—stupid system, Nohar's home comm erased anything more than a month old to avoid memory problems.

Nohar wondered what kind of messages were waiting on the comm. It was clear now the intended recipient didn't exist.

"Play."

Static, then a digital low-resolution picture with every tenth pixel gone to volatile memory heaven. "Kathy Tsoravitch, I wish—bzzt—in person. Even so I wish to give my personal—bzzt—for your generous contribution—bzzt—"

Hell, it was Binder. Saturday, July 19th. The last night Stephie had seen Johnson alive.

Nohar smiled. She had last seen Johnson at a fundraiser—that Saturday. On that same night, Binder was thanking the nonexistent Kathy Tsoravitch for her generous contribution. A contribution that must form part of that missing/not-missing three million dollars.

Now he had something to play with. He wondered how well Thomson or Harrison could stonewall if he threw this in their faces.

However, this was only one message. He played the next one. "Play."

"My dear friend, K—bzzt—Tsoravitch. Even though I am unable to thank you in—bzzt—I am giving you my personal promise that I will jus—bzzt—your confid—bzzt—I intend to fulfill my promises of law and order—bzzt—waste in government, and humane laws to promote huma—bzzt—and I am glad there are still people like you in this—bzzt—"

Someone named Henry Davis in Washington D.C. Nohar didn't believe in coincidence. The first two messages were thanks for political contributions—

"Play."

Berthold Maelger from Little Rock, Arkansas, a month ago. Thanks for helping his run for the Senate, appreciating the fact transplanted natives still took an interest in Arkansas politics. He promised his best to try and eliminate pork-barrel politics and to legislate the Hot Springs federal moreau community out of existence.

"Play."

Prentice Charvat, Jackson, Mississippi, same week as Maelger. Running for the Senate. Nohar knew him. The vids portrayed him as the most abrasive and vocal anti-morey congressman in the House. He let it be known he wouldn't stop at sterilization. He wanted to deport the moreys—by force if necessary.

Nohar played every single message. With a few exceptions for junk calls and wrong numbers, the entire message queue consisted of thankful politicians. The queue went back for nearly two years. Even with the repeats, Nohar must have counted over ninety different congressmen—only two or three Senators—that owed Kathy Tsoravitch thanks for her contributions.

Between taxes and donations, it was a good thing Kathy didn't exist. Her salary barely covered her expenses.

Nohar walked back to the cab, dazed. He let himself in the back and sat in silence for a few minutes. The cabby didn't seem to mind, though after a while she asked, "We gonna sit here, or you got somewhere else in mind?"

"Get on the Midtown Corridor, go to the end of Mayfield. There's a parking garage behind the Triangle office building."

She nodded and started gabbing again as the Tory left Shaker. Nohar was ignoring her. Zips or not, cops or not, he had to empty his apartment. There were things he needed to wipe off his comm, there was the remaining ammo for his gun, and, of course, there was his cat. He was going to have to take Cat over to Manny's, since he didn't know when, or if, he'd get back to his apartment again.

Fortunately, there was more than one way in.

They rounded the Triangle and Nohar saw his Jerboa. His car was now a burned-out effigy at the base of the pylons under the old railroad bridge. He thought he caught some movement around the abandoned bus, but his vision wasn't good enough to make it out.

The parking garage was a block away and behind the Triangle. It had its own street. Two-lane blacktop ran under a bridge straight to it. Nohar's office card-key let them in. He told her to go to the fourth level and park. There, he put forty dollars on the meter. "Wait for me until that runs out."

"Sure thing."

Nohar got out of the cab and walked to the barrier at the edge of the fourth floor and looked out. The garage was a relatively new addition to the Triangle, but it was old enough to predate the expansion of Moreytown into what used to be Little Italy. Now, Moreytown surrounded the garage on three sides. For four floors, the openings in the sides of the structure were covered by chain link and barbed wire. However, years had atrophied security, and one corner of the chain link on the fourth floor had been pulled away from the concrete.

Nohar looked out of the hole now. No sign of the Zips yet. A meter away and down was the tar roof of a neighboring apartment building. The piercing smell of the tar made his sinuses ache. The building blocked his view of the street, which was good. It meant anyone on street level couldn't see him.

Nohar straddled the lip and ducked under the gap in the security fence. He reached over with his good left leg. His left foot hit the tar roof and slid a little. The tar was melting in the heat. He was glad for the boots he'd found at Manny's, tar'd be impossible to get out of his fur.

Nohar eased himself across the gap, trying to be gentle to his injured leg. He brought his right foot down on a clay tile on the lip of the roof. The tile was loose and his leg slipped. His foot followed the tile into the narrow gap between the building and the garage. He managed to hook his claws into the fence to avoid falling.

The tile exploded on top of a green trash bin below him. The sound was like a rifle shot.

For a moment Nohar could sense a target strapped to the back of his head. Once it was clear no one was going to appear at the sound, he could move again. Staying to the rear, to avoid being seen from Mayfield, Nohar crossed the connecting roofs to reach his own building, which was a floor taller than its neighbors. Five windows with wrought-iron bars stared across the roof at Nohar. He made for the rearmost one.

The bars were connected to iron cross-members that were bolted to the brick wall. However, security maintenance was even more lax here. The bolts were resting in holes of crumbling masonry and the whole iron construction came loose with a slight pull on Nohar's part.

The window was painted shut, the glass was missing, and a black-painted sheet of plywood had been nailed over it from the inside. He stood upon a wobbly right leg and kicked in the plywood with his left foot. The plywood gave too easily and Nohar had to catch himself on the window frame. It almost broke off in his claws. Tight fit, but he managed to lower himself through the opening he made. He briefly considered replacing things, but if cops or Zips were around, he might need to leave in a hurry.

He was in a broom closet at the end of the fourth-floor hallway. The sheet of plywood had landed on a double-basin sink and Nohar had used it as a step to get down from the window. The sink was now at a forty-five-degree angle from the horizontal, and rusty water was beginning to pool across the hexagonal tiles on the floor.

Nohar made for the stairs.

As he descended, the odor of tar receded. He became aware of a familiar perfume—

The Vind came out. Nohar backed toward the wall

and crept down the steps. He rounded the landing, sliding under the window to the street, and pointed the gun down toward the third floor. No one. There was the ghost smell of blood—

He was getting a sick feeling.

Bottom of the stairs, nobody in the third-floor hallway. Three meters away, his door was ajar. The frame was splintered, proving Nohar's belief in the uselessness of an armored door in a wooden door frame.

No sounds. The perfume was still ghostlike, but the blood was stronger. Nohar flattened himself against the right side of the door frame and pointed the Vind through the opening as he pushed the door open with his foot. Blood, feces, the burning smell of terror filled the apartment—

Nohar covered all the rooms in record time, but the bastards were gone.

They had left Cat in the shower. Nohar found his pet, strips of skin removed from the back and chest, lying in a pool of blood, urine, and feces. They'd hadn't even had the decency to kill the animal before they left it. Cat had bled to death, limping around the stainless-steel pit.

Shaving is a different thing to a morey than it is to a human. To a morey it is a gesture of hatred and contempt. Removal of hair is still the basis of it, but the skin is often removed as well. Survival is rare.

The Zips couldn't find Nohar, so they had shaved Cat.

They left a message on the mirror for him, in Cat's blood. "You next, pretty kitty."

Nohar put his fist through it.

CHAPTER 17

Nohar wanted to kill something.

It was an effort for him not to listen to the adrenaline and finish trashing the apartment. What was worse, every time he thought of Cat, he couldn't help picturing Stephie—

He tried to calm himself by making a methodical inventory of the damage. The Zips had wrecked his comm, along with most of his apartment. They had shredded his clothes out of spite. The couch was dead; it had been ailing to begin with. The kitchen was a disaster. It looked like the Zips had been trying to burn down the building.

But they had missed the two extra magazines for the Vind. Those were where Nohar had left them, on top of the cabinets in the kitchen. The rats weren't particularly thorough, just violent.

Once he made sure the ammo was the only thing he could salvage, he took a sheet—one they had shredded—and wrapped Cat's stiffening body in it. The blood soaked through immediately, and Nohar wrapped him in another sheet, and finally stuffed him into a pillowcase. He didn't know what he was going to do with the corpse, but he couldn't leave it here.

On the way back to the cab, Nohar had the gun out. He hoped the Zips would show themselves, but the way was clear through to the garage. He holstered the gun as he closed in on the cab.

The cabbie interrupted him before he could get in

the back. "What hit your hand? No, don't want to know—stop right there."

Now what?

"No shit, piss, or blood in the back of my cab. They lemme drive, but I clean it up." She got out of the cab and walked around to the back and popped the trunk. She pulled out a first aid kit. " 'Spect one hell of a tip for this. Come 'ere."

Nohar hadn't bothered dressing his right hand. It hadn't seemed important. There were several deep cuts on the back of it, from punching the mirror.

The cabbie cleaned off the wound and tied it up.

"There—what's in the bag?"

"A dead cat."

"Won't ask if that's a joke. Put it in the trunk."

What now? Nohar got in the back of the cab and tried to think clearly, putting his head in his hands.

"Where to now?"

"Sit tight for a minute. We're still running off the forty bucks I gave you."

"Sure 'nuff."

Damn good thing Angel didn't want to be left alone in the apartment.

Should have ditched things when he had the chance. Now he was waist-deep in shit river no matter what he did. Ziphead had a serious in for him. *Guess the limit for rodents in this towns topped off at six—*

He shook his head. That kind of thinking didn't help.

He wanted to claw the upholstery, but it wasn't his car.

The Zips had trashed his comm, that was bad. If Terin knew what she was doing, she would have dumped the call record and read or copied the ramcards before her muscle scragged them. The Zips would have his Binder database. That was public info, not too bad. They had all his photographs. Again, something he could live without.

But now they had the forensic data base, and that was bad. Nohar didn't want to think what could happen if they figured he had a contact in the Medical Examiner's office.

Worst of all, he had no idea what messages had been waiting for him.

Nohar cursed under his breath. He was looking out the cab's window, across the garage and the bridge. He was looking at the Triangle office building—

Wait a minute. He had another comm! If the calls were being forwarded—and most of them were—there would be a copy on the comm in his office. Did the Zips know about that? Were they watching his office? Did the gang even know he had an office?

"So, you want a big tip?"

She turned around and gave him a look ranking that as a stupid question.

"Like to make a quick hundred?"

"Nothing illegal?"

"No." Nohar pulled out his card-key to the Triangle. "You just go to my office and pick up my messages."

The cabbie only took a few seconds to make up her mind. She took his key and left the garage.

She took her own sweet time getting back. It gave Nohar some more time to think. As Angel would say, things were beginning to look like they were going to ground zero on him.

The Zips' nationwide spree of violence made things loom large. MLI's pet congressmen were as ominous, and scared him more than the Zips—especially if MLI was as reactionary as Binder. He wished Smith wanted to have the meet tonight. Nohar didn't want to wait for tomorrow.

The cabbie came back with a ramcard and sat back behind the wheel. "Like you, but I'm nearly off shift. Last ride, where to?"

Nohar told her to drop him off downtown, near East Side. He was going to pay press secretary Thomson a visit.

* * *

He had the cabby drop him off next to the lake.

Nohar walked out on a pier, carrying Cat. He picked a chunk of crumbling asphalt and placed it into the pillowcase. After making sure the knot was tight, Nohar picked up the bundle and looked at it. It was a shapeless mass, but blood had seeped through and the outline of Cat's body was becoming visible in red. "Good-bye, you little missing link."

He walked up to the end of the pier and looked over Lake Erie. There was an overwhelming organic stink from the reclamation algae that hugged the shore. He spared a glance to the light-green plants that shimmered slightly in the evening sun light. Then he tossed his package over the water like an ungainly shot put. Cat hit the water about five meters out, splattering algae. He watched as the pillowcase ballooned up with trapped air, then slowly sank with the weight of the asphalt, pulling the algae in behind it to cover the surface of the water again.

He looked back behind him.

A few blocks away were the massive East-Side condos. On top of one lived Desmond Thomson, Binder's press secretary. Nohar was angry enough about recent events to not even consider how the pinks would react to him. He needed to take this out on someone.

Thomson would be a convenient target.

Nohar started walking toward the condos. The sun was setting, coating the windows of the buildings in molten orange. As Nohar walked toward the building, he amused himself by picturing Thomson's reaction when he unfolded the conspiracy MLI represented, and how deeply the Binder campaign was involved. It wasn't something you could hide, once someone knew what to look for.

Nohar smiled. When this got out, the vids would have a field day. Bobby had been right, Binder *was* the congressman to involve in this.

As Nohar walked into the valley between the ritzy condominiums, reality set in. These were security buildings. How did he think he was going to get in to talk to Thomson in the first place? Bad enough, being a morey. But he was dressed like a gang member and he was armed.

If he walked into one of these lobbies, he'd be lucky if security didn't shoot him and claim self-defense. Nohar got as far as the front door to Thomson's condo before he realized his chances of talking to Binder's press secretary was somewhere between slim and none.

For one of the few times in his life, Nohar wished he wasn't a morey.

He was sitting on the biggest political scandal of the century and he couldn't even confront someone with it. He felt positively useless. What now, he asked himself. Sit here all night and wait for the guy to leave for work? Go back to Manny's?

He thought of Stephie waiting back there and decided to call it a day.

He turned away from the door and smelled something.

Pink blood, and canine musk. Nohar turned back to the door and looked through the glass, into the lobby. There was a guard station in a modern setting of black enamel, chrome and white carpeting. Nobody was behind the desk. That wasn't procedure. The whole idea of security in ritzy places like this was to be high-profile. There should be a pink guard there.

Nohar tried the door. Locked.

He tried to buzz the desk. A guard wouldn't let him in once he saw him, but the guard would have to come to the desk to see who was buzzing. Nobody showed.

Nohar looked deeper into the lobby because he thought he saw some movement. It was an elevator door. It was opening and closing, opening and closing, again and again.

The doors were blocked by a blue-shirted arm on the ground, extending out from the inside of the elevator. The arm belonged to a pink, and in its hand it held a large automatic.

"Shit." Nohar could barely produce a whisper.

There was the echoing squeal of tires from his right. Nohar turned that way and faced the exit of the condo's underground parking garage. A green remote Dodge Electroline shot out and bore to the right so hard it jumped the curb and almost ran Nohar down. Nohar jumped and his back hit the lobby door with a dull thud.

The van shot by him, accelerating, going east.

It made no sense to do so, but Nohar drew his Vind and started chasing the van. Five seconds after he started running his limp had gotten bad to the point where he was in danger of toppling over. There was no way he was going to catch the van anyway. Not unless he shot out the inductor or a tire—and that would be pointless when he didn't know who was inside the vehicle.

Nohar holstered the Vind and began massaging his hip.

Something behind him exploded. A tearing blast that made Nohar immediately turn around, jerking his wounded leg. The shot of pain he felt was forgotten when he saw what had happened.

The top of Thompson's building had erupted a ball of flame that was being quickly followed by rolling black smoke. Nohar felt a hot breeze on his cheek as he heard the distant bell-like tinkle of cascading glass. There was a secondary explosion and the floor below belched black smoke through shattering windows.

Nohar had chased the van three or four blocks away from the condos. He still backed away involuntarily. Within seconds, the top of the cylindrical building was totally obscured by thick black smoke. Nohar was starting to smell the blaze.

It was the choking smell of melting synthetics and burning gasoline.

Nohar was stunned. He stared at the burning building until, a few minutes later, five screaming fire engines blared by him. By then, the entire top three floors were belching out smoke like a trash can that had caught on fire. Nohar backed into an alley. Cops would be arriving soon, and he didn't want to be questioned.

Nohar found a vantage point on a fire escape. At that point, a dozen fire vehicles surrounded the condo, twice that many cop cars. The vids had showed, like a flock of carrion birds. Three helicopters arrived in tight formation and aimed foam-cannons at the top of the building.

The copters pulled a tight turn, carrying them over Nohar. They were flying low and the loud chopping of the rotors made his molars ache. More smells hit him, ozone exhaust from the choppers, the dry-fuzzy smell of the foam—it made him want to sneeze—above it all, the choking, nauseating smell of the burning building. Up there, with all the synthetics, the smoke was probably toxic.

Streams of foam from the cannons cut through the air in precise formation. Three thin bands of white flew from the copters in parallel ballistic arcs, expanding as they went, until all three hit the building as one stream. Nohar watched the foam hit the east side of the building and smash through a window on the top floor. The stream displaced volumes of smoke, and after a short pause, white foam began cascading out windows, dripping down the sides of the building.

Desmond Thomson, MBA, press secretary for the Binder campaign, had lived on the top floor.

Nohar doubted Thomson lived anywhere anymore.

CHAPTER 18

Nohar waited for the chaos at Thomson's condo to die down before he walked out on the street again. Harsk had called him a paranoid bastard, but he didn't want to deal with cops. Being this close to blatant arson, Nohar doubted he'd be let alone. Nohar had the feeling if he got too close to the cops now, he'd be hung out to dry.

He hung by a public comm, painfully aware of Angel's comment, "Moreys this far west *shine*." He was glad rush hour was long over. The pinks had abandoned downtown Cleveland for another day, and the cops were involved elsewhere. The only pink Nohar had to worry about was an oriental rent-a-cop staring at him from the lobby of the Turkmen International Bank. The pink's suspicion was ironic. The pink was probably a Japanese refugee—during the Pan-Asian war Japan and India would have been on the same side, and both had been nuked into a similar fate.

Species before nationality, Nohar guessed.

The cab pulled up. This time, better neighborhood, the cab company sent a remote Chrysler Areobus. Nohar got into it, to the visible relief of the pink rent-a-cop. The van was brand new. Nohar could still smell the factory scent from the upholstery. No one had pissed in this one yet.

"Welcome to Cleveland Autocab. Please state your destination clearly."

The computer started repeating itself in Spanish, Japanese, Arabic—

"Detroit and West—" not too close to Manny, just in case— "63rd. Ohio City."

"Five point seven five kilometers from present location—" Nohar would have walked if not for his leg and the neighborhood. "ETA ten minutes. Please deposit twenty dollars. Change will be refunded to your account."

Nohar slipped the computer his card, punched in his ID, and deducted the twenty dollars. There was a slightly overlong pause while the computer read his card.

"Thank you, Mr. Rajasthan."

The cab rolled out onto the Midtown Corridor, passed through downtown, and got on the Main Avenue bridge, heading west. Night had wrapped itself around the West-Side office complex. The buildings had shifted from chrome to onyx. Traffic was dead with the exception of Nohar's cab and the endlessly running cargo-haulers.

The cab reached the Detroit Avenue off-ramp—

The cab passed it, still doing 90 klicks an hour.

What the hell? "You missed the exit."

The computer was mute. Nohar tried typing on the keyboard provided for passengers. It was dead. So was the voice phone sitting next to it. Nohar began to worry about that pause over his card.

The cab passed the Detroit on-ramp, and two cars pulled off the ramp to follow it. Even in the dark, with his vision, he knew their make. Late-model Dodge Havier sedans.

Unmarked police cars were always Dodge Haviers.

Stupid. Of course the cops would put a flag on his card. They were probably going to have Autocab dispatch send the cab straight to police headquarters.

As if the cab was reading his mind, once it had picked up the shadows it took the next off-ramp, circled around under the bridge, and got back on the bridge—going east, cops in tow.

If he was going to do something, he'd better do it quick.

Now he wasn't so glad he'd gotten a new cab. An older cab would have been fitted with a seat and controls for a driver. This cab's interior was totally filled with pseudo-luxury passenger space. Nohar had little chance to override the controls.

He got down on one knee and felt around the carpet between the forward two seats and the passenger console. When he found the edge, he clawed it up. There had to be a maintenance panel in here. The cab had no hood, and the design people didn't have hatches on the outside to mar the plastic-sleek lines of the vehicle. The only other place for a maint panel would be under the damn cab, and if that was the case, Nohar would be in trouble.

Nohar held his breath until he saw the maint panel under the carpet. It had a keypad, and a red flashing light. A breach would alert the cab's dispatcher. Nohar looked back at the two Haviers behind him. Alerting dispatch wouldn't be a very big problem.

Nohar unholstered the Vind, wishing for the standard teflon-coated rounds, and fired a point-blank shot at the keypad. The gun bucked in his hand and the keypad exploded under him. Little plastic squares with numbers on them went everywhere in the van. It set off the car alarm. He looked back at the cops and saw them activate their flashers.

Where the keypad had been was now a smoking rectangular hole. The sour odor of burning insulation filled the cab. The magnetic lock had only been on the maint panel for the deterrence value. The dumdum had scragged it. Nohar hooked his hand into the remains of the keypad and pulled out the panel.

From the light of the flashers, he could tell the cops were pulling up next to him. He kept low. If the cops had heard the shot, they wouldn't hesitate to blow his head off.

Under the maint panel were the electronic guts of

the computerized driver. Now he had to think fast. The sky was suddenly visible out the side windows. He was passing over the Cuyahoga River. The three cars were hitting downtown Cleveland, and soon after would be at police headquarters.

The circuit boards were labeled and color-coded. Nohar pulled the one labeled "RF Comm." That should cut the signals from dispatch—he hoped.

The Haviers were pacing the cab, one on each side of the center lane. The second the three cars hit downtown, the cab pulled a hard left—against the light. There was a skidding crunch as it clipped one of the Haviers on the inside of its turn. Nohar was thrown against the right wall. He grunted as the impact reawakened the wound in his hip.

It seemed he'd done two things in addition to cutting contact with the Autocab dispatcher. He had activated a homing program—the cab was no longer heading to police headquarters. It was probably returning to Autocab itself—and the collision with the Havier showed that he had cut the cab's ability to pick up the transponders of other cars.

He heard the long blare of horns and the screeching of brakes—

Fuck the cover—the sides of the cab wouldn't stop a bullet anyway. Nohar sat up so he could see what was going on. The cab had run a red light without stopping. The cab wasn't picking up on transmissions from the lights anymore. Or the street signs—it was accelerating. Nohar had blinded the robot cab as well as deafening it. It was following the streets from its memory.

Nohar looked behind him. Only one Havier was following—the one the cab had violently cut off wasn't in sight. The cop had to slow to weave through the chaos the cab had left in the previous intersection.

More horns, another crunch. Nohar was thrown flat on his back. Now his hip sent a crashing wave of pain that made his eyes water. Somehow, he managed to keep hold of the circuit board. He saw the front wind-shield split in half and fall out onto the road. Nohar staggered up and looked out the back. The cab had plowed through the front end of a slow-moving Volks-wagon Luce. The Luce had spun out and almost hit the pursuing cop.

The cab must have been moving over a hundred klicks an hour now. He was actually losing the cop. Even so, he wondered if pulling the circuit board had been a good idea.

He turned around to see where he was going. Down the road was a row of sawhorses dotted with yellow flashers. The city was digging up another hunk of road—

The cab's brain had no idea the flashers were there. They were topping one-twenty. . . .

Nohar slammed the circuit board back home and dived for one of the rear chairs, trying to get a seat belt around himself. The cab suddenly knew what was ahead of it and how fast it was going. The brakes ac-tivated, almost in time.

Whack, one sawhorse hit the front. The flasher ex-ploded into yellow plastic shrapnel. The rest of the sawhorse flipped over the top of the cab. There was an incredible bump, thrusting Nohar into the seat belt. The belt cut into his midsection as the nose of the cab jerked downward. The front-right corner of the cab slammed something in the hole, and the rear of the van swung to the left. The left rear wheel lost pave-ment and the van tumbled into the hole. It rocked once and stopped on its side.

The seat belt and the brakes had saved his life. The cab had hit the hole only going thirty or thirty-five klicks an hour. Nohar was lying on the left side of the van, which was now the floor. Nohar was still for a moment, letting the fires in his right leg fade to a dull ache.

After the cops were done with him, Autocab would probably want his balls for breakfast. Hell, it was their own fault—a remote that gets disabled like that ought to stop.

Nohar unbuckled himself and smelled the dry ozone reek that announced the inductors had cracked open and melted. The cab was dead. Nohar stumbled out the remains of the windshield. Outside was knee-deep mud that smelled of sewer and reclamation algae. Nohar faced the round, three-meter-diameter, concrete mouth of a storm sewer buried in the wall of the hole. He didn't hesitate. He knew providence when he saw it.

He limped into the echoing darkness under the streets.

It seemed like an eternity in the colorless dark, slogging through the algae, listening to the echo of his own breathing, unable to smell anything but the sour odor of the water. The only redeeming feature of his slog through the storm sewers was the fact the air was cool. The water itself was cold, and after a while his feet had numbed to a dull throbbing ache that matched the pulse in his hip.

For once he was worried about Manny's admonitions about infection.

The one big problem he was facing now was that not only had he lost the cops in the sewers, he had also lost himself. From the Hellcats, he knew every inch of the storm sewers under Moreytown. But, of course, he had no idea where the storm sewers were under downtown Cleveland. He had lost his sense of direction a while ago, so he was going upstream—had to be away from the river or Lake Erie. The direction was somewhere between east and south. Eventually he would find an inlet and get his bearings.

The few times he was tempted to go into a smaller branch off of the main trunk he was following, he decided against it. While the trunk was arrow-straight, and an obvious subterranean highway for the cops to follow, he would have plenty of warning before pursuit caught up with him. The slight phosphorescence from the algae was enough light for him to see a couple meters in any direction, the pinks would need a flashlight—that would give them away a hundred meters before they ever saw him.

It was also the only route that gave him enough clearance to stand upright.

Nohar's time sense was screwed. He'd gone for what seemed like hours without sign of pursuit. He kept glancing at his wrist, but his watch was still with whatever Young's explosion had left of his clothes at University Hospitals.

After an interminable period, the world began to lighten. At first Nohar thought it was pink cops with flashlights. However, even though the light let some blue back into his monochrome world, it was much too dim for pink eyes.

He drew the Vind and slowed his approach to the light ahead. It wasn't an inlet. It was a line of holes, large and small, that had been drilled through the concrete wall of the storm sewer. He ducked under a small one that was halfway up the wall, and crept up on a large ragged hole he might fit through.

A glance through the hole only showed him a metal-framework scaffold that was draped in opaque plastic from the other side. The tiled floor outside came to Nohar's waist. Under the scaffold he saw a jackhammer, a small remote forklift, a portable air compressor, and someone's hard hat hung up on one of the struts forming the scaffold. Nohar holstered the Vind and hauled himself up with his good arm.

He climbed in, crouching under the scaffold. He paused and looked back over his shoulder. He sensed something was wrong, even though he didn't hear or smell anything. He turned around, kneeling on his good knee, and leaned slightly back out the hole. He was waiting the split second for his eyes to readjust to the darkness beyond.

He heard a splash and his hand went for the Vind.

A hand shot out of the darkness, much too fast, and grabbed a handful of T-shirt and fur, while a shoulder hit him in the right thigh. He wasn't well balanced, and the way his leg was, it buckled immediately.

Things were going too quickly. He barely had time to recognize the arm belonged to a pink. Nohar tumbled through the darkness and splashed into the green algae water. His hand had only gotten halfway to the Vind.

His head went under for a moment . . .

Nohar came up sputtering. His eyes had adjusted to the darkness. Facing him, and pointing his own Vindhya at him, was a pink female. She had short, dark hair—black as the jumpsuit she wore. She was only 160 centimeters or so, *maybe* 50 kilos. Despite her size, the way the cords stood out on her wrists as she held the 12 millimeter told Nohar she was prepared to take the massive recoil of the weapon.

"FBI." One hand left the gun, whipped a pair of cuffs at him, and was back bracing the Vind before Nohar could react. "I am placing you under arrest. You have the right to remain silent . . ."

The cuffs fit.

As she mirandized him, he noticed something. Her eyes, pupils dilated all the way, were reflecting light back at him. Her pupils glowed at him. He hadn't noticed at first, since a lot of morey eyes did that.

Pink's eyes did not have that catlike reflection.

She was a frank.

He stared at this small woman who held the Vind like it was a Saturday night special, and he realized he was scared shitless.

CHAPTER 19

Nohar didn't know much about human standards for such things, but he was pretty sure that this frank agent was the "babe" the Fed sent to Bobby. He went with the agent quietly. He had no desire to test her capabilities. Despite a probable resisting arrest charge, he could claim he'd pulled the circuit because he'd thought they were Zipheads out to kill him. Wouldn't convince the cops, but it was enough to keep the charges down to reckless endangerment, discharging a firearm, and whatever Autocab wanted to lay on him.

She called in on her throat-mike and wasted no time getting him to the surface. Despite the long walk alone with the agent, Nohar smelled nothing from her that made him think she was worried about him escaping. He noticed she put on a pair of chrome sunglasses as soon as they left the underground. They didn't seem to affect her vision at all, even though it was close to midnight. They came out by the shore of the Cuyahoga River, in the Flats close to *Zero's*. There was still a ghostly smell of carnage to the place.

The pink law was there, in force. A few dozen uniforms had scrambled down to the shore and taken up positions covering the exit from the tunnel. They seemed almost disappointed when Nohar didn't come out, gun blazing.

She led him up the rise next to the river, toward the congregation of parked black-and-whites. The pink cops gave her a wide birth and Nohar detected a slight odor of fear from them. He wondered if the uniforms knew the agent wasn't quite human.

She ignored the uniforms and headed right for the one puke-green Havier. Harsk was sitting on the hood, drinking a cup of coffee that smelled synthetic. She smiled, first time her face showed something other than a hard, expressionless mask. It stopped short of being a sneer.

"Detective Harsk, when I say I have the target in custody—the target's in custody. I was assigned to this for a reason."

Harsk grunted and got to his feet. "Isham, don't dick me around. I don't tell the Fed how to blow its nose. Don't tell me how to wipe my ass."

So her name was Isham. Nohar had thought he detected a slight Israeli accent.

"These men would be of better use elsewhere."

Harsk was steaming. Isham's smile was widening. Nohar wouldn't be surprised if she could smell Harsk's irritation herself. Harsk grabbed Nohar by his good arm and addressed Isham in a tone of forced civility. "I appreciate you helping us with your expertise." That was a blatant lie, Nohar could tell. "But I am still going to do things by the numbers. Especially with moreys. Especially after yesterday."

For a brief moment they were both hanging on to his arm. Harsk had a firm grip. He was strong for a pink. But Isham's hand felt like a steel band. When her hand left—it didn't release his arm so much as vanish—there was an ache where it had been. He suspected she had left a deep bruise there.

Harsk squeezed him into the back of the unmarked Havier, algae and all, and slammed the door shut. Soon Nohar was headed to police headquarters.

The two DEA pinks had fallen into a good-cop, bad-cop routine and didn't seem to realize they were stuck in the middle of a cliché. The bad cop was the fat one. His name was McIntyre. Good cop was a cadaverous black man named Conrad. From every indication, both their first names were "Agent."

Nohar had already gone through the numbers with Harsk, who was, if not civil, at least businesslike and professional about things. These two acted like they were going for first prize at the annual asshole convention.

McIntyre was into rant number five. "We got you by the short-hairs, you morey fuck. There's over thirty grand in *cash* deposits to your account. You expect us to believe it ain't morey drug money? You suddenly get that kind of *cash*, in the middle of the burg with the biggest flush manufacturing center we've found to date—*and* you show up in a firefight with the biggest distributors. Tell us what's going down, tiger, because we're going to trace those bills no matter how well you laundered them."

So far, Nohar had gotten more information from the pinks than they'd gotten from him. Apparently, somewhere in Cleveland was a major flush industry. Somewhere, the DEA didn't know where, was the lab, or labs, that manufactured the flush for the drug trade throughout the center of the country. The Zips were the major dealers of flush on the street level.

Conrad was doing his variation on being reasonable. "We don't want you. We want the labs. Tell us where they are, or give us some names we can work with. We can intervene with the local judicial system, make it easy for you."

He had already protested his ignorance. So he ignored them and studied the acoustic tiles, silently counting the holes that formed abstract patterns in the white rust-stained fiberglass. He wanted to go home, forget about Zips, Binder, MLI. Worse, he was beginning to worry about Stephie. Someone torched Thomson. Of the people with access to the finance records, that only left Stephie and Harrison.

It was going to be a long night. At least he knew

McIntyre was blowing smoke out his ass about the cash. If the money was dirty, they'd know by now, and he wouldn't be in an interrogation room at police headquarters. He'd be in a cell in the federal building. As it was, all they had was the fact any morey with that much cash had to be guilty of something.

When Nohar didn't respond, rant number six was on the horizon. McIntyre never got to deliver on the steaming invective he must have been considering. Harsk opened the off-white metal door and let in Isham, who was still wearing her mirrorshades. Harsk smelled angry. He pointed at the agents and hooked his thumb out the door. "McIntyre, Conrad, get out here. I have to talk to you."

McIntyre wasn't impressed. "We aren't done here."

"Out, *now!*" Harsk was pissed. The DEA pinks obviously didn't expect this from someone they saw as a local functionary. They collected their recording equipment and left.

That left him alone in the room with Isham. She skidded a key ring at him across the formica table. It came to a stop right in front of him. She indicated his handcuffs.

"Take those off."

She didn't wait for him. She turned around to face the large mirror on the wall opposite Nohar. She took off her sunglasses, knocked on it twice, and pointed back toward the door. "I'm waiting."

The comment wasn't addressed to him.

Nohar didn't want to be alone in a room with this woman.

He thought he heard a door open out in the hall. She had just dismissed the cops stationed behind the one-way mirror. By the way her head nodded and moved, he could tell she was watching the cops leave.

"Now we can talk in private." She turned around to face him and smiled. He finally saw her eyes in the light. They looked like a pink's eyes at first, with round iris and visible whites. But there were few, if any, pinks with yellow irises, and none with slitted pupils.

"Aren't you going to remove those?"

He had forgotten about the cuffs. He picked up the keys and fumbled them off. "What's a frank doing working for the FBI?"

She put her sunglasses back on. Now there was no visual cue to her nature. But she was still not a pink. For one thing, she didn't have a scent. For another, her breathing was silent. This woman could be behind him and he would never know she was there.

She paused a moment before she spoke. "The executive isn't as picky about humanity as some people would like. If it wasn't for the domestic ban on macro gene engineering, they'd build their own agents."

Nohar slid the cuffs and the keys back across the table. He tried not to let his nervousness show, but she could probably smell it as well as he could. "So they pick up whatever trickles over the border?"

"Let's get down to business. I want information."

Nohar sighed. "I told the DEA I knew jack—"

That evil smile widened. If she had been a morey, the display of teeth would make him fear for his life. "Those schmucks never dealt with moreys before. They're convinced all moreaus know each other *and* are involved in the drug trade."

She reached into a pocket and tossed a grainy green-tinted picture on the table. It showed a shaggy gray canine in desert camouflage. It had been taken with a light enhancer.

Even with the rotten resolution, there was no question it was Hassan.

"I am searching for a canine calling himself Hassan Sabah. Contract assassin, specializes in political killings. Started in the Afghan occupation of North India. Works for every extremist cause you can name. Japanese nationalists, Irish republicans, South African

white supremacists, Shining Path social humanists in
Peru—''

Every group she mentioned was punctuated by a
picture dropped on the table: the car bomb that took
out the Chinese political director in Yokohama; the
hotel fire that killed three UK cabinet ministers in Belfast; the half-dozen Zulu party leaders hacked apart by
machetes in Pretoria; the barracks of lepus-derived infantry taken out by a remote truck filled with explosives in Cajamarca . . .

''Hassan smuggled himself into the country last year
with the Honduran boatlift. The Fed didn't know he
was in the country until a native of Belfast living in
Cleveland recognized this canine.'' Isham tapped
Hassan's picture with one of her slightly-pointed nails.
''He's in the country, and he's involved with the Zipperheads.''

''Why aren't you talking to your tip?'' Nohar had
an idea why. A morey from Belfast meant a fox.

Isham flipped out another picture, confirming Nohar's suspicion. The picture showed a morey vulpine,
very dead. The fox had a small-caliber gunshot wound,
close range, right eye.

''She was our witness. Whelp fox from North Ire-
land. Had the bad luck to be in a street gang that
called itself Vixen— I see you know what happened to
Vixen. Never got the chance to contact her.''

She leaned back and glanced, over her sunglasses,
at the one-way mirror. Then, satisfied, she went on.
''The Fed only has suspicions of what Hassan is doing. But it scares Washington. Joseph Binder's Senate
campaign seems to be his latest target. The Fed thinks
a radical morey organization is operating out of Cleveland. The terror attacks by the Zipperhead gang give
credibility to the suspicion.''

''You want information on Hassan.''

''We put you and Hassan in the same area on at least
three separate occasions. When Hassan killed a local
pimp named Tisaki Nugoya. During the attempted as-

sassination of Stephanie Weir, former assistant to the late Daryl Johnson. And the arson attack that killed Desmond Thomson.''

''Hassan was there?''

''One of the security guards lived long enough to give us a tentative ID.''

Maybe he could bargain. ''What do I get for talking to you?''

Isham took off her glasses and looked at Nohar as if she was examining a corpse to determine the cause of death. ''You'll get my good will.''

The smile was gone. ''Nohar, you are going to walk. Make me happy.''

Nohar scratched his claws across the linoleum and decided he didn't want Isham as an enemy. ''I'll tell you, but it's mostly second-hand . . .'' He gave her the story, as he saw it, leaving out the MLI angle in deference to client confidentiality. Saturday the 19th, Young had let Hassan into Johnson's house. Johnson gets whacked by Hassan's Levitt. Thursday the 24th, while Stigmata is being wiped up by the Zipheads, Hassan takes position up on Musician's Towers during a thunderstorm and blows Johnson's picture window. Thursday the 31st, Young empties the Binder finance records, torches them, and himself, on the 1st. Monday the 4th, the Zips attack the coffeehouse. Hassan and Terin are together in the four-wheeler.

She completed the list. ''Today, Desmond Thomson is a victim of a firebomb in his condo and Edwin Harrison's BMW explodes on the Shoreway—''

''Harrison's dead?''

''Haven't you followed the news?'' Nohar remembered the cabbie mentioning something about a bomb on the Shoreway. ''Him and twelve other commuters during the morning rush hour. So far, because of you, Weir is the only one to survive an attempt by Hassan. Do you know where she is?''

''No.'' He didn't want to lie. He didn't know how far he could push Isham, but he didn't want to get

Manny involved with this. "She gave me a lift to my old neighborhood. I don't know where she and the rabbit went after that."

Isham seemed to know it was a lie. "I want to know if you find out where she's hiding out. The Fed would like to put her under protection—"

The conversation stopped because a muffled yell was coming from the hall. It was McIntyre. *"What?"*

The room was supposed to be soundproof, but Nohar could hear the conversation if he concentrated. From the pause in Isham's speech, she was eavesdropping as well.

"I said," Harsk's voice, "the tiger walks. Your own fault. Screwed your own collar, if there *was* a collar to begin with. Acted worse than a couple of rookies."

"You can't talk like—"

"Maybe if I put it like this. *Fuck* you, *fuck* your little proprietary DEA investigation, and *fuck* interagency cooperation if you're going to fuck up like this around here!"

"Detective Harsk—" That was Conrad.

"Shut the fuck up! DA sent the word. No prosecution on the coffeehouse, self-defense. None on the gun. Check your files, he's had a license since 2043. As far as recklessness is concerned, *you're* the glorified dimwits that stormed into Autocab dispatch and not only disabled the override comm, but the emergency shutoff as well. DA's position is, since you didn't identify yourself, and the emergency shutoff was disabled, Rajasthan was justified."

"You don't understand," Conrad again, "this is our first lead—"

"The charges from Autocab—"

Hask almost sounded pleased. "*You* don't understand. You have shit. Autocab *is* going to press charges—*against you two*. It might come as a surprise, but not everybody likes to have the DEA walk in and take over. Not to mention the fact the Transportation Safety Board is upset with you. Cutting the override on a remote vehicle is a felony. Because you two goobers couldn't identify yourself to the suspect, the cab goes flying blind into traffic. You're lucky you don't face kidnapping charges. You're not too far from assault with intent.''

''You don't really believe he thought it was the Zips—''

''*You unbelievable shits!* Just because it's a morey, doesn't mean you can forget all that bothersome civil rights crap. The collar *still* has to fly in court. You blew it. Now get the hell out of my station and back to your stakeout in Moreytown—or better, back to the rock you crawled out from.''

''Your superiors are going to hear about this.''

''What a coincidence, your superiors already have. A district chief named Robinson would really like a word with you two.''

That ended the conversation. Nohar turned back to Isham. He was confused. ''IF DEA started this, why were you the arresting officer?''

''Only one with experience tracking moreaus. Trained by Israeli intelligence.'' The evil smile was back.

Harsk burst into the room. ''Agent Isham, where the hell you get off dismissing the observing officers? It's against operating procedure for an officer to be left alone with a suspect—''

''I'm not one of your officers, and Rajasthan is no longer a suspect.''

''Christ, woman, are you pulling this shit just to piss me off? Nohar, you're walking. The DEA guys are fucked worse than a ten-dollar whore, and the DA doesn't want to press charges.''

Nohar stood up. ''Thanks.''

''Don't thank me yet. Because of you, and Binder, I got internal affairs clamping down on my ass—even if it was those Shaker cronies of Binder's that dicked around the Johnson murder. This Ziphead crap has got City Hall in a panic, the vids are having a field day—

And I got suspicions it's all because you stuck your nose where it don't belong. If it was my choice, I'd lock you up and never let you go.

"As it is." He turned to Isham. "If the special agent would kindly leave me and the tiger alone. Nohar, we have things to discuss, in private."

Harsk led him out of the interrogation room.

CHAPTER 20

Harsk's office was in the basement of police head-quarters. It smelled of paper, dust, and mildew. When Harsk led him in, Nohar had to duck the pipes that snaked along the ceiling. There were two chairs opposite the rust-dotted green desk. They were water-stained chrome pipe with red-vinyl seats that were held together with silver-gray duct tape. Neither one looked like it'd survive him, so Nohar stood.

Harsk took a seat behind the desk. He picked up a cup of old coffee that had been sitting on one corner of the desk. It was one of many cups that occupied various open spaces in the room. Harsk took a sip, grimaced, and finished it.

"So, Nohar, you think you just walked out of all that crap because of a clean life-style and goodness of heart—"

Nohar wrinkled his nose. He thought he saw something floating in the coffee Harsk was drinking. "You're about to tell me otherwise?"

The left corner of Harsk's mouth pulled up. The closest the pink cop would ever come to a smile. He drained the cup and tossed it in the corner of the room, near a wastepaper basket that was awash in a tide of old papers. "Good. Your bullshit detector is working. I'm going to tell you *why* you're walking. It has little to do with the DEA's incompetence—"

Harsk opened a drawer and took out the Vindhya. "How many people know who your father is?"

That was the last thing Nohar expected to hear from Harsk. "What has that got to do—"

Harsk started taking out the magazines for the Vind. He arranged it all on the desk in front of him. "Everything, Nohar. If you don't see that, you're dumber than most people give moreys credit for. Do you realize what the Fed, much less those dimwits at the DEA, would do if they knew you were your father's son?"

"It isn't my fault who my father is."

Harsk gave Nohar a withering stare. "If that ain't a load of bullshit, I don't know what is. There's a good chance that half the tigers descended from the Rajasthan Airlift were sired by him. You're the fool that had to track down your paternity. There's a few hundred Rajasthans out there that left well enough alone. You brought Datia's history on to yourself. Now you got to deal with it."

Nohar wished he had a good argument for that. He didn't. "What do you mean, if the Fed knew?"

"They don't, yet. I'll answer my first question for you. Perhaps a half-dozen people in the department know that Nohar is Datia's son. The DA's one. I'm another. All of us were at that last showdown at Musician's Towers. He held off a SWAT team with that gun." He motioned to that Vind. "When the Guard showed up, they torched the building to get him out."

Nohar didn't want to hear this. He was grateful that Harsk was a pink and couldn't smell the emotions off him.

"Datia was a dyed in the wool psycho who left about half his mind in Afghanistan. A lot of humans don't understand why hundreds of moreys followed the bullshit he spouted. Datia, at the end, didn't believe it either. Could've been anyone, though, That August was too tense, too hot, too unstable. Moreytown was primed, anyone could have touched the spark— A lot like it's been lately."

There was a silence in the room. It stretched out for a long time. "What are you getting at, Harsk?"

Harsk shook his head. "You blind SOB. Do I need to spell it out for you? Six people in the department and two National Guardsmen were with your dad when he croaked. He mentioned you. His ramblings are in the official transcripts. It's just that no one has cross-referenced them yet. It is only a matter of time before someone in the Fed is going to see how closely this Ziphead thing was engineered to look like the riots, and look up your dad. Poof, all hell breaks loose."

Harsk stood up. "Does the word scapegoat mean anything to you? What you think McIntyre and Conrad would do if they knew this?"

Nohar felt the world slipping away from him. "They'd think I was . . ."

"—running the show, you shithead. It's damn lucky me and the DA know different. Though, if it wasn't for two things, I'd lock you up just to be on the safe side."

"What two things?"

Harsk sat back down. "Me and the DA think you'd make a great martyr. If you get locked up, or shot, or anything, and word got out of your parentage, that could be the spark that blows everything up again. Right now, we have to deal with the rats—that's enough."

Nohar could feel his own past bearing down on him. It felt like he had spent a decade running away from his own tail. "You said, 'two things.' "

Harsk turned the chair away from Nohar. "The other reason is your typical interagency departmental screwup. Agent Isham seized your weapon and didn't turn it over to property. Somehow the Vind got lost in the shuffle and never got tagged as evidence. You can't have a weapons charge without a weapon—"

Nohar looked at his gun, laid out on the table. He didn't need more of a hint. He holstered the Vind and pocketed the magazines. "Is that it?"

"Fucking enough, ain't it? Do me a favor and stop being one of my problems."

Nohar left Harsk's office.

When Nohar got to the lobby, dawn was breaking across a slate-gray sky. He was glad that they didn't make people pass through the weapons detectors on their way out.

The public comms in the lobby of police headquarters were in better than average condition—which meant maintenance spent at least one day a week cleaning off the piss and graffiti.

He called Manny collect, hoping to catch him before he left for work.

Angel answered the phone. "Fuck you be, Kit?"

"What the hell are you doing answering the phone? Nobody's supposed to know you're there—"

"Chill, Kit." Angel looked chastened. "Whafuck happen to you? Pinky's been up all night—" Nohar felt guilty for the way his spirit lifted when he heard Stephie was worried about him. "—and Doc's been riding a pisser ever since he got back last— Speak of the devil."

Manny came on the comm, pushing Angel aside. "Do you have any idea how lucky you are? I told myself I shouldn't ask where that hole in your hip came from—I was just about out the door to do more autopsies on rodents you shot—"

"Sorry, only place I could go."

Manny sighed. "I know, and I can't well turn you away. I hear that no one is pressing charges."

"It *was* self-defense."

"Next time would you go through the process? Where are you? You look like hell."

"Is that a professional diagnosis?" Nohar was still coated with algae. He probably smelled like the pit, but his nose had long ago gotten used to it.

"When am I going to get the full story on what's going on?"

"You don't want to know if you like to sleep nights. How's Stephie?"

Manny shrugged. "Better than most humans around a group of moreaus. She's been asking me a lot of questions, about you mostly." Manny looked off to the side of the screen and lowered his voice. "Stupid question, but did you—"

"Yes." And he'd do it again in a minute. Manny took a few seconds to respond.

"Damn." There were a few more seconds of silence while Manny recovered. "Well, did you know that they've reopened the Daryl Johnson murder investigation? Internal Affairs got wind that the Shaker division dropped the ball on purpose. Congressman Binder might get called before the House Ethics committee. Half the cops involved rolled over on him. It's all over the vids."

"I got some idea of that from Harsk."

"My office is pissed. They've been given a court order to exhume Johnson's body, even if it wasn't the autopsy that got fugged."

They talked for about ten more minutes. The rest of the conversation consisted mostly of Nohar's stories of the DEA, and Manny's inquiries after his injuries. Neither of them raised the subject of Stephie Weir again.

Then Nohar called for a cab. He specified one with a driver.

Fifteen minutes later, a familiar Nissan Tory pulled up in front of the building. Same driver as yesterday— Autocab probably only had the one.

" 'Spected it was you."

Nohar climbed in the back and slipped his card into the meter. She pulled the cab away and started west toward the Main Avenue bridge. "Busy night. Clocked in this mornin' and, whoa, the rumors. Narcs bust into dispatch and take over a remote. They ain't no drivers. They trash the van with some poor fool inside it. Never trust those remotes . . ."

The patter went on and Nohar dozed off.

She woke him up when they got there, probably after copping a few dollars from the timer. He didn't begrudge her and gave her a fifty dollar tip. "Thanks. Any time you call you can ask for me special. Tell 'em you want Ruby. Shit, you're not bad—for a moreau."

Nohar stood in front of the whitewashed bar with no name and watched the Tory go. The heat was beginning to bake the early morning pavement, as well as the algae caked in his fur. But, for once—though clouds threatened—things were dry. He paused a moment where they had parked the Antaeus. The only trace of the car was one of his own bloody footprints on the asphalt.

He walked to Manny's and had barely limped up to the door when Stephie yanked him inside. Nohar followed, stumbling slightly. He could smell fear and excitement as she pulled him into the living room. Angel was there. Manny had already left for work.

Stephie was breathless. "They started broadcasting it five minutes ago. It's on all the stations. All over the comm—"

Angel pushed her away from in front of the comm. "Shhh—"

Nohar watched the newscast. There was a pink commentator standing in front of the video feed. "We are now going to see exclusive footage of the disaster. Tad Updike, our Channel-N weatherman for the Cleveland area was on the scene. We now give you the uncut video as we received it."

The commentator faded, leaving Tad Updike there, in a safari jacket. He *looked* like a weatherman, slick black hair, insincere smile. He seemed to be standing on top of one of the terminal buildings at Hopkins International Airport, on the far west side of Cleveland.

"—it promises to be another record scorcher. Today, a high close to 33, and the National Weather Service is announcing the third UV hazard warning this sum—*cut it.*'' A plane was approaching, rendering Updike nearly inaudible. ''[bleep] damn planes, didn't anyone look at the flight schedu—''

The cameraman had panned to the plane, over Updike's right shoulder. It was a 747 retrofit, the huge electric turbofans clung to the reinforced wing like goiters. Something streaked up from the ground and hit the plane, behind the front landing gear—

A cherry-red ball of flame engulfed the lower front quarter of the aircraft. It was still over a hundred meters in the air. The nose of the 747 was briefly engulfed in a cloud of inky-black smoke. The right wing dipped and the camera started shaking as the cameraman tried to follow the plane. Updike was screaming. *''My God, someone shot it! Someone shot the plane—''*

The wing crumpled into the runway, pulling the nose of the plane into the ground. It skidded like that for a half-second and the camera lost the plane off the right of the screen. The cameraman overcompensated and swept the picture back to the right, losing the tumbling plane off to the left.

The picture caught the plane center frame again. The focus was fading in and out. In the meantime, the plane was skidding on its side down the runway. The left wing pointed straight up, reflecting the sun back at the camera. The image briefly resembled a chromed shark. The camera followed the plane as it twisted and started to roll. The left wing crumpled and the tail section separated, letting the body roll twice before it broke in two as well. The nose kept going the longest.

Updike's voice-over was useless, so the commentator took over for him as the camera panned over the trail of wreckage and bodies that was scattered over the length of the runway. ''Casualty estimates are still coming in, but there are at least one hundred dead. It has been confirmed that among the dead is Ohio Congressman Joseph Binder—''

Nohar felt like someone just kicked him in the stomach.

"—Binder was returning to Cleveland from Columbus, where he was reorganizing his Senate campaign which has been in chaos ever since the assassination of campaign manager Daryl Johnson. Also, sources say Binder's return was to answer allegations that there was a cover-up involving the Shaker Heights police investigation of Johnson's death.

"The FAA will not comment on the possibility that a surface-to-air missile was involved in the crash . . ."

Nohar slowly sat down. Someone, it had to be Hassan, had killed a few hundred people just to kill Binder. Nohar could feel that events had steamrollered way past him. Everyone who had any connection with the Binder finance records was dead now—

With one exception.

Nohar reached out for Stephie, and pulled her into his arms. They watched the plane explode a few dozen more times.

Nohar turned off the water in the shower. He had finally gotten the baked algae out of his fur. He stepped out and unkinked his neck. Stephie was sitting on the john and drying her hair.

Nohar faced her, dripping, and asked, "What do you mean, I've been 'too hard on Angel'?"

Stephie looked down, shaking her head. Nohar could tell she was smiling. She picked up a washcloth and cleaned off a streak of algae on the inside of her thigh that her shower had missed.

Nohar was getting impatient. "Come on—"

Stephie handed him a towel. "I just think you haven't seen how bad this has all been for her."

Nohar started squeezing the water out of his fur, wishing for a dryer. "Stephie, this whole business has been bad for everyone."

"I know. But she's taking it hard. I know she puts on a brave face—" *You mean an irritating, obnoxious one*, Nohar thought. "But she's scared, Nohar. Scared and alone." She stood up and helped him towel off. "She has nightmares."

"Look, she should have known better than to answer Manny's comm. And I'm sorry if her wiseass attitude gets on my nerves."

"She's only fourteen."

Nohar sighed. "Stephie, for a morey, that's adult."

"Physically adult. She's still just a kid. How do you think you'd handle her situation if you were her age?"

That hit close to home. When he was that age, he was still with the Hellcats. Back then he was probably worse than Angel—

"What do you want me to do?" He mentally added, *fuck her?* He congratulated himself on not actually saying that.

"I think she needs some respect. She needs someone to show some confidence in her, reassure her. Most of all—" Stephie looked up at him, her hands knotted in a towel resting on his chest. "I think she needs you to like her."

"I do like her, sort of."

"She needs to know that."

Nohar shook his head. He supposed he had been treating Angel like a liability. Angel didn't deserve that. He changed the subject. "Stephie, I think we better get both you and Angel out of town."

She cocked her head to one side. "Is that necessary?"

"You're not safe in Cleveland. You're the only one left from the campaign that could have seen those records. Hassan blew that plane just to take out Binder. God help you if Hassan, or the people he works for, finds out where you are."

"Thought you were an atheist."

Huh? Nohar mentally ran through what he'd just said. "Figure of speech. Anyway, we can't have you anywhere near me until this is over. I'll have Bobby reserve a car rental and a motel room somewhere.

He can fudge the records so no one will see your name—''

''Why me *and* Angel?''

Nohar put his arm around her. ''I want someone to be around to keep an eye out for you when I'm not there. Also, you pointed out, Angel needs a friend. You fit the bill better than I do.''

''When do I leave?''

''Soon as possible. Sorry.''

She turned around and started wiping the condensation from the mirror. ''Why is Hassan killing everyone in the campaign?''

Nohar saw the two of them together in the mirror. She was so damn small. ''I still think it's the campaign finance records—the Fed thinks some radical morey group is behind the killing. The *target* makes sense, but I'm not convinced.''

''Why?''

''Daryl Johnson wasn't a terror hit. It was precise, to the point, with no collateral damage. Doesn't fit. There's a motive for Johnson's death beyond some ideology.''

Stephie shrugged. ''You're the detective. You talk to Bobby and I'll try and see if any of Manny's clothes fit me—''

She walked out of the bathroom, leaving behind the pile of her old clothes. He watched her naked back recede down the hallway and realized that she *was* adjusting well to living with a bunch of moreaus.

Nohar limped downstairs and headed for the comm. Angel was still stationed in front of it. She seemed to have a growing addiction to the news channels. She was flipping through the stations with the keyboard.

Morey this, morey that . . . The nonhuman population was getting top billing everywhere across the board. It wasn't just the Zipheads either now. Harsk was right about the summer being explosive. There were already reports of retaliatory human-morey violence from New York. A Bensheim clinic in the Bronx had been firebombed, killing three doctors and three pregnant moreaus.

He thought about what Stephie had said about being curt with Angel. "Angel, I need to use the comm."

Angel turned around, like she hadn't heard him approach. She looked a little surprised. "Sure, Kit."

Angel got up and Nohar slid in and started calling Bobby.

"Nohar?"

She called him Nohar? He turned around and Angel was looking at him, "What?"

"Do you mind when I call you Kit?"

Huh? "No, go right ahead—"

The comm spoke up, "Budget Surplus."

From behind Nohar heard Angel. "Thanks for not minding."

Angel left him alone with Bobby. Nohar watched her leave.

"What do you want, Nohar?"

Nohar turned to face Bobby and explained his problem.

After he was done, Bobby nodded. "Simple enough. I'll get back to you in a few hours with some specific instructions. By the way—"

"What?"

"Are you ever going to want that data on Nugoya? It took a little effort to dig up . . ."

Nohar had totally forgotten about that. "What could I possibly want out of that now. He's dead."

"Well, Daryl Johnson's name pops up in it."

Nohar sat bolt upright, ignoring the protests of his hip. *"What?"*

Bobby displayed his evilest smile. "I *knew* that would get your attention."

CHAPTER 21

The wait while Bobby's electronic gears whirred into motion gave Nohar a chance to think. For the most part he thought about Daryl Johnson. He now had a connection, however tenuous, between Johnson and the Zipheads.

But then, there was so much junk in Johnson's system when he died, he had to be hooked on something. It was too bad flush addiction didn't show up on an autopsy unless they looked for it. That's what it must mean—had to be flush.

Bobby had traced one of Nugoya's financial threads and it led back to, of all people, Johnson. There were only two reasons why Nugoya would be receiving money from Johnson. Since Nugoya only pimped female morey ass, it probably wasn't sex.

Nugoya was offed for reselling the flush he got from the Zips.

Johnson was buying that flush.

Was he? Nohar wondered. If he was, Young had taken all trace of that drug from Johnson's ranch. Bobby had only found three weekly payments—if it was the sign of an addict, it was a recent one.

Blackmail? No, the deposits were much too small for Nugoya's taste had he known anything damaging. There was plenty of information that was damaging. . . .

It was another piece of the puzzle that didn't quite fit.

The comm beeped. It was time for Bobby's ride to show up.

A familiar Nissan Tory pulled in front of Manny's house, Ruby again. It would be a long time before Nohar would trust a remote van. Nohar opened the front door and waved at the cab. Then he turned to Angel and Stephie. Stephie had somehow made some of Manny's clean clothes fit her even when the proportions were all wrong.

She still looked good in them.

"You both know what you're supposed to do?"

"Sure, Kit, no prob."

Nohar shook his head. He was trusting the rabbit, but he wanted to be sure she got it right. "Let me hear it."

Stephie and Angel looked at each other. Stephie cocked her head and motioned with the palm of her hand, Angel first. "Right, Kit, um, we go to the Hertz counter at the airport—"

"Hopkins."

"Lady above, I know that. There's a prepaid '51, ah—"

"Maduro, it's a black, General Motors Maduro sports coupe." Stephie gave him a critical look and Nohar reined himself in.

Angel rolled her eyes so the whites could be seen. "Lemme finish the rundown, Kit. Paid for with Pink— Stephie's—new name." The little scar pulled into a smile at Stephie's expense. Stephie didn't seem to mind.

The name was Bobby's doing. He had programmed a shell identity over Stephie's card. It wouldn't fool a real close scrutiny. However, it would run up false data trail on any casual ID scan. It was a total software construct—Bobby didn't even need to see the card. The software would self-delete when its usefulness was expired.

"—then we blow to the other end of the country, and shack up together across the line in Geauga—she drives so pink law don't stop us. Woodstar Motel is in Chesterland, off highway 322.''

"Good enough. I'll get word down as soon as the shit clears.''

Nohar smiled at the rabbit, and, to his surprise, he got a full smile back.

He piled them into the Tory and paid Ruby. The cabby must have been getting used to moreys. She didn't even comment on Angel, who was buried in one of Nohar's old concert T-shirts.

Stephie mouthed, "I'll miss you," out the window as Nohar shut the door.

The cab drove west, toward the airport. Nohar was left alone in front of Manny's house. He kept looking down the road long after the Tory had passed from view.

He yawned, walked back into the house, and planted himself next to the comm. The chair still smelled of his blood.

Tonight was the meeting with Smith. He'd pretty much decided he was going to tell that blob of flesh to go straight to hell if he didn't get the full story on MLI. Things were too dangerous now to cater to his client's sense of secrecy. Smith's lockjaw might have already cost a few hundred people their lives.

He stretched and tried to make sense out of it all.

Johnson's death had an air of precision and forethought about it.

Staring with the 4th, the deaths in the Binder campaign were loud, messy, and seemed to fit into a nationwide spree of violence by the Zipheads. Violence that seemed engineered to resonate with the riots of eleven years ago. Up to and including starting the violence on the generally accepted anniversary date, August 4th. It was a coordinated effort by the Zips to scare the pinks shitless.

Nohar raked his claws across the armrest of the chair. The upholstery ripped.

The Zips weren't making sense. The Zipperheads

were drug dealers, not terrorists. What kind of profit would there be in encouraging the pinks to clamp down? If there's a new wave of morey riots, nobody wins.

Somehow, it also seemed MLI was involved with the Zips. That made little sense either. It was also hard to deny. The rats'd kept showing up, ever since he'd discovered Hassan. He wouldn't be surprised if MLI was using those green remote vans to smuggle the rats back and forth. Especially after he saw that van shooting out of Thomson's building. There was also no denying that there was some higher authority than the Zips, represented by Hassan. From Angel it sounded like Terin was under somebody's thumb—her supplier?

Was it MLI?

And, even embedded in a wave of rodent terrorism, the deaths were going to focus everyone's attention on the Binder campaign. If there was some information buried in the campaign *they*—Young's nebulous *them*—were trying to cover up, this would be counterproductive—wouldn't it?

Nohar fell asleep feeling like he had forgotten something.

Manny woke Nohar up. He was home early.

"Where are the girls?"

Nohar yawned and sat up. "I sent them to a motel out of town, out of harm's way—"

"As opposed to you . . . and me."

Nohar was stung by that. "I've been trying to keep you out of this. That's why I sent them—"

Manny sighed and sat down on the couch, across from him. Manny formed his engineered surgeon's hands into a peak before the tip of his nose. "Has it ever occurred to you that I don't want to be left out?"

Nohar didn't respond.

"Why do you think I told you you could come here if things got rough? Why do you think I help you with all those missing persons investigations? Why do you

think I took that slug out of your hip?'' Manny shook
his head. ''When you left home and disappeared with
that gang, I knew there was no way I would ever talk
sense to you. But I have the right to know what you
get mixed-up in. I promised Orai I'd keep an eye on
you.''

Manny stopped talking. The only sounds now were
the faint buzz of a fluorescent and Nohar's own breathing.

''I've already involved you in enough to lose your
job—''

Manny cast a glance out the window, toward the
driveway where the van was parked. ''I was trained to
save lives. Today, we had an emergency, the 747. So
damn many bodies to identify. We needed all the help
we could get. *They dismissed me from the scene because there weren't any morey dead.* You think I really
care about conflict of interest?''

Manny deserved to know.

Nohar told him everything, including the money, the
frank, Hassan—everything. Manny didn't interrupt,
didn't ask for elaboration. He just sat and listened.
Nodded a few times. Fidgeted a little with his hands.
Otherwise he let Nohar explain the last week—

By the time Nohar was done, the sky outside had
turned blood-red.

Manny seemed to weigh his response before he said
anything. When he spoke, it was in the even tones of
his professional voice, as if he was describing a corpse
he had dissected. ''You're right. Your frank is not from
South Africa. All their franks have been cataloged
since the coup d'état in Pretoria. What you describe
isn't anything *they* came up with, and it doesn't sound
Israeli or Japanese. On the other hand, the way you
describe Isham, it's pretty clear she's a Mossad assassin strain, something they co-opted after the invasion
of Jordan. Hassan's Afghani, a strain they abandoned
after the war, likes killing too much—''

Manny put his hand to his forehead and stopped

talking. "I knew this would be bad. You should have seen that 747—"

"Are you all right?"

"I'll be fine, it's nine-thirty, you better read your messages if you want to meet your client on time. I'll drive you to Lakeview."

Nohar had forgotten about the messages he'd had the cabbie fetch for him. So much had happened since—

He turned on the comm and got the ramcard out of his wallet. He put it in the card-reader. He called up the messages. There was a predictable—and out of date—message from Harsk about how, if he turned himself in, things would go easier for him. In retrospect, Harsk wasn't lying. Then there was a message from the late Desmond Thomson, the press secretary.

Thomson's face was sunken. The skin looked hollowed out and the vid anchorman's voice had turned into the voice of a jazz musician who smoked too much. "I have no idea what your interest in this is. Whatever you've uncovered, I am supposed to request that you refrain from making it public until Congressman Binder's press conference tomorrow."

Damn, if Terin copied this message some time Tuesday night, when they wrecked his home comm . . .

He played the next message. It was John Smith, the frank, in the same unidentifiable location.

Light was glistening off the frank's pale polyethylene skin. The glassy eyes stared straight ahead. A pale, mittened hand adjusted the comm. Manny stared at the screen, fascinated by the figure of Smith.

"It is worse than I think before. We meet in Lakeview and we must go public. I discover it is not one individual responsible. The whole company is involved and condones the violence. I cannot let them do this, the organization is not supposed to physically intervene. MLI is corrupted and we must make it known who they are and what they do here. I bring all the evidence I can carry to the meeting tomorrow."

Nohar sat back. It looked like he didn't have to threaten the guy to get the full story.

Manny was looking at him now. "Didn't you say these Zipperheads had probably copied your messages off your home comm?"

Oh shit, Terin had that message! They knew the meeting was at Lakeview, *today*. They blew a 747 to get Binder. They'd certainly be willing to ambush the frank—if MLI hadn't dealt with him already.

"Manny, we got to get to Lakeview now!"

The green Medical Examiner's van sped down the Midtown Corridor. Manny drove.

Manny had wanted in. He was in, and God help him—Nohar caught the thought and told himself what he had told Stephie, figure of speech.

He almost missed telling Manny where to take the turn. It was the opposite side of Lakeview that he was used to using. Nohar yelled, and Manny skidded the van into the driveway of the Corridor gate. There was an immediate problem in that this was the Pink entrance, so the gate was closed and chained shut. Nohar's normal entrance was the gate on the Jewish section, which was rusted open.

It was ten-fifteen. They didn't have time to circle around East Cleveland to get to the right gate.

In a pinch, Manny's van could double as a rescue vehicle—a half-assed rescue vehicle, but a rescue vehicle—so, it had its share of equipment to deal with these situations. Nohar pulled a pair of bolt cutters and got out of the van. He walked up to the wrought iron gate and looked through.

No pinks, no security, nothing but darkness, graves, and the surreal image of a tarnished-green bronze statue of a natural buck deer. It stared at the Corridor gate. Nohar cut the chain. They had twelve minutes to beat the frank. He pushed the gate open and waved Manny into the cemetery. The headlights targeted the statue, and for a moment it looked like luminescent jade.

Nohar jumped into the passenger seat—pain shot through his right leg—and started yelling directions at Manny.

Lakeview was a large place, and it was a good thing Nohar knew its layout by heart. They were racing through at the maximum safe speed, and it felt to Nohar as if they were crawling up the hill that formed Lakeview's geography. When they crested the bluff where President James A. Garfield resided in his cylindrical medieval tomb, it was ten-twenty.

They rounded the turn on the other side of the concrete barrier on the Mayfield-Kenelworth gate, and Nohar saw a familiar green van in the distance. *The bastard was early.*

CHAPTER 22

Smith's remote was pulling up to Eliza's marker, and the damn headlights were fucking with Nohar's night-vision.

"Manny—kill the lights."

There were still the lights on the remote, but they were pointed away from them. Nohar could start making things out in the gloom, like the pneumatic doors opening on the frank's van. The frank stepped out carrying a briefcase. Almost immediately, the remote drove away.

"Stop here." Nohar had a slight hope, maybe they'd be lucky and there wouldn't be an ambush. "Radio the cops."

Nohar got out and limped up to the frank.

Smith stood alone, clutching a briefcase to his flabby chest. Now that Nohar saw him standing upright, Nohar realized he was looking at a creature that wasn't designed for bipedal motion. The frank's mass seemed to slide downward, reinforcing the basic pear shape. He still smelled like raw sewage, but in the open air, Nohar could make an effort to ignore it.

Nohar stared into the frank's blank, glassy eyes. "If I'm going to help you, Smith, you have to tell me everything, *now.*"

"Please, let us move. We tell everything to media. We must—"

Nohar put his hand on the frank's shoulder. Even under the jacket, a jacket much too heavy for the weather, Nohar could feel his hand sink in and the flesh ripple underneath. "You're going to tell me first. You've been using me, withholding information—if you'd told me abut MLI up front, that 747 might not have been shot down."

Smith said something that must have been in his native language. It was low, liquid, and sounded like a dirge. Then he went on. "Do not say that!" There was the first real trace of emotion in the frank's voice, even if it didn't register on his face or in his odor. "They do not let me know what they do. You must understand, violence is anathema. Murder is unforgivable. They do this without me—"

Nohar shook his head. "What are they doing, and why are you out of the loop?"

"We must go—"

"Look, the cops will be here any minute. So calm down and tell me why you set me up in this mess."

"No, I do not intend, you do not understand—" More words in that odd sounding language. "When authorities find out what goes on, they will not let us go public. You must make this public." Smith handed Nohar the briefcase. "It is mostly in there. I tell you what is not."

Smith loosened his tie, and the roll of fat around his neck flowed downward. The frank was trembling, as if he was in pain. "You know our purpose is to support politicians. We do so fifteen years for the benefit of our homeland. I am not just an accountant, I am—" The frank let out a word that sounded like a harsh belch. "Perhaps the right term is political officer. I enforce our laws not to physically intervene. We do not engage in violent acts. To do so will prelude a war."

The frank sounded despairing. "Fifteen years in a foreign land is too long to do such work. Laws from so far away become less binding. I am supposed to prevent this. I fail. An operation has left its controls. They try to isolate me and accelerate things beyond safe limits."

The frank pulled a letter out of his pocket and handed it to Nohar. "This is the proof I find when I search our files. It is a filing mistake. I am supposed to handle the letters, but they cannot let me see this. The files are not their job and they make an error filing this paper too early. I do not know what other mistakes they make by keeping this from me—"

It was a letter from Wilson Scott, dated August tenth. The same letter Angel had found at Young's. Only, this copy was intact. It went on mentioning moreys offing pinks, moreys taking hostages, morey air terrorism. It was dated August tenth—

This year.

"Oh, shit."

"English is a difficult language for us. We compose letters months in advance. But I am the one who is to deal with the outside world. I conduct the business. I handle the money. Without me it becomes easy for them to make mistakes of sending letters too early."

"They are telling the Zips what to do?"

"Yes. They do not pay in money, to avoid me."

Flush. Nohar shook his head. "But why?"

"They are impatient. They feel control progresses too slowly. They want our men in the Senate, and they can't wait—"

Nohar could see now. "They want to panic the pinks so anti-morey candidates like Binder get elect—"

He shifted the briefcase and the letter to his left hand. He had heard something moving out in the darkness. He started drawing the Vind. "Smith, there's a van right behind me. Get to it."

"But I have to tell you where—"

"Move!" Nohar could smell canine musk in the air now. Something was approaching, fast. Smith started running. The poor frank bastard seemed to have trouble moving. He was wobbling on rubbery legs. Why the hell would someone engineer something like that?

The bulk of the frank was moving toward the van

when Nohar heard the rustle of some leaves above them.

It was no louder than the crickets or the gravel crunching under his feet, Nohar could smell a rank canine odor now—a wave of musk that overwhelmed the frank's sewer smell. The canine was riding a wave of excitement sexual in its intensity.

The smell hit Nohar too late, because the canine, Hassan, was already in the air, falling out of a tree and on to the frank.

Hassan landed on the frank. Nohar whipped around, aiming the Vind at the canine, but his knee and bad hip fought him. Smith hit the ground, his flesh rippling. The canine sank his right knee into the frank's chest and he was jabbing a rodlike weapon deep into the folds of flesh where the frank's neck should be.

Nohar fired. A hole appeared in the chest of Hassan's jacket. The slug carried the canine over a monument—Eliza's monument—to collapse behind it. Nohar ran up to the marker. The air near it was now ripe with the odor of burnt flesh as well as the frank's sewer smell. Nohar glanced at Smith, who lay on Eliza's grave, unmoving, eyes staring upward. There was a circular purple discoloration on the frank's neck.

Nohar rounded the monument, and Hassan wasn't there. He whipped around, dropping the briefcase to brace the Vind with both hands, and a foot came out of nowhere and hit his right hand. The Vind tumbled out into the darkness. Nohar kept turning to face Hassan. Hassan's jacket hung open now. He was wearing a kevlar vest. The dumdum had only knocked the dog over.

Nohar dived at the canine. Hassan spun sideways, letting Nohar pass over and slam into the ground. Nohar's right knee hit a low-lying monument and spasmed with an excruciating wave of pain, blurring his vision. He could hear and smell the canine approach. He dodged blind.

He went through a line of hedges and started to roll

down a steep hill. He caught himself before he rolled all the way down.

Hassan was hunched low, tongue lolling. He leapt over the hedge and started bounding over the monuments that dotted the hillside. Nohar knew he couldn't move that fast, even with a good leg. He braced himself defensively to receive the canine's charge. Hassan didn't seem to have a gun. Hand to hand, he had a chance to take the assassin.

Nohar felt his heartbeat accelerating. The adrenaline was kicking in.

Hassan passed him and Nohar tried to pivot to follow him. Nohar wasn't quick enough. He felt a kick slam into his lower back, above the base of his tail. He tried to roll with it, but the blow still sent him to his knees.

The Beast was roaring—

"Time for death, cat." A shaggy canine arm hooked around his neck, and there was a fiery tingle under his left armpit. He smelled his own fur burning.

He could feel the rush as The Beast was triggered. But he couldn't move. Hassan was using a stun rod— Nohar was paralyzed. When Hassan pivoted Nohar's body around on his bad knee, pain fogged his sight again. When he could see again, he was propped in front of an open grave. The canine arm began to choke him.

"Your final reward. Make your peace, cat."

Why didn't the sick bastard just shoot him and get it over with?

Manny said they were exhuming Johnson's grave. Apparently, they had. The open grave he was looking into was Daryl Johnson's less-than-final resting place. Lack of oxygen was making him begin to black out. The effects of the stunner were beginning to wear off, but his muscles felt like mush. He didn't want to have to smell Hassan's musk when he died.

Suddenly, there was a bright light. Nohar saw something—a bullet?—ricochet off Johnson's marker. They were both bathed in white light, their shadows extending forward into infinity. Hassan was quick, and the arm around Nohar's neck disappeared. Hassan's shadow jumped out of the light to the sound of another bullet.

Nohar's muscles weren't under his control. He tumbled forward, into the grave.

He splashed facedown in an inch-deep layer of black mud. His whole body cramped up on him. The stunner had been military-style, not a street or a cop version. His muscles had been through a blender and felt predigested.

It took an interminable time for him to recover. As he fought to get his body under control, he could hear sirens in the distance. It certainly took them long enough. By the time he could get up on his hands and knees and look up, the grave was surrounded by Manny and three nervous pink medics. All backlit by red and blue flashers. They were about to climb down into the rectangular hole. Nohar waved them away and stood up. His right knee nearly buckled, and from the loose way it felt, the support bandage had torn off.

Standing, he could reach the lip. It wasn't a good idea in his condition, but be damned if he was going to a hospital. He grabbed the edge, buried his left boot in the side of the grave, and hoisted himself up. His bad shoulder protested and he nearly slid back into the hole—but he clawed his way out.

There was some fear from the medics, but the strongest smell of emotion was coming from Manny. He was worried. Nohar tried to allay Manny's worries by walking—without any help—back up the hill, to where all the cops were. Manny followed. "Are you all right? What did he hit you with?"

Nohar answered through gritted teeth. The walk up the hill was sending daggers of pain through his knee and his hip. "I'm fine. Hassan was using a stun rod—" Nohar noticed a bandage around Manny's right hand. "What happened to you?"

Manny handed Nohar the Vind. "This thing has one hell of a kick."

Nohar stopped. "Oh, hell, Manny, your hand. You broke your fucking hand to shoot—"

"Calm down, it isn't like anyone's going to die from it."

Manny, Nohar thought, *your hands are your life.* "How's Smith?"

"Smith's dead."

They passed the broken hedge Nohar had fallen through and were on level ground again. "*Dead?* He only got hit with a stunner, I saw it."

Manny shrugged. "Then that's what killed him—"

There were a half-dozen black-and-whites parked around Eliza Wilkins' grave. There was also Manny's van, an ambulance, the predictable unmarked Havier, and, of all things, a black Porsche. The frank was still there, looking like an inert lump of flesh only vaguely molded into a humanoid form. Cops were all over, planting evidence tags and yellow warning strips. Harsk was yelling into a radio, alternately cussing someone out for losing Hassan, and trying to hurry the forensics guys. The only nonhumans were Nohar, Manny, the frank—and Agent Isham, FBI, who left the Porsche and walked toward him and Manny.

She still wore the shades. "Doctor Gujerat, I've cleared it with your office. We want you to make a field ID of the deceased."

Manny nodded. "No promises with just the equipment in the van—"

"Do it."

Manny gave an undulating shrug and walked toward the van. Nohar started to follow, but Isham grabbed his arm. "We talk, Mr. Rajasthan. Sit down, your knee will appreciate it."

Nohar found himself sitting on one of the cold granite monuments. She was right—taking the weight off his leg was a relief. It had been in constant pain. Isham pointed to the dead form of Smith. "So, who has Hassan killed this time?"

He didn't have any reason left to be recalcitrant. "He called himself John Smith. He's an accountant for a company called Midwest Lapidary Imports. Apparently the board of directors consisted of franks like him. Claim to be from South Africa, but they aren't."

Isham nodded. "Not South Africa. The frank's much too xenomorphic. Doubt his type is anywhere in the catalogs. Why did Hassan hit him?"

Client confidentiality was irrelevant now. "Until the killings started, MLI was a quiet little covert operation buying influence in Washington. The company has over eight thousand false identities they funnel the money through to avoid the limits on individual campaign contributions. The amount runs into the billions. Smith hired me to find out if someone in MLI was behind the Johnson killing."

"Was there?"

Nohar waved at the dead form of Smith. "The papers in the briefcase are evidence with which he wanted to go public. The MLI organization seems to have slipped out of the control of whatever government was backing them. They're in direct control of the Zips."

Isham lowered her sunglasses. "What government?"

"Hassan showed up before Smith told me. He implied that information isn't in those paper—"

Nohar turned to face the corpse. She was already watching. Manny had come out of the van with a large hypodermic needle. He was trying to take a fluid sample and do a field genetic analysis. He was kneeling over the body, removing the needle from the frank's doughy chest. As Manny withdrew the needle, odors erupted from the corpse—evil bile and ammonia smells. A few cops covered their mouths and retreated into the darkness. From somewhere behind him, Nohar heard the sound of retching. While the cops backed away, he, Manny, and Isham watched in horrified fascination as fluid began leaking from the hole Manny's needle had made.

Manny had ripped the frank's shirt open to get at the chest, and now, cloudy liquid was seeping from a tear in the otherwise featureless skin. The tear was widening with the pressure of the escaping liquid—Manny seemed to realize what was happening. He ran back to the van. Fluid was now pouring from the frank. The smell had driven back all the pinks, and Nohar's nose was numbing. The frank's clothes were soaked with the cloudy liquid, and there was a growing dark spot on the yellow lawn. Nohar thought he could see steam rising from the corpse.

The rip was no longer tearing open. The edges seemed to be dissolving. Manny was racing back with an armload of evidence jars. He was barely in time. The frank had already spilled half its mass on to the ground, and the pace of the dissolution was accelerating. Manny began shoving jars through the hole in the frank's chest—Harsk's eyes widened and he turned around, falling to his knees. Manny got three of the specimen jars into the body before holes began spontaneously erupting in the frank's skin. The skin dissolved like an ice cube in boiling water. Manny tried to get a solid piece of the frank's skin into one of the empty jars. He scooped it up, and it melted into more of the cloudy white fluid.

The body was gone. It left only a pile of clothes, a pair of pink dentures, and a pair of fake plastic eyes.

"Holy Christ." One of the cops was crossing himself.

Manny looked at the puddle surrounding the clothes where John Smith had been, and said, in a tone of epic understatement, "This wasn't a normal frank."

Isham walked over to Harsk. She seemed to be listening to her earplug. "The Fed's taking this over, Harsk. National security."

CHAPTER 23

The trip to Metro General, down the Midtown Corridor and I-90, was a convoy. Nohar didn't want to go to the hospital. In fact, just the idea of it made him nauseous. But Isham was clamping down and the Fed was going to keep all the principals in one place. Manny's van was led by Isham's Porsche. The black-and-whites followed, and downtown they were joined by a group of five dark-blue Haviers.

The convoy converged on Metro General. The cops were shunted into quarantine, Isham shouting down Harsk's objections with talk about waiting for a delegation from the Center for Disease Control. Isham had most of the cops believing the frank was some bio-weapon delivery system.

Isham knew it was a crock, Nohar could tell, but it gave her a convenient excuse to lock up the local law enforcement. It was her show now. Nohar decided she could have it.

She didn't quarantine him. She wanted the cops isolated, and she didn't want him telling them about international conspiracies to control the U.S. government. She took him and Manny to the brand-new genetics lab on the fifth floor of the new Metro wing. The floor was dotted with her agents, and Manny was given lab assistants who were not on the normal hospital payroll. The Fed had dived in with both feet.

Isham spent a half hour in someone's day office, poring over the documents in the briefcase. She had

Nohar sit across from her, getting graveyard mud all over some poor doctor's leather couch.

Occasionally Isham would shoot a question at Nohar. The questions were instructive in themselves. A hundred and fifty members of Congress had received MLI's money. Over seventy had been supported enough to have a massive conflict of interest. Thirty-seven congressmen had received enough money to owe their careers to MLI. Half of these people MLI bought had made it into the various House committees. Three of them held chairs—including the chair of the Ethics committee. There were records of outright bribes to dozens of people in the executive.

And all of this had been done indirectly.

MLI's money *did* come from wholesale dealing in gemstones—massive dealings. They moved so many rocks that the whole lapidary industry was suffering a depression. The devaluation of diamonds and lesser stones didn't seem to bother MLI's balance sheet. They simply moved more rocks to compensate. There was no sign of where their inventory came from, but its volume justified the eighty billion in assets MLI claimed.

In with the accounting information was a collection of letters.

Isham asked about a few of them. None came from MLI itself. They were all forgeries from the hands of MLI's nonexistent employees.

A Jack Brodie from South Euclid, Ohio, wrote to ask a California legislator to consider helping to eliminate federal morey housing in that state. Just a simple request from someone who contributed twenty-five grand to his campaign.

Diane Colson, allegedly living in Parma, Ohio, "informed" a committee member on House Appropriations of all the waste in the federal budget. In the military and NASA in particular.

There was that August 10th letter—Wilson Scott from Cleveland was urging support for Binder's moreau control package, "in view of the recent violence." The smoking gun as far as the Zips were concerned. The proof the violence was engineered to get certain people elected to the Senate.

Isham dispensed with most of this with a few questions. She seemed to be in a hurry to assimilate the information. She only slowed once, over a letter from the familiar name Kathy Tsoravitch, written to Joseph Binder back in the Fall of 2043.

Isham looked up at Nohar. Her sunglasses were off and her retinas cast an orange reflection back at him. "What's NuFood?"

Nohar shrugged. "A little R&D enterprise MLI bought out. My friend with the computer thinks it's only there to smooth out the loss column of their taxes. Some sort of diet food."

"Why a food company?"

Nohar really didn't care. It wasn't his problem any more. "Diversification?"

To his surprise, Isham actually laughed a little. Her laugh was as silent as her breathing. "They went to a bit of trouble to get this particular company—"

Isham slid the letter across the desk and Nohar glanced it over. Kathy was positively adamant Binder prevent NuFood's enterprise from being approved by the FDA. If he remembered correctly, MLI bought out NuFood only a few months after this letter.

Isham riffled through the papers. "NuFood's ten million in assets is barely a ripple in MLI's finances. The patents are nearly worthless. It doesn't seem to have an income at all."

"I told you it was a tax dodge. A money pit the IRS would buy."

Isham looked at length of computer printout. She seemed to be talking to herself. "Then why would they be piping money into it *before* it failed?"

The comm rang. Even though it wasn't her office, Isham didn't hesitate. "Got it."

When the comm lit up, only showing black, she said, "Bald Eagle here. This isn't a secure line."

An electronically modified voice came back. "We have the go."

The caller hung up.

Isham smiled and gathered up the papers. "Well, I'll ask these franks about NuFood when we have them in custody."

She locked the case and gestured to the door as she put on her mirrored sunglasses. When Nohar stood up, his knee began throbbing again. He had to grab the door frame to help himself move outside. Isham walked by him and started down the hall. She paused to turn and say to him, "I'm afraid we're going to have to keep a close eye on you until this clears. You're probably going to be stuck here for a while."

"I don't have anything better to do at the moment."

Nohar hobbled down the corridor and collapsed in a chair in a waiting room across from the lab where Manny was working. Isham passed him, going toward the stairs. She looked at the red-haired FBI agent who was sitting across from Nohar. She pointed at Nohar and the agent nodded.

It seemed Nohar now had his own personal pet FBI agent. The agent didn't wear shades, a normal human—

Even with the pet FBI guy, for once, Nohar was thankful for the Fed. With all this, MLI was blown open. There'd be nothing left for them to cover up. The violence should be over. He was sorry for Smith, but Nohar was glad *his* part had ended.

The agent looked vaguely uncomfortable. Nohar wondered whether it was because he was guarding a morey, because the morey he was guarding was still covered with graveyard mud, or because FBI agents were trained to look constipated as a matter of course. Nohar yawned and struggled his wounded leg up on a table.

Manny came out of the lab across from the lounge,

trailing another agent. He carried a black bag in his good left hand. "Seems to be my eternal duty to patch you up. Let me see that knee while the lab techs troubleshoot the chemical analyzer."

Nohar's agent walked up so the two FBI guys framed Manny like human bookends. Manny was ignoring the agents as he felt along Nohar's right leg. Nohar tried not to wince, but Manny knew when he got to the tender area. "Damn it, you should have gone to the emergency room."

"And make the Fed divide their forces?"

"Very funny." Manny slit the pants around the knee, which was swollen a good fifty percent. Even under the mud and the fur, Nohar could see the discoloration. "You need an orthopedic surgeon. You may have done yourself some permanent damage."

Manny reached into the bag and got out an air-hypo and slipped in a capsule. "This is a local—" Manny shot the hypo into the leg and the pain left Nohar's knee, leaving no feeling at all. Then Manny pulled out a hypodermic needle, a large one. Manny found the needle impossible to maneuver with his bandaged right hand and shifted it to his left. When he did, the color leeched from the face of Nohar's agent. "I'm going to drain this and put another support bandage around it. And if you don't see a specialist about this, I swear I will hunt you down, trank you, and drag you there myself."

Manny slid the needle home. Nohar only felt a slight pressure under his kneecap. Nohar's agent, however, began to look ill. The guy got worse when Manny started withdrawing blood-colored fluid from Nohar's knee. Manny filled the hypo, put it in a plastic bag, and repeated the process with another hypo. The agent turned away, looking out the window at the hospital's parking garage.

Manny sponged off Nohar's knee with alcohol and a strong-smelling disinfectant that made Nohar want to retch. As Manny scrubbed, Nohar tried to get his mind off the smell. "What's with the analyzer?"

"Every new piece of equipment has some bugs—" Manny sounded like he didn't quite believe it. He looked up at the agent who'd accompanied him. The guy stayed expressionless. "Your client was one weird frank. If frank is even the right term—nothing to indicate the gene structure even has a remote basis on the human model. It looks like it was engineered from scratch. I don't know what we got here. There was no cellular differentiation in the samples I salvaged. Through and through this guy was made of the same stuff."

Manny pulled out a bandage, a white plastic roll this time, not clear. As he wrapped it tightly around Nohar's leg, he continued, "No organs, nerves, skeletal system . . . all I can think of to explain it is all the constituent cells are multifunctional, able to do duty as anything the body needs as it needs it."

That was just plain weird. "No organs? Nerves? It—he had to have a brain. He was intelligent. He talked to me—"

"His identity, his 'mind,' would be distributed in electrical signals over his entire body. Just as all the other functions would be diffused within the creature. Eating, excreting—probably reproduces by binary fission."

Manny stood up and watched the bandage fuse and contract in response to Nohar's body heat. Nohar was still having trouble accepting what Manny was telling him. "Smith was just a huge amoeba?"

"In essence. Though a multicellular one. Just looking at the little sample we have is fascinating. The gene-techs that built this thing were geniuses."

"Great— *Why* would someone build something like that?"

Manny produced his undulating shrug again. "I'm only making inferences from a limited sample. But these things would be incredibly tough. Having all their vital functions distributed throughout their mass, there's very little you could do to hurt them. Fire, acid maybe—''

"So how the hell did he die?"

"Electricity. The stunner is intended to temporarily paralyze a normal nervous system. Neural paralysis to *this* creature rendered the entire mass inert. Once that happened, the mass dissolved, from the inside out.''

Manny closed up the black bag and picked up the used hypos. "They have a set of showers here for the staff, use one. I left you some hospital greens that might fit you. I better see if they've 'fixed' the analyzer yet.'' He turned and started trailing his agent back to the lab.

As Manny started back down the hall Nohar called after him. "What's wrong with the thing anyway?"

"Nothing much." Manny sounded like it was pretty major. "We'd just started to catalog amino acids and the display keeps coming up backward.''

Once Manny had disappeared back into the lab Nohar waved at his redheaded agent, who still looked a little queasy. "You heard. Doctor's orders—shower.''

As Nohar limped toward the showers, he tried to talk to his agent. "So, what do you think of Agent Isham?''

He answered in a voice as colorless as he was. "She's a good agent.''

Talk about your stock answers. "So where is she now?''

"I've been encouraged not to speculate.''

"Loosen up. You sound like the voice-over for a hemorrhoid commercial.''

That got him. Nohar could swear he got a ghost of a smile from the guy. He looked down at the agent who was afraid of needles. "You bothered by guarding a morey?''

The agent shook his head. "I've worked with moreaus before. It's what our division is trained for.''

Nohar stopped in front of the doors to the changing area. "That's not what I asked you."

Now there was a smile. A small one. "I suppose not. Perhaps I'm bothered, a little. This is my first assignment, and all the moreaus I've trained with were federal recruits. Mostly Latin American—"

"Never prepared you for a tiger?"

"They can't train you to deal with everything. I apologize if I've seemed remote. You're an important witness, not a suspect—"

"My *name's* Nohar Rajasthan. What do I call you?"

The agent held out his hand. "Agen—Patrick Shaunassy."

Nohar gripped it and decided there was hope for him. "Pleased to meet you."

Shaunassy gave Nohar's hand a healthy shake. "Ditto. You're going to be taking a shower here?"

"Like I said, doctor's orders . . ."

Shaunassy opened the door. "Well, once I secure the area why don't I go back to the vending machines and get us some coffee?"

Nohar usually detested coffee, but he was feeling the lack of sleep catching up with him. "Do that, I could use a few cups."

They entered the changing area and Shaunassy stopped him at the door. Shaunassy made an economical search of the room and the shower stalls as he spoke. "Sugar, cream?"

"Both."

He checked the toilet stalls. "Anything to eat?"

"Hate hospital food."

He returned to the door and made sure it had a lock. "Lock this until I come back. Shouldn't be more than ten minutes. If you're in the shower, I'll wait."

Shaunassy left and Nohar locked the door as requested. Amazing, scratch an FBI agent and there might be a person underneath.

The changing area was a study in white. White plastic lockers with recessed keypads, white fiberglass squares in the ceiling, white tile on the floor, white fluorescents—the only things in the room that weren't white were the greens Manny had left folded on the bench, and the chromed fixtures in the showers. The glare was irritating, so Nohar killed the lights, letting his eyes adjust to the darkness.

The disinfectant was bad here. It was killing his sense of smell. He wished there was a window in here he could open.

He breathed through his mouth as he removed the latest set of clothes he had destroyed.

He got into a shower, turned on a blast of cold water, and let the mud melt off his body. He found himself thinking, not of the FBI or the whole MLI business, but of Stephie Weir. All he wanted, right now, was to be in that motel room in Geauga. He was exhausted and had had enough of this bullshit. He just wanted to hold somebody—her—and get some sleep.

There was thirty grand in his account. He wondered if it was worth it.

He killed the shower and stood there, dripping, listening to the drain gurgle and wondering why he had taken the case in the first place. Did he really, subconsciously, want to go to California after Maria? Did he just want enough money to leave this burg? And where was that coffee?

He stepped over to the dryer—he was going to be done before Shaunassy got back—and slapped the large button with the back of his hand. He was enveloped in a nearly silent column of warm air. His abused muscles appreciated it.

Nohar nodded off a bit.

He slipped against the cold tiles and woke up. He shook the sleep from his head and walked out to the changing room. He spared a glance out the little rectangular windows into the hall. He hoped Shaunassy didn't see the lights off and assume he'd left already. He decided he wasn't going to wait behind a locked door just for Shaunassy to get back. The disinfectant smell in here was getting to him.

He unfolded the bottom of the greens and pulled them on. They fit around his waist, and they came down to a dozen centimeters past his knees. Nohar still had to split the seam on the bottom of the right leg to fit around the swelling.

The top that went with the pants—came short above the waistline and both arms—looked just plain silly. Nohar left it. While the boots he had been wearing were still intact, he left them. His feet needed to air out and it felt good to give the claws on his feet a chance to stretch.

Still no coffee, damn it.

Nohar opened the door and was no longer immersed in the disinfectant smell. Now he could smell fresh coffee, the same synthetic-smelling stuff Harsk drank.

Nohar also smelled blood.

He grabbed his Vind from the pile of his clothes and ran—limped, really, the drug Manny had shot into him was keeping him from feeling his knee, but didn't make it work any better—down toward the vending machines, the waiting area, the labs. The first corner he rounded brought him to the vending machines—

Shaunassy was dead.

He had slid halfway down the wall between the micro and the coffee dispenser. His right hand had knocked over a brown plastic tray, scattering small bulbs of cream and packets of sugar into the widening pool of blood. Three cups of coffee had spilled on the linoleum tile floor. The edges of the spill mixed with Shaunassy's blood, pulling swirls of red to mix with the tan—

Nohar's heartbeat was thudding dully in his ears.

Nohar pulled him away from the wall. Shaunassy hit the ground with a boneless splat. His throat hung open and his shirt was drenched with red. He was still warm.

The canine's musk hung in the air.

Hassan had done this. Probably with a straight razor.

Nohar kept up his limping run to the genetics lab, his breath a furnace in his throat. Why? Why was Hassan doing this?

The hall smelled like an abattoir. The smell of blood seemed to adhere to the back of Nohar's sinuses.

Nohar passed another agent. This one was crumpled in the middle of the hall. Hassan had sawed through the windpipe and had held the throat open. Blood had splattered halfway up the walls. Nohar stepped over the body, and his left foot slipped in the agent's blood. He ignored it and kept running, his foot making little tearing sounds each time he pulled it away from the linoleum.

He took the safety off the Vind and cocked it. The blood smell was getting worse. There was no question in Nohar's mind that Hassan was heading for the lab.

Nohar took in a deep breath, sucking in the smell of blood. His heart hammered in his ears, his head, and neck. Nohar raised his left hand to his mouth and tasted Shaunassy's blood.

For the first time, Nohar willingly invited The Beast into his soul.

The Beast came out and sniffed the air. Blood, it smelled human blood from at least five different people. It smelled the discharge of someone's gun. It smelled an excited canine. It smelled blood from a morey—

From Manny.

Nohar would have roared, but he was stalking now. Hassan didn't know he was here. The canine had passed by the changing area and the room had looked empty, the disinfectant had covered Nohar's smell. Nohar closed on the lab. It formed a T-intersection at the end of the hall. Ahead were a pair of fire doors, an agent crumpled against them, one arm hooked through one of the crash bars. To Nohar's right was the lounge. An agent was sprawled across the table.

To Nohar's left were the swinging doors to the genetic lab. He could hear someone moving in there. He could smell Manny's blood.

Things slowed down as the adrenaline kicked in. One of the doors was half open. And this time Nohar recognized the smell of gasoline—

He crept up on the open door and listened, smelled the air. Hassan was in the rear of the room, to his right—

He burst through the door. Hassan turned, very quickly. Not quickly enough. Nohar's first shot hit him. Hassan's right shoulder exploded into a shower of blood. The canine dropped the package he was carrying and spun off to the left. Nohar, still moving toward the rear of the room, followed with another shot. That one missed and hit a large piece of equipment— probably the chemical analyzer—the impact exploded a picture tube and caused the body of a dead tech to roll off it and hit the floor.

The third shot followed Hassan, missed again, and slammed into a stainless steel sink. Water shot up in a mini-geyser.

Nohar was moving slowly, dreamlike. Hassan took cover behind a large, stainless steel object, an oven or an autoclave. Hassan was drawing a gun. Apparently the need for the stealth of a razor was over. Hassan took too long to aim, and Nohar's fourth shot hit his cover. A white jet of steam blew from the side of the machine, hitting his gun arm. Hassan's wild shot hit the ceiling, taking out a light fixture, and his gun sailed into the middle of the room.

The gun slid and came to rest next to the corpse of another FBI agent, sprawled facedown in a pool of blood in the center of the room. Nohar looked up and Hassan was hidden behind something—a cabinet, the chromed oven, or the other lab-tech, who was slumped over a cart, giving some cover.

Nohar covered the door and backed toward the corner where Hassan had started. His foot stepped on something soft—

Manny.

Manny was facedown on the ground. The slashing wounds on his throat were multiple, violent.

Nohar roared. He screamed rage as he advanced on Hassan's cover—

"Cat—"

Where did that voice come from? Behind the lab cart?

Nohar pumped four shots at Hassan, through the corpse of the lab-tech. Blood sprayed the white lab coat and the cart rolled across the floor with the impact, bottles rattling. There was scrambling, perhaps the smell of canine blood.

Nohar walked up and kicked over the cart. The tech thudded on the ground and the glass bottles shattered. The smell of alcohol filled the room. Hassan had moved behind a counter, closer to the exit. "Cat, thirty seconds and the place goes up. We both go. Still time to leave."

Nohar replied by pumping a shot into the base of the counter. Cabinet doors under the sink splintered.

The canine bolted for the door. Nohar bolted after him, firing. He missed and hit the light switch. The fluorescents winked out as a few anemic sparks leapt from the wall. Next shot was an almost. He could see the shell slam into Hassan's back, pushing him through the door— But the bastard wore a vest. The third shot slammed into the door, blowing a perfectly circular hole in it.

Nohar slammed through the door after the canine. Hassan was still picking himself up from the impact in his back. He had rolled into the lounge. Three shots in rapid succession—

Hassan would be dead if the gun wasn't empty.

Hassan stood up and backed toward a window. He started to open it. "Ten seconds, cat. You can make it down the hall—"

Hassan warded off Nohar with a blood-soaked straight razor in his left hand. His right was trying to fumble open the window in time . . .

The Beast didn't give up that easily, and Nohar wasn't going to stop it this time.

Nohar shifted the weight off his bad knee and leapt at Hassan, claws extended, roaring. Hassan cocked back with the razor to slash at Nohar's neck, but he was wounded, using his off-hand, and he was trying to do too many things at once. In peak condition, he might have hit Nohar. Instead, his forearm hit ineffectively against Nohar's right shoulder. Nohar grabbed Hassan's neck with his teeth as the window gave way before his weight.

Hassan's blood was the sweetest thing he had ever tasted.

The lab exploded.

CHAPTER 24

The window was blown apart by the explosion. They fell onto the top floor of the adjoining parking garage.

Hassan's back slammed into a car below them. The fiberglass underneath them gave and Nohar felt his knee sink into Hassan's chest. Something inside it broke. The canine coughed up blood.

Hassan cocked back with the razor again. Nohar responded with a backhand slash. The fully-extended claws of his right hand hit Hassan's left arm, slicing open Hassan's wrist. The razor went tumbling into the darkness.

Nohar's teeth were still buried in the flesh of Hassan's neck and canine blood spilled into his mouth.

Hassan jerked underneath him. The canine's flesh ripped out of his mouth, and Nohar heard a collarbone snap. Hassan spilled out on the concrete drive and backed away, toward the other end of the garage.

Somewhere a pink screamed.

Debris from above began to rain down on them.

". . . cat." Hassan spat a gob of bloody phlegm at the pavement. He seemed to be laboring to breathe and his voice had a breathy, bubbling quality to it. Nohar thought a rib must have punctured a lung. "Too bad, you didn't go . . ."

Hassan paused to get his breath as Nohar jumped from the car and advanced. "To Geauga with everyone else . . ."

Nohar was barely a meter from the canine and Hassan actually smiled. How—no, he couldn't have. There wasn't enough time.

But where had the Zipheads been when Smith got hit at Lakeview? Where were they now?

Hassan had backed all the way to the railing. Behind him was only space.

Nohar—The Beast—roared and swung his right hand. He aimed at the soft part of the skin under Hassan's lower jaw. The claws, and his fingers, dug in through the skin under Hassan's muzzle. Nohar's claws pierced the skin and crushed Hassan's tongue against the inside of the jaw. Hassan's eyes went wide with shock. Warm blood streamed out of the wound, soaking Nohar's arm.

Nohar put his whole body into the follow-through. He grabbed hold of Hassan's jaw from inside the mouth and his arm continued the swing. Hassan's weight barely slowed it. The swing carried the canine out over the edge of the roof. He was actually thrown upward before he started falling. Hassan slid off of Nohar's hand and followed a near-perfect ballistic arc to the ground.

Hassan crashed into an ambulance that was in the process of pulling out of the driveway below. The roof caved in with his weight, and the siren and flashers— for some reason—kicked in. The ambulance slowed to a stop and a pair of medics piled out to see what the hell had happened.

The Beast retreated but didn't leave. Nohar was shaking as he ran through Metro General's parking garage. No one stopped him as he made his way down, even though his arm and his face were streaked with Hassan's blood—or perhaps because of it. Good thing. Nohar was in a dangerous state of mind. Even an innocent bystander who got in his way would find himself in trouble.

Manny's van was still where they had parked it less than an hour ago. It cut diagonally across three parking spaces and was surrounded by a flock of dark-blue

Haviers. One of the Haviers' doors hung open. The agents from it must have rounded the building to see Hassan's splat.

Manny had never bothered to hide the van's combination from Nohar. Nohar punched it in, opened the door, and got in the driver's seat. The feed ripped out as he floored the van out of the Metro lot.

He could still taste Hassan's blood and it didn't do a damn bit of good. Manny was dead, pointlessly.

"WHY?"

MLI was finished. It was all blown open. *Why?*

Nohar smelled Manny off the driver's seat and he wished the Indian techs had made his strain able to cry.

He was already pushing the van at one-twenty klicks an hour when he hit the I-90 on-ramp. He was dodging slower-moving cars when he remembered this van had a siren. He found the switch and turned it on. He stopped dodging. The other cars were pulling to the side.

He maxed it out at one-fifty as he shot through the exit on to the Midtown Corridor.

Even blowing down the Corridor, going twice the speed limit, gave him time to think, time he didn't want. He didn't want to know Manny was dead. He wanted The Beast to handle it. That's what it was for, damnit.

However, invoking his bioengineered combat-mode didn't help him a bit when it came to dealing with the death of the closest thing to a father he had ever had.

He needed to hit Mayfield, and fuck the barriers. He put on the seat belt.

He shot past the city end of Mayfield and took a right toward the Triangle parking garage. Between the bridge over Mayfield and the one over the driveway, there was a small hill that sloped toward the tracks. Nohar left the driveway and shot the van over the mostly dead lawn, up the hill, and over the dead tracks. A Dodge Electroline wasn't intended to take that kind of grade, but the velocity carried it over. The van started spilling over the other side of the hill, only going seventy now, headed for the side of an apartment building.

Siren still going, Nohar skidded the van to the right. The rear left corner clipped the building as he bumped on to the crumbling Moreytown section of Mayfield. The van rolled to a near stop, scattering the nocturnal population off of the street.

Nohar floored it again, feeling the uneven road in his kidneys.

After the first block, he was going eighty.

He passed the abandoned bus going a hundred.

Third block, he was going one-twenty—

Three concrete pylons blocked the road ahead of him, each three meters tall. The hulk of the dead Subaru was still wrapped around the center pillar.

He pulled the van all the way to the left, on to the sidewalk. On one side was now a concrete wall to Lakeview, and, coming up on the right, one of the pylons. Nohar hoped the gap was big enough.

The front end screeched and the van bucked forward with a crunch—

He was through.

He'd made it. There was now a wobble on the front left tire, and he'd left both front fenders behind him. But now he was shooting east down Mayfield.

He was back to going one-fifty when he passed by Coventry. The cop on the riot watch only took three seconds to decide to give chase. Good for him. Nohar saw the first 322 marker when he passed the minumum-security prison. So far, the cop was the only shadow.

As long as the cop didn't try to stop him.

The vibration from the front wheel was getting worse, but he didn't slow. Malls and suburbia shot by him, a ghostly gray blur under the streetlights. His headlights had been taken out by his squeeze through the barrier. He drove by his night-vision and the infrequent streetlights.

Some shithead going through an intersection didn't get out of the way. Nohar wove a tight arc around the vehicle without hitting the brakes, and raked the side of the van across the rear end of the new BMW. It spun out and hit a light pole.

Suburbia vanished in a wave of trees. The Cleveland cop was still the only shadow, and they were now three suburbs out of his jurisdiction. The streetlights vanished with the malls and the split-levels. The only light now was the van's red flashers, turning the world ahead into a surrealistic image in pulsing-red monochrome.

He hit the county line and could see the blurred lights of the motel coming up on his right. Bobby had chosen a fifty-year-old relic to stash the girls—all tarnished chrome and flickering neon. Nohar saw the lights when he was about a klick away from the hotel and cut the siren as he slowed the van.

When he passed the entrance, he spun the van into the parking lot. The van was going seventy. The first thing he saw in the parking lot was a Ziphead with a submachine gun. The rat was standing guard outside a familiar-looking remote van. Nohar aimed his vehicle at him.

The ratboy's reaction time was just too slow. He jumped to the side too late to avoid being hit. Nohar heard a burst of ineffective gunfire as the wobbly front tire bumped up over the rat.

The front end of Manny's van plowed into the side of the remote. The remote tumbled forward like it had been jerked on a cable, the sudden deceleration throwing Nohar against the seat belt.

There was the sound of shattering glass. Then more gunfire. He felt a wave of shots strafe the rear of the van. He heard more gunfire, not aimed at the van.

Where the hell was his Vind?

Nohar felt the bottom fall out of his world when he realized he had lost it somewhere in the fight with Hassan.

Something inside him smelled the rat-blood under

the van and told him it didn't matter. He was the hunter, they were prey—

And Stephie was in there.

He loosed a subliminal growl as he popped the seat belt and tumbled out the driver's side door, away from the motel. When he hit the ground he shuddered in pain. He was beginning to feel his knee again. He let the pain jack up the adrenaline.

He took cover behind the van—most of the shots were coming from the hotel. He looked at where the shots seemed to be going and saw the Cleveland cop car. The cop was huddling down behind the front fender. The flashers were going, but a bullet had taken out the plastic covering them—the flashers were now giving off a stark white searchlight glare. The cop looked like he had taken a hit or two. Nohar recognized him. He was the pink cop who had looked so scared when he and Manny had passed him—the night all this shit started.

The whelp had better've called backup.

The ratboy who'd guarded the remote was a smear on the pavement. When he looked at the corpse, he could feel his time sense telescoping. The rest of the Zips were holed up in the motel. The Zips weren't paying attention to him yet. The cop must've rounded into the parking lot just after he had plowed in.

The wreck of the remote offered him some more cover. Nohar hunkered down and ran along the side of the wreck on all fours, right leg barely touching the ground.

The motel was simply a line of rooms facing the parking lot. The nose of the remote was only a meter in front of a door—the room next to the Zips. Nohar tackled the door, and the cheap molding splintered. He kept going, tumbling onto a twin bed. The legs on the bed snapped off and spilled Nohar onto a synthetic rug that smelled of mothballs, rug shampoo, and old cigarette smoke. The room was empty.

Nohar could hear the gunfire and the Zip's chittering

Spanish through the thin drywall. He stood up and looked for a weapon.

The room's comm was bolted to its own table. His shoulder protested as he lifted it. The cable connection ripped out of the wall, taking a wall plate and ripping a hole up the drywall for nearly a meter before it snapped free. Knee shaking, he lifted the comm over his head—it had to weigh thirty kilos—and listened to the Zips.

One was near the wall. It sounded like he had a nine-millimeter. Nohar aimed the comm at that one—

The comm and attached table flew in an arc that intersected the wall. It hit dead center at a fake painting—some anonymous landscape—and crashed through the drywall separating the two rooms. The mylar wallpaper tore away in sheets, following the comm through the hole.

Perfect hit on the rat—bandage on the face marked this guy as Bigboy—the side of the comm hit the rat in the face and the picture tube imploded, adding a small cloud of phosphor powder to the plaster dust.

The comm kept going, knocking away a table another rat was using for cover. The rat—dressing on his arm marked him as the one with the chain—turned to face Nohar. That was a stupid mistake. The cop was still covering the picture window from behind the cop car.

The cop put a .38 slug through the rat's neck before the ratboy realized he had lost his cover.

The hole in the wall was a meter square.

Nohar jumped through without any hesitation. He aimed at the third rat, who was hiding behind a set of dresser drawers.

For a moment Nohar bared his entire flank to the cop, the kid had a perfect shot through the long-ago-vaporized picture window. Nohar didn't care.

Nohar landed on the third rodent, Fearless Leader. Fearless had a revolver, a forty-four. An old gun but powerful. He tried to turn it on Nohar, but Nohar grabbed the ratboy's wrist—it was in a cast—and slammed it into one of the open drawers of the dresser. Then he crunched the drawer shut with his entire weight. The gun went off inside the dresser, blasting chunks of particleboard over the rat the cop had shot.

Fearless was looking at Nohar with wide eyes, going into shock. Somewhere, under the growling, Nohar found his voice. "So, 'pretty kitty's' next?" The rat tried to shake his head.

Nohar slashed Fearless Leader's throat open with his claws, opened the drawer, and removed the gun from the sputtering rodent.

The gunfire had ceased.

He could smell perfume coming from the bathroom, over the cordite. Nohar could also smell blood that didn't come from a rat. He gave the cop a great shot at his back as he bolted for the bathroom door at the rear of the motel room.

Somewhere, where his rational mind was hiding, he prayed to Maria's God he wasn't too late.

He kicked the door open, sending a piercing dagger of pain through his right leg. Terin turned toward him. She was picking up a nasty looking assault rifle. It looked too big for her. It was certainly too big for the small bathroom. Terin couldn't sweep it to cover the door.

There was a bloody knife sitting on the sink. Something small and blood-covered was hanging in the shower—

"I'll give you the fucking Finger of God."

The first shot hit her in the chest, slamming the rat into the white tile wall.

The second got her in the face.

The third clicked on an empty chamber.

There was a weak sound from the shower ". . . way to go, Kit . . ."

CHAPTER 25

Angel's voice brought him back. The Beast didn't go back to its mental closet—the closet didn't seem to be there anymore—but it did let his rational mind take over. For the first time Nohar felt the full impact of what he had put his body through. Glass had been ground into his left foot. The falls and the leaping had strained his back. His knee couldn't hold his weight anymore. Any pressure on it was agonizing—

He grabbed the sink and pulled himself into the bathroom. He looked into the shower. Angel's hands were tied to the showerhead. Her feet didn't touch the floor. She was still conscious, and her face was recognizable. Terin had been working from the bottom up. Terin was experienced at shaving moreys—the process was supposed to be long, painful, and the victim was supposed to live up to and, hopefully, a little past the end.

Angel's legs had become strips of bleeding meat.

"Kit, you look like hell . . ."

Nohar gritted his teeth and knelt slowly to examine the damage. It was bad, Angel was probably in shock. He dropped the forty-four in the toilet and grabbed Terin's knife. He stood on his left leg and circled his right arm around, under Angel's armpits, as he cut the bonds on her hands. Her weight nearly toppled him over. He pulled himself along, out of the bathroom, with his left hand. The three rodents that had been covering the picture window didn't move. Every half-second the room was bathed in the searchlight glare of the cop's flashers. Nohar wondered where the cop was.

He laid Angel out on one of the twin beds. Her legs began to stain the white sheet. "I'm calling an ambulance—"

Her head was cocked toward the front of the room. "Only one?"

Nohar went to this room's comm, it was intact. He called emergency. "I need a half-dozen ambulances, Woodstar Motel off route 322 in Chesterland, humans and moreys—cops, too, some of these people are dead—"

The dispatch cop nodded. "What's the problem there?"

Nohar spun the comm to face the carnage. "That's the problem."

He didn't bother to hang up. He turned to Angel. Somewhere along the way he had screwed up, badly. "Where's Stephie?" He almost didn't get the words out. He was too afraid of the answer.

"Back in our room, last in line. Talked about having a hostage. Left a Zip with her . . ."

Oh, shit. If a ratboy was left with her, the bastard would probably kill her once he saw how the fight went. Nohar hobbled over to the picture window; still no sign of the cop. He reached and turned Bigboy over. The rat had been using an Uzi. Nohar grabbed the gun and crawled out the window. Once outside, he saw the cop. Fearless had got off one well placed shot. The cop was unconscious or dead.

Because of his knee, he had to advance on Stephie's room while leaning against the wall. His progress was agonizingly slow. He passed the wreck of the remote and the door he had busted in. He passed an unoccupied room. Slowly, he came upon the last in the line, the black GM Maduro parked in front.

He checked the clip on the Uzi. Good thing Bigboy wasn't spraying the cop. There were a few shots left. He hit the ground and scrambled under the picture window—his right knee was beginning to make popping sounds every time he moved—and rolled in front of the door.

With the feeling this was going to be it for him, he shouldered the door open and covered the room with the Uzi.

And there was Mister Mad Bomber, looking like he was about to wet his pants. The rat's twenty-two thumped on the carpet.

Stephie was alive, and apparently unhurt. She had been stripped naked and tied to the bed. She turned her head toward the door when it burst open. She had never smelled so good to him.

The Beast wanted Nohar to shoot the rat. To Nohar's surprise, he still had control. Even though the mental door was no longer there.

"Kid, second chances are rare, use yours. Get out of here."

The rat carefully approached the door, where Nohar was still half-sitting, stepped over him, and ran into the night. Stephie's eyes were wide as she watched Nohar pull himself into the room and on to the bed. Nohar didn't waste time. He bit through the rope.

As soon as Stephie was free, Nohar found himself on the receiving end of an embrace that smeared her with blood. "God, what's happened to you—where's Angel?"

"Angel, I called an ambulance for her— and everyone else. They killed Manny—"

Stephie broke off the hug. "Oh, Christ, I'm sorry—"

"Can you find me something to use as a cane?"

The curtain rod was stainless steel, and not as cheap as everything else in the motel. It made a halfway decent cane. Stephie found a robe and followed him out to the parking lot. He asked aloud the question that had gnawed at him ever since he had smelled Shaunassy's blood—

"Damn it, why?"

He hobbled to the wreck of the remote. The power

plant was still alive. The wheels were trying to drive it away despite the broken axle. He walked up to the vehicle. Green, just like Smith's van. Hell, it could *be* Smith's van. "The whole thing was *blown*. The Fed has *everything*."

He slammed his left fist at one of the dangling pneumatic doors. There was a slow hiss, and the door slid aside with the smell of leaking hydraulic fluid. There were guns and a dozen white plastic crates in the back. Most of the crates had burst open. Little vials of red liquid rolled out the rear of the van. Hypo cartridges— flush, a few million dollars' worth.

The DEA would be happy.

Nohar leaned in and looked at the crates more closely. They were labeled. "NuFood Inc. dietary supplements—MirrorProtein(tm)"

MLI was using NuFood as a drug lab.

There had to be another reason for NuFood. The Zips had only come on the scene recently. MLI had been dealing with NuFood ever since MLI's inception.

MirrorProtein?

What was it Manny said about the chemical analyzer? They had been cataloging amino acids and the display was reversed. Nohar had thought the picture had been coming up backward.

What if it was the amino acids themselves that were coming up reversed?

"Stephie, do you know any biochemistry?"

Stephie was already at the Zips' room checking on Angel. *"What?"*

Nohar hobbled after her. His thoughts were flying, trying to remember things, put them into place. "This is important. Really important. Biochemistry, proteins, amino acids, what do you know?"

"Next to nothing." She had her hand on Angel's neck. "She's still alive— What the hell are you talking about?"

"I need to remember if we're based on levo or dextro amino acids . . ."

"Derry was the chemistry major. Where the hell are you getting this from?" Stephie was looking worried, as if she thought he had gone over the edge.

Far from it. Things were making sense. "I don't know if you'll understand this." He was racing to get it all out. "I lived most of my childhood with Manny—a doctor and an expert on moreaus. I got a biology lesson every time I asked a question like, 'Why am I different from the other kids?' "

Even to him he sounded like he was rambling. He slowed down. "You can't live like that and not pick up on biological trivia. Like the fact our amino acids all have their mirror image versions." He finally remembered. "Almost all the life in this world is based on levo amino acids—"

"So?"

Nohar shook his head. "Just tell the cops when they get here. You have to talk to an FBI agent—Isham. Tell her the franks aren't at MLI's office building. It's just a front, like everything else. If they're anywhere, they're at NuFood's R&D facility. Tell her the MLI franks are based on a *dextro* amino acid biology. Got that?"

"Yes, but—"

Nohar was hobbling back to the Maduro. He stopped at the remote. An Uzi wouldn't do much to one of the things Manny described. He looked in among the crates of flush and saw a pump shotgun. He'd take that, and hope.

He was beginning to hear sirens in the distance. Stephie ran after him. "Where are you going?"

"NuFood. This isn't over—"

He slumped up next to the car. "Did they wire the car?"

"No—"

"What's the combination?"

"Nohar, you can't! You're in no condition . . ."

"The damn combination!"

Stephie backed up a bit at Nohar's growled command. Nohar shook his head. "*Please,* God damn it."

Stephie heard the sirens now as well.

She stepped up and punched the combination on the driver's door. Nohar watched the numbers. She looked up at him afterward. She was crying. "You are not going to die on me."

Nohar hugged her with his good arm. "I don't intend to."

The Maduro had pulled out of the parking lot and was going down Mayfield by the time a convoy—Chesterland and Cleveland local cops, sheriffs from Cuyahoga and Geauga, six ambulances, two police wreckers, a fire rescue vehicle, and three Haviers—shot by going in the opposite direction. Everything but the National Guard.

Nohar drove by them going a sedate sixty klicks an hour. He was squeezed in the sports car, but the gentle ride of the undamaged suspension made up for it.

Everything came together for him when he saw that NuFood label. He had been right along. Despite the hyped violence, the morey terrorism, the Johnson killing came down to one little piece of information in Binder's financial records.

The precognitive letter from Wilson Scott was only part of it. That only proved MLI had a hand in planning the Zipheads' terrorism. MLI was trying to hide something else.

Their origin.

Johnson used to be a chemistry major. It made sense he would figure this mess out.

It had all started thirteen years ago. Midwest Lapidary would have approached Young, Binder's new finance chairman. It would have been a very tempting offer. Young took the offer, and the bucks poured into the campaign.

And Binder's position became more and more reactionary.

Over the next few years, other, similarly unpopular candidates had made some sort of deal with the shadowy diamond merchants working out of Cleveland—candidates that weren't supposed to win. Their positions would evolve as well.

Then, in 2042, morey communities across the country exploded into a week of riots and burning that took the National Guard to control. Led by the psychopathic rhetoric of a morey tiger named Datia Rajasthan.

The violence created a convenient wave of antimoreau sentiment that catapulted most of MLI's candidates to office.

MLI had about seventy hard-core puppets in the House now, all incumbents. They only had a few men in the Senate, though, and a large percentage of their men, including Binder, wanted to be Senators.

The rogue agents in MLI, without Smith's knowledge, recruited the Zipheads to step in to create their own "Dark August." The Zipheads were happy to comply, considering the profits they made on flush on the street level.

Daryl Johnson knew or suspected all of this. At first he must have condoned it. You couldn't keep that kind of conspiracy secret from the campaign manager. The whole Binder inner circle must have known about the illegal financing. That's why it was so tight. Harrison, Thomson, Johnson, and Young stuck with Binder through his radical shift to the right. They *all* had been bought.

Johnson was the first to have second thoughts. Nohar suspected that it would probably have originated with the whole duplicitious situation with Stephie. It must have grated badly. He stewed for years. Even tried to drug himself out of an untenable situation.

MLI must have thought they had him under control because he was hooked on flush that they supplied—though indirectly. If he did anything to break the silence, his supply would be cut.

Three weeks before his death Johnson found a new supplier. Nugoya.

That wasn't what got him killed. The flush still came from MLI, they still controlled his supply even though Johnson didn't know that. What killed Johnson was *why* he was trying to get out from under the thumb of his supplier. Johnson's problem was curiosity. He thought too much.

He had thought too much about NuFood.

He thought too much about Kathy Tsoravitch's letter.

Johnson made the mistake of wondering, as Isham had just a few hours ago, why MLI would be interested in preventing NuFood from succeeding. Tsoravitch lobbied to prevent FDA approval. Denial of that approval bankrupted NuFood.

Whereupon, MLI bought out the company, and the patents.

Why?

The question must have nagged at Johnson for years. Especially when MLI simply sat on the company. He might even have realized that MLI was using NuFood as its flush lab. A very expensive drug lab.

He finally figured out the real reason. When he did, he made his second, and last, mistake. He told Young. And Young had told the creatures running MLI—

That's when the shit went ballistic. That's why Young was so scared, as well as guilty. He *knew* MLI's secret—they would have killed him once he had served his purpose, IDing the people in the campaign whom Johnson had talked to, those who read the letter.

But Young toasted himself, so MLI had to use their agents—Hassan and the Zipheads—to waste anyone who could have read that letter.

All from Kathy Tsoravitch's letter, and her pleading that the DA reject NuFood's application to mass market their dietary supplements. Supplements that were based on synthetic proteins derived from mirror image dextro amino acids. Proteins a creature based on a levo amino acid biology—like the fat pinks at whom the food would be targeted—couldn't metabolize.

Johnson had looked too closely at MLI's agenda. He saw NuFood, moreys as a hot issue to be counted on to get MLI's people elected, and the budget. And the letters about government waste always mentioned NASA.

Johnson must have seen the creatures running MLI— the humanoid things that could only be franks. Otherwise, Nohar doubted Johnson would have come to the conclusion he must have. Because the truth was quite a leap.

Nohar's Maduro had glided into the suburbs again. He began watching the left side of Mayfield. NuFood's R&D complex was at 3700 Mayfield, near the minimum security prison he had passed earlier. NuFood's plot was cheap property, little-traveled.

The conclusion was simple, if hard to accept. Johnson must have asked himself the same question as Nohar did when Smith told him MLI supported Binder.

Why were a bunch of franks backing right-wingers like Binder?

They weren't franks.

Why the hell were they involved with something like NuFood?

Johnson must have inferred what Nohar had told Stephie. These things were based on a dextro amino acid biology. Manny had discovered that from Smith's remains. Manny had known, but he had never gotten the chance to double-check the results. He never got the chance to make sure the analyzer wasn't broken.

That was what MLI had to cover up.

The prison came up on the left.

Nohar pulled the Maduro over and parked on the sidewalk across from it. NuFood was next to the prison's barbed wire topped chain link. It sat in the midst of a grove of trees and bushes that nearly hid the two lab buildings from sight.

They couldn't let anyone know they were based on

a mirror image biology. It was because of that *they* needed NuFood. *They* literally couldn't live without it. Normal living things couldn't metabolize NuFood's products, but the converse was true. NuFood's production was the only thing *they* could eat.

No gene-tech, even as an experiment, would give their work such a bizarre handicap. Johnson would know that. It left one conclusion.

These things *weren't* bioengineered.

They had evolved naturally.

It was a fifty-fifty chance life on Earth ended up stabilizing around the one type of amino acid. Life elsewhere, if it evolved as it had on Earth, would end up stabilizing around one form or the other, dextro or levo. Same chance, fifty-fifty. Even odds. It was just bad luck, for everyone concerned, that these guys came from a planet that was based on the wrong type.

They were aliens.

Nohar hobbled across the street.

CHAPTER 26

The storm that had been threatening all night finally came as Nohar crossed Mayfield. It was a sudden deluge that washed some of the blood off of him. His makeshift cane was thumping an erratic counterpoint to the click of his claws. It was slow progress, but it was nearly three in the morning and there wasn't any traffic. The street was dead.

He made it across. To his right was the prison hiding behind its electrified chain link. Its yard was bathed in arc lights.

To his left was a line of shrubs and trees that almost hid an old, low slung, office complex from the street. Ahead of him, between the overgrown shrubs and the five-meter-tall electric chain link, was a dirty-gravel driveway. It looked like a landscaping afterthought.

He began worrying about the pink guards at the prison. They weren't involved in this, but it wouldn't be good if they noticed a morey with a shotgun skulking just outside their grounds.

He limped a dozen meters down the gravel path, all the while cursing his knee and wishing he could move faster. He made it to a point where the hedges got sickly. He turned away from the prison and pushed through a small gap between the bushes. He immediately tripped over a rusted "No Trespassing" sign. He managed to land on his left side, but the fall still hurt his knee.

He was sprawled on a shaggy, uncut lawn, looking across at a parking lot of broken asphalt. The only light came from the arcs of the prison behind him. Half the NuFood complex was wrapped in glaring blue light, the other half in the matte-black shadows of the surrounding trees.

Two remote vans were parked in the lot, the only vehicles there. There were two buildings in NuFood's complex, both old two-story studies in metal, glass, and dark tile. The tiles had been falling off in clumps, helped by ill-looking ivy. The glass was sealed shut from the inside. A few panes were cracked and broken—real glass—allowing Nohar a good look at the white plastic that covered the windows from the inside.

Between the two buildings were an overgrown lawn and a crumbling driveway. A fountain was choked by an advancing rosebush—and even in the rain, he could smell the stagnant water filling it.

These guys weren't big on maintenance.

Nohar pushed himself up and got unsteadily to his feet. The makeshift cane sank about half a meter into the sod when he put his weight on it. He squished to the asphalt parking lot.

The remotes were parked next to each other. Nohar hobbled between them. He decided if the guards back at the prison started hearing gunfire, the worst thing they could do was call the cops.

He eased himself down on the ground and looked under the chassis of one of the vans. The inductor housing was nestled in front of the rear axle. Nohar leveled the shotgun at it, the barrel a few centimeters from the housing. He turned his face away, closed his eyes, and pulled the trigger.

The blast popped the pressurized housing, and the air was filled with the smell of freon, ozone, and the dust from a shattered ceramic superconductor. There was a wave of heat as the housing sparked and began to melt.

He did the same to the other one.

There went their transport. If *they* were still here, they'd *stay* here.

The guards back at the prison had heard the gunfire. Sirens began sounding behind him.

Nohar hauled himself upright and limped up the circular driveway to the first NuFood building. The door was glass and black enamel. Gold leaf on the glass announced this was indeed NuFood. Its slick modern logo was flaking off. A chain was padlocked around the handle, the one thing that looked new and well maintained.

Locks on glass doors made about as much sense as an armored door in a wooden door frame.

Nohar hunched up against the wall for support and raised the curtain rod. He put the end of the rod through the logo, shattering the glass—real glass again. There was another plastic sheet sealing the window. It tore away from the frame, loosing the bile-ammonia smell Nohar associated with Smith.

Bingo.

There was a crash bar on the inside of the door, halfway up. The plastic caught and bent over it. Nohar had to lean the curtain rod up next to the doorjamb so he had a hand free to knock the plastic out of the way. In response to Nohar's break-in, an alarm inside the building did an anemic imitation of the sirens at the prison.

Because of his leg, Nohar put down the shotgun and scrambled under the crash bar on both hands and his good leg. He sliced open his right palm on a stray piece of glass.

Once he pulled the cane and the gun after him, he pushed himself up to a standing position.

Inside, the place was much better maintained—and strange. He could smell *their* odor, as well as the odors of chemicals—there was a strong hint of sulfur and sulfur dioxide—and disinfectant that had a fake pine odor. The hall he was in was brightly lit with sodium lamps. They cast an unnatural yellow glow over the hallway. There were filters on the lamps that seemed to increase the effect. The floor he was hobbling along had been stripped to the concrete. It had been polished and felt slightly moist under his feet. Not water. It was damp with something more viscous that made it hard to keep his footing.

The first door to his right was open. He looked in and saw a storage area. The room must have filled half the building, both floors. It was stacked with white plastic delivery crates. It was lit with normal fluorescents, and to the rear was a rolling metal door that must open onto a truck-loading bay. Nohar could smell the flush—even through the packaging, there was so much of it—a rotten, artificial fruit smell, like spoiled cherries.

Nohar continued to limp down the hallway. The doors he passed on his left were new, solid, air lock doors. He looked through the round porthole windows, and saw clean rooms containing glass laboratory equipment filled with bubbling fluids. Here was the damn flush lab the DEA wanted. Nice sterile environment. The stuff must be real pure.

He kept walking, following the ammonia smell. *They* were here. He could feel it. He kept going down the corridor. It took a right turn near the far wall. More labs, older, not behind air lock doors. Nohar noticed familiar items that matched the genetics lab at Metro General. Especially the hulking form of the chemical analyzer. This had to be part of the food production, R&D anyway. Any real volume processing must happen in the other building.

Nohar rounded the corner and faced a stairwell, up and down. Same slick polished concrete. The sulfur and the ammonia were worse going down. That's where he went.

The steps went slowly, one at a time. Each step felt like he was going to slip and break his neck. As he descended, the atmosphere became thicker, denser. The sodium lights faded to a dusky red, and Nohar was beginning to feel the heat—the temperature down here must be around 35 or 40. The atmosphere was heavy with moisture that clung to his fur.

The heat and the heavy atmosphere were making his head throb.

He could feel his pulse in his temple.

Down, he was in the basement. Here, there was no pretense at normal construction. The hall was concrete that had been polished to a marblelike sheen. All the right angles had been filled in and polished smooth, giving an ovoid cross section. The walls were weeping moisture that had the viscosity of silicone lubricant.

There were pipes and other basement equipment, but all had been molded into the walls. Nohar looked up and saw a length of white PVC pipe just above his head. Concrete had been molded around the ends where it came in through the wall so the wall's lines melded smoothly with the length of pipe. It looked like some organic growth. Nohar looked at one wall, and from the discoloration he could make out where the lines of the old cinder block wall used to be.

There was only one way to go. He followed the hall. He hobbled down and left the last of the yellow sodium lights, and entered the world of green-tinted red. The ammonia smell was very close now.

He rounded a very gradual turn in the hall. It felt like he was hobbling through a wormhole in the bowels of the earth. He completed the turn, and saw a perfectly round door. Out the door was pouring an evil bluish-green light and that bile-ammonia smell.

Nohar stumbled through the opening and covered the room with a shotgun held, clumsily, in his left hand. He didn't realize the floor was a half-meter lower than the floor in the hall until it was too late. His good foot slipped away. He tried to catch himself with the cane in his right hand, but the pipe was slick with blood from his palm and slid off into the room, beyond his reach. He slid down a steep concrete curve sitting on his bad leg. He heard a crack. A shiver of agony told him he was not going to walk again for a long time.

He did manage to keep a grip on the shotgun.

Through his pain-blurred vision, he realized that if there had been any doubt Smith wasn't the product of some pink engineer, one look at this room put all doubts to rest. The room was a squashed sphere nearly ten meters in diameter. Eight, evenly spaced, round holes were in the wall, doors like the one he had come through. In the center of the room was a two-meter-tall cone, molded of concrete, shooting up a jet of blue-green flame. From it came most of the oppressive heat in the room, and the smell of burning methane.

The wall had niches carved into it. Hundreds of them, all the same size, a meter long by half a meter high. They were concave, oval pits that angled down into the wall slightly. From nearly half of them came the glitter of MLI's wealth, diamonds, rubies, emeralds. Thousands, perhaps hundreds of thousands, of stones—

And, of course, there were Smith's kinsmen. The creatures that ran Midwest Lapidary. Four, in all, were facing him. They were wearing pink clothing, like Smith had. They all had the same blubbery white humanoid form that Smith wore.

"That's why," Nohar managed through gritted teeth. "The hit in Lakeview. Couldn't tell who he *was* over the comm . . ."

One of them addressed him in Smith's blubbery voice. "We do not do such things lightly. We must be certain of the right when we do such irrevocable acts. A waste you must be here—"

The pain in his leg was making him dizzy. He was beginning to feel cold, clammy. In this heat, he must be going into shock. *"Right?"* It was a yell of pain as much as an accusation. "I talked to Smith." Nohar caught his breath. "You were breaking your own rules when you cut him out of the loop." Nohar wished he had one of Manny's air-hypos.

"He is a traitor. He knows not that the mission is paramount. He clings to propriety as if we are in—" A word in the alien's language. "And not in this violent sewer."

Another one continued. "We do not allow ourselves to perform physical violence. The traitor does not understand our circumstance is dire and requires an exception."

Nohar was beginning to have trouble feeling his leg. The dizziness was getting worse. "End justifies the means?"

A third one, near the cone, spoke. "It is a waste. The tiger understands."

The first one—perhaps the leader, but Nohar was having trouble keeping track of these similar creatures—continued. "The traitor, perhaps, understands or suspects our plans when he hires you. It is intended you lead the new unrest—"

The one by the cone, "—like your father leads the convenient rebellion eleven years ago. The traitor anticipates us and hires you against us—"

"The traitor," one of them went on, "knows what kind of resonance there is when he hires you—"

"—Datia is a useful charismatic figure to keep unrest going, Datia's son is useful as well. A waste the traitor talks to you before us—"

The one by the cone bent—no, oozed—over to turn a valve that was recessed in a concave depression near its base. The flame sputtered out. "It doesn't matter. We go, take our supplies and begin elsewhere. We have done well to prepare for the time the plan is uncovered—"

Nohar shook his head too quickly. He felt faint.

He couldn't tell them apart. They all looked like Smith, all smelled like Smith, talked like Smith. "You guys blew it—"

"Who are you to judge? We achieve our end—"

"It was the vote to scuttle the NASA deep-probe

project, wasn't it? It will hit the Senate after the election and you just couldn't wait . . .''

All the *things* stopped moving. They didn't say anything, didn't move. Nohar slowly raised the shotgun.

''Enough of your pet congressmen were supposed to win Senate seats to tip the scales on the vote. Then the shit hits the fan and MLI falls apart. You designed the whole thing to be uncovered eventually. The phony identities are just *too* damn phony. You want the scandal and the indictments that would follow to throw the Congress into chaos—''

Nohar paused to catch his breath. He couldn't feel his leg at all anymore.

They were regrouping to face him. He still had the shotgun covering them, and he hoped desperately it would do some good. ''The Fed was about to follow up all your false trails. The DEA was about to find its flush manufacturing center. But you blew it. Forensics was not supposed to get to Smith's body that fast. There wasn't supposed to *be* a body. You tried to have Hassan erase that mistake. It was too late. I know, and now, the Fed knows.''

That got them. They were looking at each other. One spoke, ''Then we must end it—''

''End us—''

One of them headed back for the cone while another addressed Nohar. ''We complete our original mission. We end ourselves. Nothing is left but speculation and pieces of paper. Without physical evidence, no probes are sent. Your violent races will not contaminate our star systems. We need those new worlds, you will not take them away—''

Nohar was leveling the shotgun at the one that was at the cone. ''No, you're not getting off that easy. No suicides. And you call us violent. How many people have you managed to kill because of those probes? A tac-nuke on the moon would have done the same thing, and not killed anyone—''

''Law requires we act indirectly in covert activity.''

Nohar gagged on that one. "*Law?* You screwed-up bastards—no wonder the only one of you with a shred of morality ended up a 'traitor.' "

It kept moving. They were going to flood the room with methane. Nohar pumped the shotgun and shot the creature. Bile and ammonia filled the air, and the creature was knocked back to the far wall. A chunk of the creature's translucent flesh splattered against the wall. But it didn't bleed, didn't even leak. The shot had passed right through it.

It stood up, none the worse for wear.

"Unnecessary display, such things do not hurt our kind. Useless since we end now anyway."

The thing went back to the valve and started turning. "You, and others, may know we originate from a different biology. But without us to examine, your ethnocentric culture never accepts the idea of an extraterrestrial culture."

Nohar lowered the shotgun.

What were they going to do, asphyxiate or ignite? Didn't matter, he was dead either way—his leg wouldn't let him move.

CHAPTER 27

The one at the valve had finished his job, and Nohar could hear the hiss of the methane.

The creature had half-turned toward him when Nohar heard a soft "phut" from the hole behind him. A small tube had planted itself in the folds under the creature's chin. There was a bubbling groan from the creature, and it raised a flabby white arm to the tube stuck in its neck.

Three more "phuts" and similar tubes embedded themselves in the other aliens. There was a shuddering moan from the first one. Its arm had stopped halfway to its neck. There was a tearing sound as the pink clothes gave way and the thing collapsed into a shapeless white mass. There was a clatter as its eyes, fake plastic orbs, rolled off the mound of shuddering flesh. A pair of pink dentures followed.

The others collapsed as well.

They weren't dead, so much as reverted to some natural state. They still moved, though in a shuddering, rhythmic fashion—occasionally throwing out a multitentacled pseudopod from their mass, only to be reabsorbed into the mound of flesh a moment later. They now *looked* like the amoebic form of life Manny had described.

Isham came through the hole behind Nohar and went to the valve on the cone, shut it off. She was talking to herself. ". . . cave dwellers, lots of heat vents and volcanic activity. Dim red-yellow sun, thick atmosphere, probably high gravity. They could survive very heavy acceleration. Could have ridden in on a nuclear rocket not much more advanced than our own. Gems are probably synthetic . . .''

Nohar hadn't realized how tightly he was holding the shotgun until he tried to drop it. His hands didn't want to move. ''Damn it, Isham. Where did you come from, and what took you so long?''

Isham squatted and was looking at one of the quivering mounds of alien flesh. She poked it with the end of an air rifle she was carrying. The white flesh rippled like a water balloon. ''We were staked out at Midwest Lapidary 'headquarters.' NuFood seemed too small to rate notice. Our team got word from the DEA. McIntyre and Conrad have been two steps behind the Zipperheads all night, ever since the rats jumped a cabbie at the airport. They radioed your message, and my team had to scramble all the way from downtown. I was point, got here about two minutes after you did—''

''What?'' Nohar had spoken too loudly. He was suddenly out of breath and felt faint.

She activated her throat-mike. ''Aerie, this is Bald Eagle—nest is clear, send the Vultures in with the cleanup. We need a local ambulance, with our own medics. Out.''

She stood up and looked into one of the niches in the wall. She reached in and took out a diamond. It glinted red facets of light.

''I had to tape them just in case the drug killed them. Otherwise, their rapid decomposition would be hard to explain to Washington—''

''You were there.'' Nohar was fighting alternating waves of pain and nausea. ''All that time?''

She tapped a lens hanging off her belt with the diamond and dropped the gem back in the niche. ''Two meters behind you. All the way through the building.''

Nohar sighed.

''That D amino acid information was vital. But you threw the tac-squad for a loop. We had stunners, but we wanted the 'franks' alive. And because of you, we discovered the trank we were using wouldn't have worked right on their biology—''

Nohar looked at the pulsing forms of the aliens. ''What'd you use?''

''The only thing I had access to, flush. It's a symmetrical molecule. Probably use the same stuff, wherever they come from.''

Talk about poetic justice. ''What happens now?''

''The cleanup crew'll be here in about three minutes. They'll pack these things up. The Fed will take over the processing plant here, keep them alive. If we're lucky, these will lead us to any more covert cells these guys have set up in the country. You *do* understand this is a national security matter. These *are not* aliens. This didn't happen.''

The Fed and its passion for secrets. It was becoming difficult to remain conscious. ''What about the Zipheads, and the politicians?''

''The DEA has the Zipperheads. They can have them. The MLI plot was designed to unravel, so we'll let it unravel. We've done extensive computer searches into MLI's background, much more thorough than your hacker friend. These things seeded a money trail that leads back to the CIA. It's going to look to the vids, and everyone else, like this was just another rogue Agency operation—''

Nohar sucked in a breath. ''You're not really FBI, are you?''

Isham smiled. It didn't look like a grimace this time. ''Only on loan.''

''Just let the CIA take the heat for this?''

''That's what it's for. The CIA's designed to take the heat for the NSA, the NRO, and a half-dozen other organizations in the intelligence community. We'll gladly let them fall to the wolves to keep this bottled up. Justice will prosecute a good percentage of Congress, Congress gets to flay open the CIA. Executive hits Legislative, Legislative gets back at the Executive—''

Nohar leaned back on the curved concrete, ignoring the sudden dagger of pain that erupted from his leg. it was just too much effort to stay upright. ''Checks and balances, right?''

''The way it works in practice anyway.''

''What about NASA's deep-probe project?''

''Congress will scuttle them. The NSA will black-budget them, launch, and eventually, we'll find out where these things come from.''

Nohar closed his eyes. It felt like he was losing consciousness. ''We're going to do the same thing to them, aren't we?''

''Not my decision . . .''

Figured . . .

Nohar slipped into darkness.

It was Friday, the 26th of August, and the weather was deigning to cool down a little. That, and it looked to be the first week of August with no rainfall. Nohar had just closed the deal on Manny's house, and he was feeling emotionally exhausted.

He sat down on a box in the center of the empty living room and looked at the comm. He wanted to call Stephie, ask her to go with him. However, he couldn't muster the courage—he'd been avoiding her ever since he made the decision to leave this burg. He knew if she said no, he wouldn't leave. And staying in this town would kill him. Too many memories.

He sat on the box in the middle of Manny's living room, realizing he was going to do to Stephie the same thing Maria had done to him. That decided it. He *was* going to call her.

He had just reached for the comm when someone at the front door rang the call button.

Their timing sucked.

Nohar grabbed a crutch and hoisted himself up to his feet. He was getting good at maneuvering with the cast. He managed to get all the way to the door without bashing it into anything. He didn't bother with the intercom. He just threw the door open.

There she was, carrying a huge handbag, smelling of roses and wood smoke.

Nohar fell into the cliché before he could stop himself. "I was just about to call you."

There was a half-smile on her face. "Oh, you were? I've been looking for you ever since you left the hospital. You moved out of your apartment—"

"Transferred the lease to Angel—"

Stephie nodded and patted him on the shoulder—the left one where the fur had come back in white. "You going to let me in?"

Nohar stepped aside and let her through. She surveyed the empty living room and sighed. It echoed through the house. "So you're moving out of here, too—how is Angel, anyway?"

"She's lucky rabbits are common. They had skin cultures to match her. The fur on her legs is white now, but she can walk. She got a job."

The concept seemed to shock Stephie. "As what?"

"Cocktail waitress at the *Watership Down*. A bar on Coventry—"

She pulled up a box and they sat down, facing each other.

"So how are you taking things?"

Nohar slapped his cast. "They had to weave some carbon fiber into the tendons, but the cast comes off in a month, and with a few months of exercise—"

She shook her head. "That's not what I mean and you know it. You're still blaming yourself for Manny, aren't you?"

That hit home. "If—"

Stephie put her finger on his lips. "I talked to Manny a lot about you. He was your father for five years, and because of school you ran away to Moreytown and joined a street gang. When your gang got involved with the riots and you found out what your real father was, you ran away from them. Now you're going to run away from this life, right?''

Nohar shook his head. "I can't live here anymore . . ."

"I suppose not. But you aren't going to run away from me. I won't let you."

They sat, looking at each other.

"I suppose not."

She smiled and shook her head. "At least he doesn't object. Well, I got myself a new job, demographics for Nielsen."

Nohar had a sinking feeling. He forced a smile. "Great. Where?"

"Santa Monica."

Nohar was speechless for a moment, and she seemed to enjoy his reaction. "You *knew* I was going to California?"

" 'California is a lot more tolerant,' " she quoted.

"Where did you hear that?"

"Those rodents had more than drugs and guns at that motel. The white one left this on the comm." She reached into the overlarge bag and pulled out a ramcard. Nohar noticed the bag kept moving when she took her hand out of it. The bag emitted a slightly familiar smell. "Seems to be a copy of whatever you had on permanent storage on your comm. I *was* going to give this to you when you got out of the hospital. But you slipped out without telling me. So I played it."

Nohar took the card wordlessly.

"That Maria is one stupid cat for walking out on you."

"No, she isn't."

The handbag was still moving. Nohar couldn't hold it anymore. "What the hell do you have in the bag?"

Stephie broke into a wide grin. "I still remember that line you gave me in the parking garage, about your cat."

Another thing Nohar wanted to forget. He sighed. "Yes?"

Stephie reached in the bag and pulled out a small, gray-and-black tabby kitten and handed it to Nohar. Nohar had to collect himself enough to cup his hands under the little creature. It barely fit on his palm. Nohar watched as it stumbled a little, disoriented, and circled around. Then, finding the new perch satisfactory, it curled up, closed its eyes, and began to purr.

Nohar stared at the little thing in his hands. "Damn it, Stephie. That isn't playing fair."

"I know."

She began scratching the little thing behind the ears.

Science Fiction Anthologies

☐ **FUTURE EARTHS: UNDER AFRICAN SKIES**   UE2544—$4.99
   Mike Resnick & Gardner Dozois, editors
From a utopian space colony modeled on the society of ancient Kenya,
to a shocking future discovery of a "long-lost" civilization, to an inge-
nious cure for one of humankind's oldest woes—a cure that might cost
too much—here are 15 provocative tales about Africa in the future and
African culture transplanted to different worlds.

☐ **FUTURE EARTHS: UNDER SOUTH AMERICAN SKIES**
   Mike Resnick & Gardner Dozois, editors   UE2581—$4.99
From a plane crash that lands its passengers in a survival situation
completely alien to anything they've ever experienced, to a close en-
counter of the insect kind, to a woman who has journeyed unimaginably
far from home—here are stories from the rich culture of South America,
with its mysteriously vanished ancient civilizations and magnificent
artifacts, its modern-day contrasts between sophisticated city dwellers
and impoverished villagers.

☐ **MICROCOSMIC TALES**   UE2532—$4.99
   Isaac Asimov, Martin H. Greenberg, & Joseph D. Olander, eds.
Here are 100 wondrous science fiction short-short stories, including
contributions by such acclaimed writers as Arthur C. Clarke, Robert
Silverberg, Isaac Asimov, and Larry Niven. Discover a superman who
lives in a *real* world of nuclear threat . . . an android who dreams of
electric love . . . and a host of other tales that will take you instantly
out of this world.

☐ **WHATDUNITS**   UE2533—$4.99
☐ **MORE WHATDUNITS**   UE2557—$5.50
   Mike Resnick, editor
In these unique volumes of all-original stories, Mike Resnick has created a series of science fiction mystery scenarios and set such inven-
tive sleuths as Pat Cadigan, Judith Tarr, Katharine Kerr, Jack Haldeman,
and Esther Friesner to solving them. Can you match wits with the
masters to make the perpetrators fit the crimes?

Buy them at your local bookstore or use this convenient coupon for ordering.

PENGUIN USA P.O. Box 999, Dept. #17109, Bergenfield, New Jersey 07621

Please send me the DAW BOOKS I have checked above, for which I am enclosing
$_____ (please add $2.00 per order to cover postage and handling. Send check
or money order (no cash or C.O.D.'s) or charge by Mastercard or Visa (with a
$15.00 minimum.) Prices and numbers are subject to change without notice.

Card #_____ Exp. Date _____
Signature_____
Name_____
Address_____
City _____ State _____ Zip _____

For faster service when ordering by credit card call **1-800-253-6476**

Please allow a minimum of 4 to 6 weeks for delivery.

Tanya Huff

VICTORY NELSON, INVESTIGATOR:
Otherworldly Crimes A Specialty

Kate Elliott

The Novels of the Jaran:

☐ **JARAN: Book 1**   UE2513—$4.99
Here is the poignant and powerful story of a young woman's
coming of age on an alien world, a woman who is both player
and pawn in an interstellar game of intrigue and politics, where
the prize to be gained may be freedom for humankind from
long-standing domination by their alien conquerors.

☐ **AN EARTHLY CROWN: Book 2**   UE2546—$5.99
On a low-tech planet, Ilya, a charismatic warlord, is leading the
nomadic jaran tribes on a campaign of conquest, while his wife
Tess—an Earth woman of whose true origins Ilya is unaware—is
caught up in a deadly game of interstellar politics.

☐ **HIS CONQUERING SWORD: Book 3**   UE2551—$5.99
Even as Jaran warlord Ilya continues the conquest of his world,
he faces a far more dangerous power struggle with his wife's
brother, Duke Charles, leader of the underground human rebellion against an interstellar alien empire.

DAW

Elizabeth Forrest

☐ **PHOENIX FIRE** UE2515—$4.99

As the legendary Phoenix awoke, so, too, did an ancient Chinese demon—and Los Angeles was destined to become the final battleground in their millennia-old war. Now, the very earth begins to dance as these two creatures of legend fight to break free. And as earthquake and fire start to take their toll on the mortal world, four desperate people begin to suspect the terror that is about to engulf mankind.

☐ **DARK TIDE** UE2560—$4.99

In 1968, a freak accident at an amusement park saw three boys drowned, and the only survivor pulled from the ocean in a terror-fueled, near catatonic state. Years later, the survivor is forced to return to the town where it happened. And slowly, long buried memories start to resurface, and all his nightmares begin to come true.
